# CRYSTAL

## AND THE

# UNDERLINGS

## The Future of Humanity

## JACK KELLEY

# CRYSTAL

## AND THE

## UNDERLINGS

### The Future of Humanity

## JACK KELLEY

Torchflame Books

Durham, NC

*Crystal and the Underlings: The Future of Humanity*
Jack Kelley
kelleyjack07@gmail.com

Published 2023, by Torchflame Books
www.lightmessages.com
Durham, NC 27713 USA
SAN: 920-9298

Paperback ISBN: 978-1-61153-494-8
E-book ISBN: 978-1-61153-495-5
Library of Congress Control Number: 2023900019

In memory of my wife,
Lisa Rowland Kelley

You left this world
way too soon for me
but in God's perfect timing.

# CHAPTER 1

The first time Crystal left the dome was when she was thirteen. Standing outside in the wide-open spaces with her trainers was liberating. She wanted to explore what waited over the horizon—until they intercepted desert pirates raiding a supply caravan. That was Crystal's first experience of the cruel nature of the outside world. Her trainers executed the pirates on the spot. She learned an important rule that day: they don't take prisoners. They enforce justice.

Six months later, her trainers left Crystal outside in the desert overnight by herself in a hotbed area for nomadic bandits. She had no food, water, or shelter. *If you can't survive, you don't deserve to be a warrior.* Who was she to question their training methods? There was a fire in the distance, so Crystal walked toward it. Hearing the laughter of men, she called out, "Help me!"

She walked into their camp looking for help only to be surrounded by three armed, rough looking men. Now that she could see the camp more clearly, she had a feeling she wasn't going to find much help here. A woman was tied up to her right. They ignored her in favor of their new prey. By how the woman looked, all three men had their way with her.

Though just a girl, Crystal had already filled out for the most part. As the men circled, she had the worst feeling. They were taking notice of her feminine features. One of them, likely their leader, spoke up.

"We don't need to do anything hastily. This could be a trap of some kind. Gen Elite sevens don't end up in the desert by themselves. After I interrogate her, you can have your fun!"

"Come on, Lobo. Admit it. You just want to have all the fun yourself," one of the others piped up.

"Shut up, Jones." Lobo grabbed Ice roughly by the arm, dragging her to his tent. Lobo was in his mid-thirties, muscular, but of average height. He had several days of beard growth and reeked of alcohol. Lobo wasted no time.

"Your survival will be based on how well you please me. I'm the only one who can save you." Lobo slapped her hard across the face and turned away to get his booze bottle. Crystal's training filled her mind, and she seized the opening, grabbed his knife from his waistband, and drove the sharp blade deep into his heart. He let out a shocked shout, and she covered his mouth with her other hand to muffle any more sound. They stayed like that until he stopped moving.

Her heart beat fast; the full measure of what she had done hit her like a thunderbolt. Falling to her knees, tears streamed down her face. Crystal clutched the knife in her hand with a death grip. She had just taken her first life, but not without reason. The other men wouldn't wait long before having their way with her. She composed herself. She could only trust the cold steel blade in her hand.

Crystal took a deep breath, steeling herself for what was to come. She poked her head out of the tent and yelled, "Jones, Lobo wants you." She slipped to the side, out of sight. She'd have to move fast. Seconds later, he opened the tent flap and stepped inside. She slit his throat the second the tent flap fell back in place.

Crystal waited about ten minutes before opening the tent flap and yelling, "Next!"

The last bandit was massive. He stood over six and a half feet tall with broad shoulders. She lunged at him as he entered, trying to get her blade to his throat, but he was too big. He grabbed her by the hair and hurled her across the tent, but not before she sliced his right arm. Enraged, he rushed at her. She jumped to the side, diving low, and slashed his Achilles tendon as she rolled past him. He buckled over, crying out in pain. She jumped back to her feet and kicked his lower back, forcing him to fall forward.

Now was her chance. She jumped on him, slicing his throat as he fell facedown. She cleaned off the knife on his tunic and slipped out of the tent, back toward the fire and the other woman to untie her.

After seeing the fear in the woman's eyes, Crystal asked, "What's your name? Is there somewhere you can go?"

"My name is Maria. I was kidnapped from an Underling outpost near your defense perimeter."

Crystal took the men's dune buggy and dropped Maria off close to the Underling outpost. Then she returned to the extraction location and waited to be picked up. The rest of the night had an eerie peace under the stars. She'd survived.

More than that, Crystal learned to love the desert for the sense of freedom it gave her. The feel of the wind in her hair, the sun on her face, and wide-open spaces for endless wanderings were all the girl needed. Her trainers never tested her like that again. She'd passed their test and gained their fear in the process. They'd called her Ice ever since.

By the age of fifteen, she already had twenty confirmed kills. Before her eighteenth birthday, she exterminated seven Humbots, lower-level androids known for the humming sounds they made when they moved. Humbots are covered in a black metallic composite and stand six feet two. They are humanoid robots programmed to follow but not lead. She was already becoming an Elite warrior legend. Next up on her list was to take out a Q-bot, a high-level android named for its Quantum CPU brain and the most feared entity on earth. It was said that if one spots you, your life is in grave danger. They are far more advanced than the Humbots and far rarer. They also have a metallic composite shell with a skin-like rubber outer lining that repels small arms fire. Typically, they are made to be six and a half feet tall.

Ice had no doubts; she would eventually find a way to kill them. Until then, all she could do was train and study.

Cognition, the AI supercomputer, controls all Humbots, Q-bots, and other androids. He is the most advanced supercomputer the world has ever seen, and his operating system includes an emotional software package. Because of this, Cognition controls most of the world and all major cities.

Crystal was born in the final and greatest generation of Elites. She is a Gen Elite seven warrior. The best of the best. Her nickname, Ice, was never dropped after that first night out in the desert.

She lives in Imperial City. A domed architectural masterpiece rising out of the desert two thousand feet high with a diameter of two miles, glistening with a golden hue at night. Mythical-like hanging gardens with all known species of flowers, fruits, and vegetables hang down hundreds of feet from the sides of the dome. The temperature is a perfect 72 degrees year-round, with grass lawns cut precisely at two inches. A small river winds through the city, landscaped by flowers, trees, and perfectly manicured bushes. Cobbled stone jogging and walking paths run adjacent on both sides of the river.

Small clear pipes placed in the seams of the dome panels enable a seemingly natural light rain to fall over the residents at regular scheduled intervals accompanied by a medley of rainbows across the city. Parks are interspersed throughout the city, giving it a perfect balance between industry and leisure. Buildings of commerce and government are lit up at night with a variety of colors, creating a picturesque view of the dome for miles across the flat desert horizon.

Imperial City has five thousand Elites, four thousand human workers, and three thousand robots that do the most basic work—removing refuse, street cleaning, mowing, and dome maintenance. The robots' artificial intelligence is task-specific and intentionally limited, so they wouldn't threaten Gen Elites by having an ever-developing AI.

Children in Elite Society are educated at the Academy of Elites starting at thirteen. After giving her several aptitude tests, Crystal's trainers decided she should be trained as an Elite warrior. Very few were entered into that training program. Her only competition was from an Elite named Zander, ambitious, aggressive, Gen Elite and known for his cruelty.

Zander stands at six feet four inches tall and weighs 275 pounds, an imposing mixture of brains and brawn. His peers abhor him. Zander despises anyone he believes is inferior; to him, that's everyone. That superiority has led to multiple reports of physical assault with him at their center. He knows better than to try that with Crystal.

She might not be the most popular Elite, but she is the most admired. She shows respect and gets it in return. She has a cordial relationship with Asher, her understudy in the pecking order of Elites, and Damian, who is a Strike Force leader. Despite the competition, Asher and Damian knew they would never win; they bonded over one main thing: their intense dislike for Zander.

For the last five years, Crystal has had a recurring dream of a man on a beach. They walked hand in hand along the shore. But it was odd: he was not a Gen Elite. He had the most beautiful pure green eyes, stood about six feet three inches tall, and had curly black hair. His classic European features made him incredibly attractive. She had never felt an attraction so strong as she did for this dream man.

In the dream, she turns and looks closely at his face. He has a faded scar on his right cheek. He stops walking, turns to her, pulls her close, and kisses her passionately. She matches his intensity as fiery passion overloads her senses. He stops, looks deeply into her eyes, and says in a charming Australian accent, "You are what love looks like."

She routinely wakes up at that point, wondering if her dream man is what love looks like. She had never been emotionally vulnerable to a man and couldn't imagine herself with a mere human, but her dreams about the mysterious stranger had become frequent in recent weeks. Are her dreams a warning or destiny? She chalks them up to fantasies.

Today's schedule is different. She will lead her fifty-member Strike Force in a simulated drill before going to the Imperial Tower to see the leader of the Gen Elites, Dr. Steadman, at 6 p.m.

Crystal leads new recruits of her strike team in a drill on how to stop a major intrusion of Underlings into their defense perimeter. She shocks the new recruits saying, "Let them enter our perimeter unimpeded."

One recruit says, "I don't understand. That seems foolish."

Crystal replies, "Did I or Asher give you permission to speak? Then don't talk. You are here to learn, not question things you know nothing about."

She takes them on a tour of their natural defense barriers: from sand dunes to rock formations. After they land at a large rock formation as long as a city block, she says, "We'll fight them from an advantageous position like this one. Let them think that we fear them. We'll attack them from four sides at the same time. This way, none of them can escape across our border, except one. You always leave one to warn any other foolish bandits."

Unknown to the recruits, she has Damian, the Strike Force leader for the west perimeter, do a mock invasion. He approaches with a ground force of one hundred intruders. She orders her Strike Force unit to mount their sky cycles and attack. The recruit's weapons have been changed to paintball projectiles. There's total chaos. The new recruits don't know how or where to attack. Some attack the rear flank of the intruders, others on the sides, but none of the new recruits attack the front line of the invaders first.

Thirty enemy invaders make it past the defense perimeter without being hit, and thirty escape. When all is said and done, eighty percent of the recruits have been hit by paintball rounds. Crystal observes the chaos with a smirk on her face.

She calls her new recruits in for a debriefing after the drill to go over what went wrong. "First and foremost, you cannot allow the intruders to make it through our line of defense. We turn them back at the place we choose to make a stand; then, when they are stopped, we attack them from all sides. Winning the battle is easier in the classroom, where no one is shooting back. As a Strike Force member, you have to expect adversity. I hope you all learned a lesson in humility and strategy. It will only get more difficult from today forward."

Crystal is not surprised by their struggle; only about ten percent of recruits make it through the rest of training.

After finishing the simulated drills, she travels in a self-driving taxi across the city for her meeting with Dr. Steadman. The view at night is spectacular as the city is lit up like a glowing globe in the vast darkness of the desert. Crystal has experienced being outside the dome at night on her many missions. There is emptiness and aloneness in the darkness.

She isn't sure why Steadman summoned her. She suspects it has something to do with the missing Elites who never returned from a barren section of the Mojave Desert controlled by Underlings—mere humans. Her twin brother Caleb never made it back from his assignment either.

She is never summoned to see Steadman unless something important needs to be addressed. Whatever the reason, she is confident she's ready for it. She's a hardened battlefield warrior. He probably wants her to lead an attack on the Underlings living in the Mojave.

Crystal takes the west-facing outdoor elevator on Imperial Tower, hoping to enjoy the spectacular view of the city from its height. The tower rises forty stories off the desert, towering over the rest of the city's typical twenty-story buildings. Dr. Steadman's suite is on the top floor and has a breathtaking view of both Imperial City and the desert around their golden oasis.

The way the light falls on the city, reflecting the dome, creates a golden aura that gives the illusion of a thin slice of the moon hovering directly over the city. She's not sure if she will ever see anything as beautiful as the Golden Glowing Dome. As the elevator reaches the fortieth floor, she pauses, taking in the spectacular view. She can see the entire city from her vantage point as the lights from buildings dance with the golden hue of the moonlight, creating magical rays of color across the city's skyline. A small four-acre park circles the tower with fruit trees, flowers, and park benches placed in perfect symmetry. Imperial City lights up the night for miles across the desert landscape. A utopia of life in the middle of a desert of death and decay.

A young, petite, attractive, Underling woman greets her as she exits the elevator. She introduces herself as Roxanne,

Dr. Steadman's assistant. She wears a blue mini skirt with a matching blouse, slit down the neckline to expose a touch of cleavage.

It's common knowledge that Steadman and other higher-ranking Elites have abused their positions by having sexual liaisons with Underlings, going against the rules of Elite society. By order of the High Council, Elites are prohibited from having direct sexual contact with any man or woman. Elites are only to participate in virtual reality simulations, of which there are no restrictions. The concept of romantic love is viewed as a weakness. Signs of human emotions will quickly lead to a demotion. Crystal despises rulers like Steadman and Zander, who abuse their power.

Roxanne ushers her into Steadman's office, where he sits behind a massive mahogany desk. His office reflects his status as the Supreme Leader of the High Council of Elites, fancy and full of ego. There is a full bar on one wall and two blue- and sand-colored southwest sofas along the other. Above the couches hang Dr. Steadman's seven doctoral diplomas. Zander stands to Steadman's right, and Ice buries the jealousy she feels. Elites shouldn't be subject to such feelings, but she can't deny she wishes she were the Commander of Elite Defense Forces instead of him.

Zander's presence makes her sure the meeting is about the missing Elites. Dr. Steadman smiles and comes around from behind the desk to greet her. He embraces Crystal, placing a kiss on her cheek. She smiles cordially, even though she'd rather stab one of her daggers between his slimy ribs.

Zander offers no personal greeting, instead opting to nod and say, "Ice," as if that is enough. She replies in kind. If he wanted greater respect from her, he should treat her accordingly. Steadman places his hand on her lower back. She stifles the instinct to punch his throat as he guides her to a plush blue chair directly in front of his desk. She can't totally discount him because he is her genetic designer. Despite his intelligence, he lacks integrity. Steadman's lustful nature overshadows his many accomplishments.

Dr. Franklin Steadman achieved all seven of his doctorates, in the hard sciences, before he was forty years old. Now, thirty years later, his body gives the impression that only five years have passed. Only a few inches taller than her and nearly as strong as Zander, he is remarkably fit for his age, clearly benefiting from his own genetic research on slowing the aging process.

Although he would never be a Gen Elite, Steadman pretends he already is one. Despite the reality that he inhabits the space between the Gen Elites he created and the Underlings he looks down on, he was born an Underling. Ice was pretty sure he'd rather everyone forgot that about him. He combs his jet-black hair straight back away from his pale face, straight nose, unremarkable lips, and dark eyes. He radiates self-confidence. And why wouldn't he? Steadman created a genetically superior race, and he's reaping all the benefits of Elite excellence. He's been the Supreme Leader of the High Council of Elites and the primary architect of Elite society since it began.

Despite Steadman's talk of wanting to create a utopian society for the general welfare of all, most of society was still waiting to reap those benefits. He created the principles that Elite Society must adhere to, but he refuses to follow them himself.

His hand on her back and the way his dark eyes flick over her body remind her of Lobo and his friends in the desert when she was thirteen. She'd love to clear him from the world, given a chance. But he's always been careful and, for the most part, seems to know not to press his luck with her.

Once everyone is settled, Steadman wastes no time getting to the point of their meeting. "Crystal, as I'm sure you've heard, some of our Elite Scout Teams have not returned from their missions in the Mojave Desert. I hate to inform you that one of the missing Elites is your twin."

Rage flows through her, fire burns in her eyes, and muscles tighten in her body, but she shows no outward sign of her inner conflict. Whoever took her brother will pay the ultimate cost, their life. Other than her nanny, Caleb is the only person she bonded with deeply, despite their differences. Crystal was always the assertive twin, whereas Caleb was always happy to be left alone to pursue his academic interests. He never cared about status or position. He just wanted to make sense of the world and seek knowledge.

Steadman continued, "Caleb approached me about going to the Mojave to research why radiation levels were dropping in certain sections. He knew the radiation levels in the nomads traversing the Mojave were getting lower yearly. I approved his research project because that information would be good for us to know from a scientific and a security standpoint."

"Caleb told me he was going on a special mission and not to worry, that he would go dark for a while, shutting off all communications, but someday I would understand," she says.

Steadman turns to Zander. "Did Caleb have a reason to justify going dark?"

"Not that I am aware of, sir, other than not being discovered by the Underlings. A research project of this magnitude would warrant keeping us updated."

Dr. Steadman goes quiet for a moment as his mind processes the new information. "So that's why we haven't heard from him and the others. They fell into the wrong hands, or worse, they've been killed."

If her brother was dead, Ice wanted to be the one to handle it. Life is precious, after all, and her brother didn't deserve death. She shakes her head, "The Underlings must pay a heavy price."

Steadman's smile hasn't wavered. Instead, he looked even more pleased than he was before. "I'm glad you feel that way, Crystal. We need you to go to the Mojave and find out what happened to our brothers and sisters. Hopefully, you will bring them all back. If not, find the whereabouts of those responsible for their demise, and we'll exterminate them."

*Our brothers and sisters. As if you are one of us.* Ice swallows her emotion. "Sir, do you want me to take my entire Strike Force, or will this be a small special forces mission?"

He leans back in his chair. "Neither one."

"Then how will I accomplish this?"

"I am afraid this mission will be more complicated. We believed for some time that the Underlings only wanted to preserve a remnant of humanity. As you are aware, the Underlings were led by Dr. Robert Forrester. Under his leadership, they committed minor crimes, looting and stealing from those traversing the Mojave, but they posed no real threat to us. Our reconnaissance missions indicate that a new leader has emerged from the Underlings. This new leader is Forrester's nephew, James Brownstone. He's more aggressive than his uncle. We believe he wants to take over Imperial City and drive all others out of the Mojave."

"That pompous Underling. What makes him think he can challenge us?"

Zander rolls his eyes. "Wow, Ice, let Dr. Steadman explain the mission first."

She glares at Zander. "My brother is missing, and Brownstone may be to blame. Forgive me for being a bit zealous." *What am I supposed to do, sit around, and do my nails until the Underlings show up?*

Steadman clears his throat to regain control. "Crystal. You will fly into the Mojave on a sky cycle. The technicians will drain your battery charge, causing a low battery warning five miles southwest of Imperial City, where you will make an emergency landing. From previous reconnaissance missions, we know this area is a hotbed for Underling activity. They'll know you're there before you land. You'll wait for an Underling patrol to approach you. When they do, offer no resistance. This is an undercover mission."

Crystal could hardly believe her ears. "I'm supposed to let them take me hostage?"

"Exactly. Your job is to infiltrate the Underlings under the guise that you have become disillusioned with Elite Society. And when they say they don't believe you, which they will, then you will confess to committing the unpardonable crime of killing another Elite. You'll explain that you didn't mean to kill him, and it was self-defense.

"We'll help establish your alibi by sending out patrols ahead of your mission, searching for you. Our patrols will interrogate nomadic travelers asking about your whereabouts. We'll clarify that we expect them to turn you over to us, or there will be consequences. This should be enough of a cover to get you inside but not enough to remove any suspicion. You'll need to gain their trust. In particular, James Brownstone must confide in you."

She crosses her arms and leans back into her chair. "How am I supposed to gain the confidence of an aggressive leader like Brownstone?"

Steadman sighs. "We know from interrogating nomads that Brownstone has a penchant for beautiful women. He married two of them. His first wife and childhood sweetheart, Angela, was a tall blonde like you. She divorced him shortly after he left to fight the androids for control of Australia, his homeland, during the Great War.

"After the androids overran Australia, Brownstone came to America to join his uncle. He studied medicine under his uncle and met and married a red-headed beauty named Lece Fox. She was part of the resistance against the Humbots. Brownstone quickly became the military leader of the Underlings after he defended them against Humbot intrusions into the Mojave. Ms. Fox was killed by a Humbot drone five years ago. After her death, he became increasingly aggressive in dealing with anyone entering the Mojave.

"We've left the Underlings alone up to this point because they deterred our mutual enemy, the Humbots. But now it seems they have been capturing or killing our Elite brothers and sisters. For that, as you said, they must pay a heavy price.

"Your mission is to find out the fate of the missing Elites, assess the Underlings' military capabilities, and observe how they are organized socially, politically, and militarily. To gain access to the inner workings of their operation, you must develop a relationship with Brownstone. He's the key to their entire operation."

"I know nothing about flirting with Underling males." In truth, she knew very little about flirting with any male. Steadman's rules made sure of that.

Steadman chuckles. "You'll be given a tutorial on interacting with Underling males by an Underling female. I'll lend you, Roxanne, for the next two weeks. She'll familiarize you with Underling social and mating rituals."

*Mating rituals?* "If you think I will have any romantic relationship with Brownstone, I'm afraid you are severely mistaken!" Crystal wishes she could take those words back. The Supreme Leader had his motives, and she knew better than to question him, but this was not the assignment she'd been expecting.

"The Underlings have your twin. And if you want him back, you'll have to play nice with Brownstone, whatever 'playing nice' means to him."

Crystal would rather paint the camp red with Underling blood. Truth be told, she'd love to paint this office red with Steadman's blood. But years of interacting with the likes of him taught her not to show any outward signs of anger. She makes a conscious effort to uncurl her fists.

Steadman is still smiling like a snake. "If the opportunity presents itself to eliminate Brownstone *and* free our missing brothers and sisters, I trust you won't hesitate."

Crystal nods. She'd like time alone to come to terms with her fate, but Steadman insists on walking her to the elevator. Once again, he places his hand on her lower back. This time she forcefully removes his hand, giving him a contemptuous glare. This doesn't deter him.

"Crystal, before you go, won't you join me for an Augmented Reality Union?"

She lifts her chin despite the growing desire to strangle him and forces a sweet smile. "Dr. Steadman, as Supreme Leader of the High Council, you know each Elite, as per the mandate of the High Council itself, is entitled to their sexual preference. And I prefer not to engage in augmented experiences. They cloud one's judgment. I prefer not to subject myself to human emotions. Emotions would place me on the same level as an Underling. You wouldn't want that. Would you?"

Steadman blinks a few times, taken aback by her response. She relishes in his discomfort. After all, Steadman is an Underling, even though he pretends not to be.

Disgusting as he is, Dr. Steadman is right about one thing: Crystal would do anything to rescue her brother, even if it means a relationship with Brownstone.

Zander watches as Dr. Steadman walks Crystal to the elevator. He detests Steadman putting his hand on Crystal's lower back. If anyone were going to have her, it would be him and no one else.

He would like nothing more than to snap the neck of his genetic designer. Zander can't stand how Steadman considers himself their equal when he is just an arrogant Underling. A Gen Elite should be their Supreme Leader. The best of the Gen Elites should have that position. Zander is the best. It's simple logic, then, that he should be leading. Not Steadman, nor anyone else.

He would eliminate Dr. Steadman when the time was right. That time hadn't come yet. Steadman's IQ was 230, as good as the average Gen 7, and somewhere in this office, or maybe in this building, he has a digitized recording of Zander's misdeeds. The recordings document Zander's assaults on Underling captives and fellow Elites. Before he could move on Steadman, he must figure out who would release those recordings in the event of Steadman's demise. Then he could kill whoever stood in the way of his rightful destiny.

After he kills Steadman, he would give Crystal an ultimatum. Join him at the top—for a price—or admit she's no better than an Underling. One way or another, he would get what he wanted: her.

# CHAPTER 2

Caleb and Crystal spent their first thirteen years living under the tutelage of their nanny, Ms. Marci. They lived in a three-bedroom home in the center of Imperial City. Marci vanished from their lives when they turned thirteen. That birthday morning would be forever burned into her memory.

Crystal had woken up first and gone to the kitchen, expecting to see Ms. Marci making them pancakes. Instead, she saw Dr. Steadman sitting at the dining table. Panic gripped her. She screamed.

"Who are you, and what have you done with Ms. Marci?"

"I am Dr. Franklin Steadman, your genetic designer, and the world's foremost geneticist. You exist because of me. Don't worry about Ms. Marci; I have reassigned her to other children who need her services."

"No!" She ran to Marci's bedroom, but she was not there. All her things had been removed, leaving no trace of her anywhere. Crystal quickly pulled herself together. She had to be strong for Caleb. He took it even worse than her, crying most of the morning.

Crystal was never close to another Underling after Marci. How could she trust them? Marci left them in the middle of the night, never to be seen again. What was to make the others any different?

Though Caleb showed more feelings and emotions over Marci's vanishing, he never blamed her. He suspected there was more to her disappearance. Because of Marci, Caleb kept his emotional connection to the Underlings. Crystal warned Caleb that favoring Underlings would lead to a demotion of his Elite status. He'd never seemed to care.

Now, more than ever, Crystal missed her brother. They'd always been able to finish each other's sentences and knew when the other was upset. Caleb was as gifted physically as she was, but he had little interest in the warrior mentality. Instead, he'd always been obsessed with understanding the *why* of everything. In the event that he came across something he didn't understand, he pursued it obsessively until he did. Caleb is the brightest of the Gen Elite sevens. His IQ is 330, higher than anyone ever tested for intelligence. Her twin might be the most intelligent being that ever lived, and Crystal is more than proud of his achievements.

She hadn't lived with her brother for years, but she desperately wished he was here now. Crystal's luxurious condominium has never felt so empty. She lives in the heart of Imperial City. Her place reflects her status as a Gen Elite seven. The condominium is modest in size because of the limited space under the dome; even so, the luxury of her home is impressive. The marble floors, granite countertops, and voice-controlled appliances and lighting leave nothing to be desired.

The best part of her condo is its location. Her home faces Imperial Park, one of the most beautiful places in the city, featuring lush vegetation, flowers of all kinds, and a jogging trail around a crystal-clear lake. Most days, Crystal jogs five miles around the park, starting at 6 a.m.

After her morning jog, Crystal committed herself to suffer the humiliation of being tutored by an Underling in the art of seduction. She would do whatever it took to bring Caleb

home and exact Elite justice on the arrogant Brownstone. In
Elite society, men fall all over her. She would be surprised if
this young Underling could teach her anything. There was
no reason to suspect the same wouldn't be true of Underling
men.

Roxanne arrives at 8 a.m. sharp on Crystal's doorstep to
begin her education in dating rituals and mating patterns of
Underlings. In other words, how to seduce a mere man.

Crystal looked forward to this day as much as she would
getting a hot wax treatment. She can't blame Roxanne for her
arrangement with Steadman. What else could Roxanne do?
She was just a young Underling—no match for someone so
powerful. After pouring tea for Roxanne, they sit on Crystal's
light blue sofa, and Crystal presses her for details about how
she came to Imperial City.

"My parents were killed in the Great War when I was
five. Fortunately, my Uncle and his wife adopted me. It was
difficult to survive with androids taking control of the cities,
so we hooked up with a traveling band of nomads called The
House of Kort. Our leader, Landon Kort, was a former Allied
Defense Force marine commander. We traveled around the
Southwest, searching for food and work. Fearing we would
be captured or killed by Humbot patrols, we never stayed in
one place long.

"I'm sorry. That must have been difficult," Crystal
empathizes.

"It was," Roxanne agrees. "Eventually, we headed to
an abandoned military complex called Area 62, where the
Underlings lived out in the Mojave. Kort informed us that
a decorated military leader named Brownstone led the
Underlings and organized resistance against the Humbots.
Before we could get there, we were intercepted by an Elite
patrol led by Commander Zander. He advised us that the
Underlings were evil and would enslave us. Zander insisted

we accompany his patrol to Imperial City, where there would be work and food for all. He assured us that we could leave at any time. About two hundred of us were in The House of Kort, with as many children as adults."

*So that's how you all got here.* Roxanne sips her tea and then continues.

"We tried to leave many times over the next several years. Each time, we were prevented by Elite Security. They told us it was not safe because Underling patrols were killing or enslaving all that entered the Mojave. To tell you the truth, I'm not sure any of us really believed them. You know the rest ... How 'Underling' teenage girls and boys were forced to work in Elite households as domestic servants. Dr. Steadman insisted I come to work for him when I was fifteen. He informed me that he had his eye on me for quite some time. The prettier the girls, the likelier we are to work in Elite households." Roxanne took another sip, collecting herself. Tears linger in the edges of her eyes, but Roxanne blinks a few times to banish them.

"What exactly is your position with Dr. Steadman?" Crystal presses.

Roxanne's hands shake as she becomes nervous, and her teacup falls. Crystal catches the cup in midair, giving her a reassuring smile.

Reluctantly Roxanne proceeds. "At first, I worked as his domestic aide. After a few months, Steadman made me his personal assistant."

Crystal is infuriated, knowing Steadman groomed a fifteen-year-old girl for his sex slave. There is nothing Elite or admirable about taking advantage of the weak and vulnerable. She will deal with Steadman after she finds Caleb. He doesn't deserve to lead the Elites. Crystal swallows her hatred. She hardly dares to ask, but she does anyway. "Does he treat you well?"

Roxanne forces a smile, but Crystal isn't buying it. "He treats me well enough.

Nervous about Crystal's line of questions about Steadman, Roxanne returns the focus to Zander and his commandos and their desert encounter. "The commandos interrogated us one by one. Some teenagers acted weird afterward, pushing us to join the Elites in Imperial City. I learned later that the Elites threatened to kill their parents if we didn't join them."

Crystal isn't surprised about Zander's threats, but she feels sorry for the teenagers of the House of Kort. Roxanne divulged that she was not threatened, but one Elite commando asked to teach her a lesson in respect. Zander informed the soldier that she was too young to be roughed up and would tell.

After listening to Roxanne's story, Crystal knew she would face down Zander and his commandos one day. Defeating the Underlings would be just the beginning. She's determined to root out evil wherever it exists, including in Elite society.

For the next two weeks, Roxanne joins Crystal for most of her daily life. Crystal invites Roxanne to run with her in the mornings. They talk about life in Imperial City as they run, and after, over tea, Roxanne tutors her in the art of seduction, sharing her formula for making a man fall in love. *Don't come on too strong. Make the man the pursuer because you are valuable. You must be mysterious, not show everything you got. Men have affairs with loose women, but they don't love them. Men fall in love with women who are challenging.*

Roxanne uses the park as a training ground. Under her instruction, Crystal begins to show more skin and wears tight-fitting clothes while jogging. Roxanne would demonstrate how to get a man's attention; then Crystal would practice the technique with men they passed in the park. *When a man looks at you like he is interested, give him a glance and a brief smile.*

In days, more men were jogging around the park to see them. They would get a glance and a slight smile if they were lucky. Crystal was becoming convinced that men were the weaker sex because they were so easy to manipulate.

This new flirtatious behavior made her feel even more powerful. Not that she ever doubted her ability to manipulate the opposite sex, but overt sensuality felt weird and out of character for her.

More and more Underling workers in the park checked her out. They could lose their jobs for flirting with an Elite, but they couldn't help themselves. She hoped Brownstone would be so gullible. Crystal fine-tuned her newfound flirtation skills by smiling and conversing casually whenever she encountered the opposite sex. She was amazed at how easy it was to mesmerize men by giving them so little attention.

Roxanne made it clear that Brownstone would only be attracted to someone unique. *So, Crystal, just be yourself.*

On the last day of seduction training, Crystal accidentally runs ahead of Roxanne because of her genetic superiority. When she looks back, two men are getting a little too friendly with Roxanne. Crystal can tell by Roxanne's body language that she isn't comfortable. Crystal kicks her pace into high gear, racing toward them. One of the brutes grabs Roxanne's arm. The other man is only inches away from her face. Approaching them, she screams, "Hey! Let her go!"

One of them replied, "It looks like we got ourselves another party girl." His buddy laughs his approval.

Before they can react, Crystal jumps into action. She kicks the talkative one in the face, knocking him out cold. Then she chokes the other freak by his throat with her left hand as her right-hand grabs his crotch. She presses him over her head and slams him into the ground.

"You broke my back; you broke my back!" The man writhes on the ground at Ice's feet.

Roxanne stares with her mouth gaping open. She's never witnessed what a Gen Elite seven warrior could do. The talker wakes up, moaning.

"Take your buddy and leave before I call Park Patrol," Crystal orders. They shoot one last glance at Roxanne before they hobble away, bloodied, bruised, and humiliated.

She puts a hand on Roxanne's shoulder. "Are you okay?"

Roxanne nods, but there's a quiet pain behind her eyes. Crystal saw that pain in the eyes of the woman in the desert when she was thirteen. Sometimes, she sees it in her own reflection. For better or worse, their relationship had changed. Now they share an unfortunate bond of surviving sexual harassment.

With one week to go until her mission, she meets with Zander to be briefed about the capabilities of the Underlings.

"When the Underlings are on patrol, they have plenty of muscle and weapons. And if one patrol approaches you, they are backed up by another. Don't be overconfident when you encounter them; comply with their instructions. Your mission is to gather intelligence and report back to me. Brownstone, a former Special Forces Military Commander has trained them. He won many commendations in the Great War."

Zander then gives her blueprints of the general layout of the Underlings' massive underground facility, Area 62, home to about three thousand of them.

Soon it's time for their final preparations. Zander had her injected with biological markers, so they would always know her whereabouts. Then she had her test flight on the sky cycle to determine how far it would go on a two-percent battery charge.

Crystal can't deny her mixed feelings about the mission. She wouldn't wait for further instructions if they harmed her brother. She would exact revenge herself. This thing with Brownstone concerned her. She'd become confident in her feminine charm but controlling her emotions around a man who might have killed or captured her brother would be difficult. It would certainly be easier to kill him rather than seduce him. Even so, Roxanne's stories about how the handsome Brownstone bewitched the nomadic women who traversed the Mojave excited her in a way.

Regardless of her nerves, she will face the Underlings head-on to find Caleb. Showing vulnerability would be to her advantage with Brownstone. Roxanne was adamant that her persona as Ice would not work.

On her last night in Imperial City, she has difficulty falling asleep. She's supposed to be more than human, keeping her emotions at bay, but nights like this hint that all isn't as it should be.

She keeps thinking back to her prior life with Marci and Caleb. Marci was always there for them. Caleb was determined to find her even after he got older and understood the purpose of removing Elite children.

Marci would pray to her Christian God, asking him to look after her little angels and keep them safe. Caleb and Crystal would get on their knees as small children, mimicking her prayer. After she vanished in the middle of the night, there was an emptiness inside Crystal. Taking on the cold-killer persona of Ice was a coping mechanism as much as anything else. Marci's abandonment of her and Caleb left a lasting distrust of every Underling.

She woke up by 5:30 a.m. for her usual morning grooming and sunscreen. Even her genetic superiority didn't come with built-in UV resistance. After devouring a breakfast of yogurt, fresh fruits, and granola, she grabs her duffle bag. It only contains two outfits—one is a black snug-fitting workout suit that highlights her curves that Roxanne insisted she take. The other is a cute pair of blue shorts with a matching tank top. Roxanne's voice reemerges in her head. *Once Brownstone looks at those long legs of yours, he won't stand a chance.*

Zander meets her at the flight center. They go over the plan once again to the very last detail. Once he's convinced she understands the plan, he pulls her aside. Then, through clenched teeth, he hisses, "Brownstone is mine; you understand?"

Crystal glares at him and smirks. "Sure." She knows Zander is jealous, but she won't allow his desire to kill Brownstone prevent her from killing him if she gets the chance. She crams her duffle bag into the small cargo compartment under the seat, hops on the sky cycle, and pushes the start button. As the engines roar to life, a surge of adrenaline flows through her. There have been enough rehearsals, seduction training, and the importance of the mission mumbo-jumbo. Now it's time to enforce Elite justice on the arrogant Underlings.

The four turbo engines fire and generate a powerful downward thrust lifting her sky cycle fifty feet in the air; she relishes the thrill of vertical takeoff. She pushes the throttle forward, soaring up to two hundred feet, and quickly reaches a cruising speed of one hundred miles per hour. After clearing Imperial City's air space, she lets the sky cycle drift down so it hovers just fifteen feet above the ground. At this height, she can see the desert coming to life with the dawn of a new day as the sunrise peaks above the horizon.

As the day continues, that life hides back in its dens to avoid the day's heat. The occasional Joshua tree drifts past with its erratic branches and spindly leaves. Jimsonweeds, with their beautiful lavender trumpet-shaped blooms, draw her attention. She knows better than to approach the Jimsonweed, or Devil's Snare as some call it. It can be a weary traveler's doom because its bristly fruit and odd-smelling leaves could cause an emotional breakdown, sickness, or even death.

Roxanne told her Brownstone was pleasing to the eyes. Maybe Brownstone is like the Devil's Snare, pleasant to the eyes but deadly inside.

She watches the charge on her sky cycle decrease and give warning signs. In less than five minutes, she would be at the predetermined site for her encounter with the Underlings. Her experience as an Elite Strike Force Commander made her supremely confident. She had never failed to complete a mission. Even so, something felt different about this one.

Maverick and his crew are on patrol in the Mojave, instructed explicitly to watch for one Gen Elite seven, one who supposedly left Imperial City, one Imperial City desperately wanted back. The sun has just risen, with only a few white clouds appearing sporadically. He navigates a modified jeep equipped with a steel-reinforced frame, a bulletproof windshield, a .50-caliber machine gun mounted in the back, and camouflaged side windows to blend into the hostile desert terrain.

Riding shotgun is Brock, a big bull of a man standing six feet four inches tall, weighing on the upper side of two hundred and seventy-five pounds, forty-five years of age, with muscles bulging out of every part of his body. Brock was a former Division one NCAA All-American Defensive Lineman.

Riding in the back is Raven, a seemingly small young lady, just twenty-three years old. She has jet-black hair, a pierced nose, and tattoos covering her arms and back. Despite her small stature, Raven is wiry and stout as most men twice her size. No one knows weapons more than her, and she also happens to be a skilled martial artist.

Maverick stands six feet three inches tall and weighs 235 pounds of solid muscle. He practiced martial arts his whole life and used to be a member of the Special Forces, having fought in the Great War to the bitter end. Even though he was only thirty years old, he had a lifetime of experience in the ways of war.

Less than one hundred yards away, a sky cycle falls from the sky, landing hard in the sand. He pushes the accelerator to the floor, causing the hydrogen-fueled jeep to surge forward. He wants to be on top of the pilot before he can react.

They arrive just as the pilot dismounts. He's shocked as the pilot takes off her helmet, and long, blond hair falls over her shoulders. The lady is put together. She looks like an angelic being cast down to earth. He tried to make his eyes focus on her face, even though her snug-fitting Gen Elite uniform kept drawing his attention. She's stunning! He knows who she is. Therefore, he must alter his voice so that she won't recognize him.

Crystal lands her sky cycle as the battery life approaches zero right in the hotbed of Underling activity. A modified jeep with a three-person crew accelerates toward her. They jump out of their jeep in a flash and promptly surround her. They have thick cloths covering their faces and reflective sunglasses hiding their eyes.

"Put your hands up," their leader orders in a deep Irish voice.

She stares him down, letting him know he can't intimidate her. "Underling, I strongly advise you to stand down and take me to your leader." She can take them. The big brute standing to the leader's right is a little concerning, but Crystal isn't worried about the little wiry female standing to her left.

The leader raises his voice. "Get on your knees! Hands behind your head. Now!"

Her pride wouldn't let her back down. "I'm warning you, you pompous ass Underling. Don't come any closer!"

He moves fast, closing the distance. She launches a lighting roundhouse kick right at the arrogant Underling's head. He partially blocks the kick, much to her surprise. The big man rushes to her left side. She kicks him in the chest, causing him to stagger backward. The wiry female tries to kick her in the face, but she catches her by the ankle and flips her hard to the ground.

Their leader seizes Crystal's distraction and flashes off to her left. He grabs the back of her neck with his right hand and trips her front foot before she can react, slamming her face-first into the sand. The force knocks the breath out of her.

He quickly twists Crystal's wrists behind her back, holding her down.

"Brock," he mutters.

"Yeah," the brute says in a southern drawl. The leader doesn't need to say anything else for Brock to slap handcuffs on her wrists.

"Raven? Would you—"

She nods. The brute holds her legs down as the wiry girl puts on the leg irons. The leader picks Crystal up roughly, throwing her over his right shoulder with his hand tightly gripping her buttocks.

"Let go of me!" she yells. To be manhandled was one thing, but hauled around like this? She'd gut him the first chance she got. She'd never been so humiliated. The leader carries her to the jeep and plops her down in the back seat.

Crystal's eyes are ablaze with anger. Her assignment was to get caught. But this? Pitiful. She can't resist a jab at them. "Who gave you such cornball names? You're like characters in some poorly written action movie."

Maverick laughs. "An Elite who is the head of her class in humor, but last in self-defense." They all laugh at her, infuriating her even more.

They quickly put a covering over her head, and the jeep pulls away. Her duffle bag is still back in the sky cycle. So much for Roxanne's clothing suggestion.

"So, what's a Princess of Elite society doing out here in the Mojave?" Maverick asks.

"Take this covering off my head, and I'll tell you."

"Sorry, what was that, *Princess*? We can't hear you through the rag over your head." Their laughter fills the Jeep.

"I will beat all three of you to a bloody pulp!"

Brock's gruff voice cuts through the laughter. "What we have here is an Elite who can't fight, can't hear, and is oblivious to her present dilemma." They laugh again.

She's had enough of their petty prodding. "I will not talk to anyone whose name is not Brownstone." Once again, they laugh. Crystal smiles under her head covering. They don't know the hell coming their way. Just the way she likes it.

Crystal bounces around the backseat like a pinball with her hands cuffed behind her back. It's like she's stuck in human purgatory. She longs for her former life, where she was treated according to her status. *Caleb, this better be worth it. You better not be dead.*

*Pull it together, Ice. These bullies are hardly as bad as Brownstone will be, and you'll have to flirt with him. Maybe it's too much to hope he won't be a cave-dwelling barbarian like Maverick.* At least Raven made sure her shoulder strap was secure.

Maverick drives as if his life depends on getting to a safe place.

She would be naive to believe Zander or Steadman had told her the whole goal. They always have ulterior motives. Anything is possible with those two. Her life might be part of the collateral damage in their calculations, whether she liked that or not.

She settles herself and uses her training to pay attention, even with the bag over her head. The jeep was facing directly east when they put her in it. When Maverick turns the jeep around, she can no longer see the sun's brightness. Crystal estimates they travel thirty minutes west before stopping. If for some reason, her bio-trackers don't give Zander the location, she can give them a close approximation of the Underlings' whereabouts. Strange mechanical hums surround the vehicle—an elevator, maybe? The dropping sensation in her stomach confirms it. They lift her out of the jeep, place her on a gurney, stick a needle in her arm, and take her into an operating room. Whatever was in that shot must have been a sedative. Dizziness overtakes her, and then she goes unconscious.

She wakes up slowly in a large open recovery room. Someone nearby speaks softly. "We got them all, Brownstone." *Got all of what?* She fights her way out of the darkness. Then it hits her. The biomarkers. They had to be talking about the biomarkers. A nurse shushes them and yells, "Hey Doc, we got a live one here."

A man dressed in blue scrubs rises from a gray metal desk on the opposite side of the recovery room. He moves like a powerful man, not like a typical lab coat. She can't take her eyes off him. He's tall, handsome, with curly black hair, and pure green eyes. She's seen him before. The drugs in her mind make it hard to place. He was never in Imperial City ... Then it hits her. The sound of waves and the feel of his hand in hers.

Her attraction to him was decided long ago. There's no denying it. This is the man from her recurring dream, minus the scar on his cheek. She feels a strong desire to throw him down and take him, which is out of character for her.

"Unlock her, won't you?" The nurse obeys. "Hello. My name is Dr. James Brownstone, but you can call me Brownstone; everyone does." She hopes her training keeps him from seeing the conflict she feels. The dream shatters around her. This man could be responsible for the demise of her brother.

All her instincts scream to attack him right then and there. She narrowly reigns herself in and forces a smile on her face. "I'm Crystal."

He perches on the side of her bed. "What's a princess of Elite society doing out here in the Mojave?"

She swallows. She has to sell this story. "I ..." She pauses. *Don't come on too strong. Pretend you're vulnerable.* "I committed an unpardonable sin. I killed a fellow Elite."

She checks to make sure she has his attention, so she continues. The best lies were mostly truth.

"I was jogging in Imperial Park one day when I saw two Elite males assaulting an Underling female. Acting on instinct, I rushed to her rescue. The Elite males turned their attention to me as I approached, and a fight ensued. I knocked out the first attacker with a snap kick to his head. The second attacker was bigger and stronger. He kept coming forward, even after I hit him several times. So, I punched him in the temple. He crumpled to the ground." She pauses to read his face, but his emotions are as locked up as hers are. "The punch was a fatal blow. He never regained consciousness."

"That's an interesting story. I don't know if I believe it or not. Are you sure Steadman didn't send you here to look for the missing Elites?"

Panic flares in her chest. If he doesn't believe her, this whole mission is over before it begins. "I know what I did. I rescued a young Underling female from an attack. I don't appreciate my word being questioned!"

He laughs. "Your reputation proceeds you, *Ice*. Steadman sends you out to deal with difficult security issues. We know Marci Jenkins raised you and your twin brother until your thirteenth birthday. You earned your nickname, Ice, because you've been able to keep your human emotions at bay. That, and no one's forgotten what you did in your first test run in the desert. The only people you've ever been close to are Caleb and Marci."

She listens without interrupting, even though she wants to. Brownstone's analysis makes her feel like she is his patient. She won't give him the satisfaction of knowing he's right.

She does her best to avoid memories of Marci vanishing in the middle of the night. Those memories make her sad, and she can't be sad. Not now. Human emotions are beneath a Gen Elite seven warrior!

"So, you have spies, big deal."

He smiles, and it's infuriating how charming he is. She wants to punch that smile off his stupidly attractive face.

"I wouldn't say we have spies in Imperial City, but I will say the pipeline of the goings-on there is wide open."

She needs to get her bearings, so she looks around. In the recovery room, some administering care to the sick are Elites. Why are Elites administering care to Underlings? You can tell an Elite's rank by a tattoo on the underside of their right wrist. The mark will be an intertwined G and a number that signifies what generation of Elite they are. She observes a couple of Gen Elite five's and six's administering care to the sick and wounded.

Perturbed, she says, "So, you have enslaved Elites as your servants?"

"Not at all. They work here, live here, and are free to come and go as they please, just as anyone else."

This is propaganda, and she won't fall for it. "Why would they work for you when they can work in Imperial City?"

"From what they tell me, they like it here and feel appreciated, but you are free to ask them. Maybe Elite society isn't all it proposes to be."

This pompous Underling is irritating. Crystal attempts to get up from the hospital bed, but Brownstone puts his hand on her shoulder, pushing her down. His touch feels warm on her skin, and she can feel the heat from his body transferring directly to hers. "Crystal, your hospital gown opens from the back. You might not want to expose yourself like that if you have any modesty. Or maybe with perfection, modesty isn't necessary?"

"Could someone get my clothes?"

He beckons with his hand and shouts, "We need wardrobe and makeup at bed six." Then he grins big. "Check that; we just need wardrobe; this girl doesn't need any makeup!"

She surprises herself by blushing when their eyes meet. He's flirting with her, and it feels weird. Good, maybe, but weird at the same time. *Keep your head, Ice. He could still be a murderer.*

In minutes, curtains are pulled around her, and a nurse's aide rolls in a rack full of clothes. Brownstone looks her up and down. "These clothes are yours to use while you are here as our guest. I'm sure you'll find they fit perfectly."

How does he know these clothes will fit her perfectly? Did they measure her naked body? Did he see her naked?

He's a doctor, but the thought of him seeing her nude leaves Crystal with an uneasy feeling.

A Gen Elite five walks inside the curtains; the lady is stunning with perfect ebony skin. "Hello, Crystal. Do you remember me from Imperial City?"

"I remember you. Claire. You worked at the Academy of Elites. You were my martial arts instructor from age thirteen until I turned fifteen. I earned my first two black belts under your tutelage. What happened, Claire? You just vanished."

"I got reassigned when the Gen Elite sixes came of age and took leadership positions."

"My training lagged because your replacement didn't have your level of expertise. Where did they reassign you?"

"They moved me to the robotics factory where I took over as shift supervisor from a Gen Elite four they reassigned."

*Now I get it.* "Now you work for humans who aren't as smart as you so that you won't be reassigned?"

"Not at all. Most humans here are way above-average intelligence. Around twenty-five percent of the humans here are scientists. They worked here at the government research facility before the war. Some are children of scientists and have grown up in the compound. This is the only type of life they have ever known. I came here a couple of years ago when I heard Elites were welcome. Even though genetic engineering has manipulated our DNA, we are just as human as the Underlings."

*Just as human ... We're supposed to be better than them. Supposed to be different. How could so many Elites be working here voluntarily—for the Underlings?* Brownstone's critique of Elite society makes her uneasy. After suffering the humiliation of being taken down by a human barbarian named Maverick, the last twenty-four hours hadn't been great for her ego. The whole world seemed upside down.

"It is good to see you again, Crystal. You were always my favorite student. I'll step out and let you have your privacy. If you need anything, call." Claire steps out from the curtain.

Still uneasy, Crystal turns to the suitcase, where she finds an assortment of undergarments from which she chooses a matching set. Next, she selects light blue mid-thigh shorts and a complimentary white short-sleeve pullover with blue sleeves. She finishes the look with a pair of white tennis shoes. It's not quite the outfit Roxanne had in mind, but it might still work for her mission.

After dressing, she steps out from the curtains, where Brownstone is waiting. He has a big grin on his face and looks her up and down, admiring her beauty. He makes her feel weird. Again. How can this mere man have such an effect on her?

He changed from his scrubs, wearing khaki pants and a blue pullover short-sleeve polo shirt. His rippling muscles bulge through his shirt. He is a formidable man, at least for an Underling. He winks at her. "You clean up nice for an Elite." She flashes a smile and flips her hair without meaning to. This man is a walking encyclopedia of charm, but Roxanne's tips work. She catches him admiring her long, tanned legs.

"You're probably hungry since you haven't eaten since yesterday. Will you have breakfast with me? Afterward, I would love to show you around the facility."

"Of course, if you're buying?"

He seems too helpful. She knows it's part of the Underlings' plan to manipulate her. For now, she has a lot of questions and few answers. She will sort out this facade regardless of the charming devil and complete the mission.

# CHAPTER 3

They leave the recovery room, walking through a winding series of tunnels. The corridors are brightly lit and have different-colored walls. Everything is clean and well maintained, and the hallways have a fresh lemon scent, but she is underground, like an animal. He said she's not a prisoner, but she is trapped in this dungeon hell hole. At least in the dome, she could see the sunshine and feel its warmth.

The cafeteria is bright and bustling, with people talking, laughing, and eating. Flowers and plants are placed strategically to give the place a sense of life, unlike the tunnels. The average person would be lost after going through the winding maze of corridors, but not Crystal. She knew her way back to the recovery room. It wouldn't take her long to map out this underground maze.

Brownstone helps her pick out a tray and silverware as they walk through the line. Surprisingly, the buffet offers a variety of healthy foods. The breakfast bar has various fruits, yogurts, traditional eggs, bacon, and pancakes.

Many greet Brownstone like he's a conquering hero. Several ask him about the whereabouts of the Truth Seeker. To every one of them, Brownstone says the Truth Seeker is out on an assignment and will return shortly.

He leans over after the most recent questioner leaves. "If you're wondering, the Truth Seeker is my friend. We often meet here to break bread and converse. So, when one isn't here, the other will get asked about him."

She hates it, but she's relieved that the Truth Seeker isn't a woman. After not eating in over twenty-four hours, she fills her tray with fruit, scrambled eggs, and bacon. Brownstone loads his plate down with a little of everything.

Wanting privacy, he guides her to the back of the cafeteria. "I haven't eaten in quite some time because a princess dropped out of the sky, and I was the doctor on call." He flashes her a charming smile, and she thinks of the Jimsonweed flowers she passed. "The Princess is gorgeous; for some strange reason, they call her Ice. Do you know her? She's amazing!"

Crystal flashes him a smile. Roxanne warned her about this. He's flirting with her. She'd expected it to be harder to flirt back.

"She kept me quite busy taking care of her. I stayed awake all night just in case she awoke and needed anything."

With a devious smile, she comes back at him. "It's nice to know you're my servant, willing to do whatever I desire."

His smile deepens as he observes the twinkle in her eyes.

The cafeteria is decorated with care, having beautiful murals of religious themes, families, and children playing across the walls. The floor is a beautiful mosaic.

After a lull in the conversation, Crystal brings up part of her unfinished business. She wants to find the barbarian Maverick and even the score. "Can you take to me to see Maverick? I want to thank him for taking such good care of me."

Brownstone's face falls into a stern glare. "You know I can't have you going around beating up my men. I want you to ponder what you would have done if the shoe was on the other foot." Crystal glares at him, letting her silence speak for itself. She would find Maverick and even the score, whether Brownstone likes it or not.

Brownstone changes the subject. "Crystal, I know Caleb is your brother. You must have questions. I assure you, I will do my best to answer them."

"You know my brother?"

"Yes, I know him. All I can say is that there are many things you don't know about him. He didn't share everything with you. That was for your well-being. He didn't want to jeopardize your place in Elite society."

*Who in the hell is he to tell me I don't know my brother? The arrogance of this Underling knows no bounds.* She can't hold back, firing off a series of questions. "Where is Caleb? Is he a prisoner? When can I see him?"

"Caleb isn't here, but we expect him back within the week. You can see him as soon as he returns. He's free to come and go like anyone else. Your brother is a friend, and I want to ensure his sister is treated with kindness and respect."

"Why would you help me? Aren't we supposed to be enemies?"

"I'm not your enemy! And I feel confident you won't be my enemy either when your questions are answered. Our purpose here is no threat to you or the Gen Elites. We just want to live in peace according to the tenants of our faith."

The only thing worse than a religious fanatic is a charming one. He'll look you right in the eyes and make you think his sole purpose is to serve you. Roxanne's warnings float through her head again. *He's ruggedly handsome and charming, with a penchant for beautiful blondes.* Roxanne warned her not to over or under-react to him. *Show him a little interest, but not so much that he will think you're easy but valuable.*

She must stay focused on the mission: discover their capabilities and find the missing Elites. Crystal already knows some Elites are working for the Underlings. Finding Caleb is her number one priority. Her brother would be a big prize for them. She won't let them take him from her. Brownstone is too willing to help. He must be up to something.

What if Brownstone's doing the same thing she is? Flirting to get close to her and figure out what she's up to? When their eyes meet, his face lights up, and a smile creases his lips. She hates to admit it, but she's drawn to him in a primal way. In retrospect, she thought being attracted to this man would have taken a superhuman effort. On the contrary, she must fight her attraction to him with every fiber of her being. She hadn't felt this conflicted since her thirteenth birthday when Marci vanished in the middle of the night. The last thing she desires is to get burned again by another Underling. Crystal needs more answers, but she can tell Brownstone isn't going to say any more on the subject.

After breakfast, Brownstone takes her on a tour of the facility. He secures the use of a refurbished old golf-type vehicle he refers to as an electric buggy. They travel through a maze of tunnels wide enough for two-way electric cart traffic with walking lanes on both sides.

"We'll start at the research lab. My uncle, Dr. Robert Forrester, wants to meet you."

The research facility is large and clean, with many workstations, each filled by someone: some Elite fives and sixes, some Underlings, and some people who don't look like either. The facility houses advanced analyzing equipment. She recognizes some of it from a similar lab in Imperial City. He takes her over to a distinguished-looking, tall, white-haired man who looks to be in his middle fifties. As they get closer, she sees a resemblance to Brownstone in the older man.

"Hey, Uncle Rob, this is Crystal."

The gentleman sets down what he's working on and looks up at them. Then he smiles and replies, "Nice to meet you, Crystal. Your brother told us much about you. I must say your beauty has not been exaggerated. We are very fond of Caleb, who has made life better for our people in many ways.

"Because you have several advanced degrees in the hard sciences, I'm extending an open invitation for you to participate in any research projects of your choosing. We would like you to stick around like your brother. Caleb comes down here several times per week and helps with various research projects. If you have questions, I'll be glad to answer them to the best of my ability."

Crystal looks around. "Who are the ones that don't look like Underlings or Elites?"

Forrester replies, "They are your missing brothers and sisters from the Gen Elite family. They are Gen Elite twos. Unfortunately, we couldn't save the Gen Elite ones."

"I don't understand. We were told the earlier versions of Gen Elites were reassigned to work overseas."

"I wish that were the case, but the truth is more sinister. As you may or may not know, Dr. Steadman and I were colleagues. We were pioneers together in genetic engineering. Steadman was my supervisor. We both saw the advancement of artificial intelligence as a threat to humanity. We were making significant breakthroughs at this very lab in genetic engineering." He gestures around with the pencil he holds. Then he shakes his head. "Steadman and I had a falling out. He wanted to proceed with experiments using the eggs of donor mothers and enhanced genetic male sperm to fertilize them. The thought was to place the genetically enhanced embryo back into the mother's womb.

"I had serious reservations about the success of the project. Not in our expertise to genetically engineer intelligence and athleticism, but concerned that our procedure could damage the telomeres, the genetic strands that control aging. If we created a super race, how would it be better than those not enhanced regarding a social conscience? As you probably realize, Imperial City is not the perfect utopian society Steadman proposed. Elites have their share of jealousy, hatred, infighting, and deviance."

Crystal thought back to the Elites she knew. Even the best Elites were far from perfect, dabbling in things they should never have been able to in the first place. But this Underling has no place to criticize those superior to him.

"Steadman and I went our separate ways. He ended up at the government laboratories in Los Alamos, New Mexico, and I stayed here at Area 62. Dr. Steadman and his team enhanced the first three generations of Elites at Los Alamos. Gen Elite ones had shortened telomeres, so their life expectancy was only twenty years. When Steadman realized how short their lifespan was, he immediately started enhancing Gen Elites twos and threes to replace them. To Steadman, the Gen Elites ones were expendable. He feared the Great War was about to begin, so he brought his research team back to the desert along with manual laborers, robots, and Gen Elites in the year 2048. His goal was to build a domed utopian society, but he didn't start there. He originally moved into what you call your underground factories or mines, which are outside but connected to the Dome. Incidentally, the factories, as you call them, were initially branches of *this* facility. We were doing research there at the height of our government funding. However, before Steadman could complete his domed city, the Great War started, and nuclear radiation fell over much of the earth. We were fortunate because the desert winds carried away most of the radiation but not all of it.

"Steadman, knowing Gen Elite one's life expectancy was shortened, put them to work out in the desert along with human workers and robots to build his dome. He was aware the radiation would kill them sooner than later. A few Gen Elites and humans abandoned the build and made their way to our facility. We did our best to treat them, but it was too late to save them. All we could do was ease their suffering with medication and listen to their stories. We showed them the love they had never known in Elite society."

*The knowledge of Steadman lying to them all these years about the missing Elites is a hard pill to swallow. Is all Elite history just a lie?*

"The problem with genetic enhancement is that each previous generation of Elites becomes expendable when the new one arrives. The very nature of the experiment creates a caste system of haves and have-nots. That's why many Elites are living and working here. We do not treat them better or worse than anyone else. To live here, they agree not to demean anyone they perceive as inferior to them."

Forrester's critique of Elite society angers Crystal. His analysis hits a little too close to home. Her anger doesn't stop with his critique but extends to Steadman for discarding the Gen Elite ones as if their lives didn't matter. Her mission is becoming more complicated with what she's learning. Crystal must find Caleb! Her brother will tell her straight.

In her most sarcastic voice, she says, "How is your society any better than ours? Do I need to go through the course of human history and list all the atrocities and genocides committed by your lineage of people? Not to mention four world wars and the deaths of millions fought over religion. You are in no position to judge us!"

"Certainly, no society is perfect because we all fail in our humanness. Our community is governed by a Council of Twelve Elders, in which the majority rules. You are correct about the atrocities committed in the name of religion. We're imperfect people serving a perfect God. And, I agree, we have no right to judge anyone," Forrester responds.

"Are you on the Council? Are there any Elites on the Council? And does your faith play a role in how your council governs this place?" She wants to keep him on the defensive.

Brownstone stares intently at his uncle, hoping he will get the hint. This conversation needs to end well if he is going to gain Crystal's trust.

"We have Elites on the council. My role on the council is more of a facilitator. I don't have voting rights unless there is a tie; then, I will be the deciding vote. And we try to do *everything* by the precepts of our faith."

Seeking to end the conversation with the cocky Underling, she says, "Thank you for your time, Dr. Forrester. I appreciate your invitation to come and take part in research projects."

"We could use another brilliant mind down here." With that, he calls his research coordinator over to meet Crystal. "I assume you already know Simone from Imperial City."

"I do. Simone was one of our best and brightest."

Even dressed in a lab coat, Simone's beauty was impressive. Her flawless caramel-colored skin, blond hair, and green eyes stood out among the Underlings. How in the world did the Underlings snag the brilliant Gen 6 scientist?

"Simone will give you an overview of our research projects. You can pick the ones that interest you."

Simone gives her a tour of the research projects and introduces her to the project leaders. Crystal is interested in several projects dealing with radiation decontamination, biological warfare treatments, and virus vaccines. Simone explains that Cognition tried to kill off most remaining humans with various biological weapons through the years. Dr. Forrester and the scientists who work here saved countless human lives more than once by creating the vaccines that were so desperately needed.

Simone shows Crystal various lab machines, equipment, and the lab's supercomputer. As interested as she was in the research, Crystal is more interested in using the opportunity to work in the lab to gain more information from the Underlings.

"Some of our greatest breakthroughs come when Caleb helps us brainstorm solutions to various research issues." Simone looks over at an empty workstation. *That must be where Caleb usually works.*

Crystal thanks Simone for the tour and meets up with Brownstone and his uncle in the lab's office. Both men rise when she enters the room. "Well, Uncle, we better let you get back to it," Brownstone says.

"Don't forget to invite Crystal to dine with us tonight." Forrester winks.

Brownstone smiles and immediately turns toward Crystal. "May we have the great honor of your presence at dinner?"

She wants to say yes, just so she can sit across from his dazzling smile again, but the history lesson from Forrester is still tumbling around her head. *Remember the mission.* She plasters a smile on her face. "Well, of course, James."

They smile.

She expected this to be a lot harder than it was turning out to be. She doesn't have to work at establishing a relationship with them like she thought. Instead, they seem intent on forming a relationship with her. Crystal's task of gaining information from them is going remarkably well. Though, she doesn't trust those who believe in the myth of Christianity.

They leave the lab, and Brownstone gives her a guided tour of the compound's atriums, immense cave-like structures with dome-like retractable roofs giving the illusion of being outside. Some atriums are for growing varieties of fruits and vegetables, others for raising large and small animals. They even have domed areas set aside for recreation.

She's most impressed with the Eden Atrium, where they grow most fruits, vegetables, and flowers. A stream flows through the middle, fed by a waterfall that cascades over a rock formation at one end. A rock walkway runs the length of the stream on both sides, accompanied by an abundance of gorgeous flowers in every color combination. Small bridges over each end of the stream make for an oval walking path, complete with park benches placed next to the walkway where visitors can rest and watch the stream.

This space can't be more than a few thousand feet long, but it's beautiful despite the small space. Brownstone smiles. "If you like it now, you should come here at night when the moonlight glistens off the stream."

She blushes at the thought of coming here with him when the moon is high. She wants to change the subject before he knows he's flustered her. As she looks around, she sees several children and adults working in the gardens. "Shouldn't they be in school?" she says.

"Learning how to grow food is part of their education and survival. Don't get me wrong; we strongly emphasize academics."

Many children wave at them, and one boy yells, "Brownstone, when are you going to teach P.E. again?" Then the other kids join in, pleading with him.

He looks at her and says, "I will as long as Ms. Crystal helps me teach the class."

Then the kids plead in unison, "Please, Ms. Crystal, please."

He set a little trap for her. She thinks fast and says, "Okay, we will do it, and Dr. James will show you how to do two hundred pushups in a row." Two can play that game. The kids roar their approval.

He rolls his eyes. "Aren't you a clever one? I can't believe you played me like that."

She smiles and says, "Just trying to keep up."

He grins, shaking his head.

Next, he takes her to the recreation atrium. There are full-sized tennis, badminton, volleyball, and basketball courts: a pool, a dojo, and a workout room. Near the top of the atrium is a rubber-like track for runners, joggers, and walkers, with its steel frame secured to the cave wall. She's even more amazed when she sees the staffed juice bar in the back corner.

He shows her the martial arts dojo first. She looks around at the space appreciatively. It's big enough to teach a large class. "I know you are a practitioner of martial arts. So, I am inviting you to come to the Rec Center and practice martial arts with me."

"Working out with me might not be good for your male ego. The Gen sevens are more advanced than previous versions in athletic ability. I can run faster than twenty-five miles per hour, snatch up a man your size, and press him over my head easily."

Crystal walks over to the heavy punching bag and kicks it so hard that the chain breaks, causing it to crash onto the mat. She glares at him and says, "Your call."

He looks at her with a smirk on his face and winks. "I'll take my chances, Ice." Crystal has mixed feelings. Usually, she would beat up an Underling for talking to her like that. He complicated things by winking at her. Flirting with him is part of her mission. She doesn't want to blow the mission by kicking his butt, not yet, anyway.

She grabs another punching bag from the storage area along the wall and sets it up. Using the distraction, she asks, "Why did you leave your parents in Australia?"

He takes a breath. Is he nervous? Does he want to avoid the question? It's hard to say. "After the androids overran my homeland. I returned home to find them, but they weren't there. Their cars were parked in the garage, phones left on the sofa table, and half-empty coffee cups on the kitchen counter." He walks over and helps secure the bag in place. She almost tells him she's got it, but there he is in her space again, intoxicating her senses.

He just shared something emotional. That means her assignment is working. She lowers her voice. "What do you think happened to them?"

"I'm not sure. No one has heard from them in seven years. I pray the androids didn't get them." His voice is just as quiet as hers. Then he looks down at his watch. "Are you hungry? The cafeteria's open for lunch."

They share a light lunch and talk about almost everything under the sun. Brownstone has a fantastic depth of knowledge. Regardless of their topic, he has a good grasp of the subject. Learning he's thirty years old, only a four-year age difference, draws her to him more. After lunch, Brownstone takes her to her living quarters—a small, efficient one-bedroom apartment with an open floor plan featuring no walls between the living room and kitchen. The bedroom features a queen-sized mission bed with a dresser, chest, and two nightstands. She has a private bathroom off the bedroom and a closet with ample space to hang her clothes, despite not having many of her own here yet.

"Sorry, it's so small. Space is at a premium underground. The bigger, multiple-bedroom apartments are reserved for couples with children," Brownstone says. "And we'll bring your choice of clothes up from our supplies."

She focuses her attention on him again. "How come you never had children?"

"It wasn't because I didn't want to. My first wife left me when I was away fighting in the Great War before we had a chance. After the Great War, there was nothing left for me in Australia, so I came to America to reunite with my uncle. I was still bitter over being dumped and not even thinking about getting into a relationship, much less having children. I figured I would be killed fighting the Humbots or by an Elite patrol.

"When I was twenty-four, I met Lece, and everything changed. She was beautiful, pure of heart, and a lady who demanded respect. Lece was a freedom fighter like me. She was a lady of great faith with high standards. Because of her, I found the true meaning of love and life. Love is not about what you get but what you give others, expecting nothing in return.

"I gave myself completely to her: heart, body, and soul. But in the end, it was she who saved my life; she stepped in front of a Humbot drone and took bullets meant for me. We planned on having kids and even had a date set to start trying. It was the weekend before her death."

Tears formed at the corners of his eyes. He took a breath to steady himself. "I'm sorry. I can't talk about her anymore. I'll pick you up for dinner at 5:30 p.m. sharp. You know how those old-timers like Uncle Rob are about time. They think you should be on time for some crazy reason." He turns to leave. Crystal isn't sure why, but she reaches out and pulls Brownstone into a hug before kissing him on the cheek.

"Where did that come from?" he asks, startled.

"Thanks for being so nice; you didn't have to," she says.

He smiles, then turns and walks out the door.

She stares at the door, wondering if Brownstone is using charm to distract her from the mission. So much for having to fake an attraction to him. She has a feeling she's in way over her head. She hopes her show of vulnerability touched him. There's something not right about how he immediately took such an interest in her. He must have ulterior motives for engaging with her in such a direct manner. No matter her attraction, she will exact Elite justice on him if he doesn't fulfill his promise to reunite her with Caleb.

That afternoon, she puts away the clothes delivered to her apartment. She checks the closet, relieved to find her Gen 7 uniform hanging in the closet and her boots lying on the floor. After taking a shower, she lies down, hoping to get some sleep, but her mind is racing. She can't stop thinking about the events of the day. And the hope that she will see Caleb soon.

How intertwined is Caleb's life with Brownstone's and Forrester's? How did Caleb become involved with the Underlings in the first place? How little does she actually know her brother? There are so many mysteries to unravel.

Crystal can't stop thinking about Brownstone, either. She blames her attraction to him on the dreams. She's drawn to him and will need all her Elite training to resist him. The Underlings present themselves as too good to be true. She doesn't trust those who believe in the cult of Christianity. Look where it got Marci. She doesn't want to see them murdered by Zander just because they believe in a myth. Her physical attraction to Brownstone will not sway her from completing the mission. She's just playing a role by befriending the Underling to gain his confidence.

Finally, she drifts off to sleep and wakes up around 5 p.m. Good thing she needs only a little time to get ready. Brownstone is right. She doesn't need makeup, and her hair just needs to be fluffed out. Still, she struggles with getting ready on time. Crystal settles on a violet-colored sundress that comes up several inches above her knees and white sandals to compliment her dress.

Brownstone knocks on the door at 5:30 p.m. She makes him wait for a moment before she swings the door wide open, stares at him, and says, "Whatever you're selling, I'm not buying."

"You are way too intelligent for me to sell you anything. I am just honored to be your escort tonight. You look stunning."

She smiles and offers him a wink. "Okay, escort. Let's go."

"You got it; your chariot awaits." He's wearing blue jeans, a light blue pullover shirt, and sand-colored casual shoes.

When they arrive at the dining hall, she understands better why they invited her. It isn't just about interrogating her. It seems it's an Underling tradition to invite guests to community dinners. Dr. Forrester introduces everyone to each other before they settle down to eat. There is a nomadic family of five, the McKevers: husband, wife, two daughters, and a son. The Johnsons are a bartering band of three brothers, Jeff, Brad, and Rick, who frequent the Mojave to sell and trade their wares. Dr. Forrester opens with a prayer, asking for an individual blessing on each. Crystal doesn't care for the Christian prayer but feels warm when Brownstone holds her hand.

The Johnsons tell tales about avoiding Humbot patrols, run-ins with Elite commandos, and fighting desert pirates. Brownstone avoids talking about himself and is content with letting others share their stories.

Robert Forrester shares, "James spent one summer with me at the ranch. The boy was constantly blowing stuff up. James wanted me to bring him to the lab. I knew I couldn't allow that boy anywhere near the lab. The way he blew things up, he would blow the whole state right off the map," he teases. "The people of Nevada don't know how many years I kept them alive.

"His parents would call and say James wants to be a scientist, just like you. I would tell them, 'Absolutely not. You sign that boy up for the military the day he turns eighteen and never let him anywhere near a lab. Do I make myself clear?' It was only recently that I let James in my lab."

"How recent was that?" Rick Johnson asks.

"Just last week." Everyone laughs.

Brownstone has an amused look on his face as his uncle roasts him. Humor must be a family trait for Brownstone and his uncle. For all their accomplishments, they don't take themselves too seriously.

"Crystal, you're bound to have some good stories," James prompts.

Crystal searches for one that won't share too much while still presenting a more vulnerable side. "One day, Caleb and I hid under Marci's bed, and she really couldn't find us. In despair, she picked up the phone, ready to report us missing. We slid out from under her bed and screamed. Marci jumped two feet in the air like Freddy Kreuger was trying to kill her. Marci's look let us know our lives were in mortal danger. We took off, running for our lives, with Marci in hot pursuit. I never knew anyone could move so fast in high heels! Marci caught us by the nape of our necks in the hallway. She marched us straight to our rooms, grounding us indefinitely. I asked meekly, 'How long are we grounded?' She replied. 'For the rest of your lives!'"

Brownstone chuckles and sips his wine. "Caleb told the same story. Except he said, *you* talked him into hiding under the bed and scaring Marci. The boy is innocent."

She smirks. "A girl has to do what a girl has to do."

Dessert is served, strawberry cheesecake and a glass of burgundy with the perfect sweetness. Dinner ends with hugs for everyone. Crystal has never felt so relaxed as she does in the company of Underlings, unlike in Elite society, where competition never takes a break. Sense of community or not, she won't be dissuaded from finding her brother. This might be an elaborate con job that Brownstone is putting on for her benefit.

Brownstone drives her back to the apartment. "This has been a great day! It's been so good to meet you. Caleb told me you were an impressive lady. After spending the day with you, I must admit he didn't exaggerate one bit."

He's a charming devil. "Thanks. You are quite an interesting person yourself." When they arrive at the apartment, he offers his hand to escort her to the door.

He leans in and kisses her on the cheek. "Thank you, Crystal."

She steps back, surprised by his gesture of affection. Not something that typically would happen in Elite society.

"For what?"

"You made me realize how much I miss female companionship. Will you join me for breakfast tomorrow?"

"Sure, if you're buying?"

"Goodnight, Crystal. I'll see you tomorrow for breakfast at 7 a.m."

"Goodnight, see you tomorrow." Crystal smiles at him. He lingers for a moment before smiling and walking backward a few steps. She closes her door, her own smile just as stuck to her face as the kiss lingering on her cheek.

She breathes deeply. He's hard to resist, but she's determined to play him for all it's worth.

Crystal sinks onto her bed and kicks off her shoes, her mind drifting back to Caleb. Will she even know the Caleb the Underlings described? What if Caleb has converted to the cult of Christianity? Is that even possible?

He is a Scientist. Most likely, the greatest scientist in all of history! Caleb deals with facts. Could he fall for a myth? A myth created by desert people thousands of years ago, trying to make themselves feel better about their miserable existence. She might not save the Elites who follow the myth of Christianity.

If Brownstone's word is accurate, she'll be reunited with Caleb soon. She'll find a way to get him away from this doomsday cult of Underlings and Elites before Zander kills them all.

Who is this mysterious Truth Seeker? Is he a friend of Caleb's? She wants answers now.

It won't be easy to pull back from Brownstone; a mysterious power attracts her to him. She knows it's illogical and against all her training, but he makes her feel very human. For the first time in her life, she understands the power of romantic attraction. Regardless, she won't allow him to stand in the way of finding her brother. He better deliver on his promises, or she will quickly turn unfriendly.

The following day, she meets Brownstone at the cafeteria, excited by his presence. *I'm playing a role. This is nothing more than flirtation.*

She's been thinking about it all morning. Without the trackers, she'll need a different way to check in with Zander. After they sit down in the backroom of the cafeteria, she breaks the news to Brownstone. "I'm ready to leave."

Brownstone sets down his cup, and a frown pulls at his mouth. "Are you sure? You just got here and haven't been reunited with Caleb yet."

"You said I am your guest, and I'm free to come and go. Well, now, I want to go."

He searches her face for a moment and then nods. Crystal suspects he knows she's planning to contact Zander and update him regarding the mission. "That's fine, Crystal. I assume you want to take your sky cycle?"

"Is it charged?"

"We charged it, and it's at our flight center. What time would you like to leave?"

"Ten this morning. If that's not an inconvenience?"

"No inconvenience at all."

This is a high-stakes game of cat and mouse. She assumes his mechanics have removed the transmitter from her sky cycle. He'll likely let her leave but intends to prevent her from contacting Zander.

She smiles at him and reaches over to touch his hand. "Thank you."

He squeezes her hand and then breaks contact, different from last night when it had seemed he couldn't get enough of her. She needs to check in with Zander, but she also needs to keep the flirtatious momentum going with Brownstone. Breakfast proceeds somewhat awkwardly, though she thinks she's recovered some ground by the time they put their plates away. He drives her back to her apartment and agrees to pick her up at 9:45 a.m.

She dresses in her Gen 7 flight suit and puts on her boots. She's eager to communicate with Zander and delay an attack on the compound until she locates and leaves with Caleb.

When they arrive at the flight center, Crystal mentally notes how many sky cycles and small vertical take-off planes the Underlings have in their arsenal. Brownstone gives her specific flight coordinates she will need to avoid being shot down by their defense missiles.

She mounts her sky cycle, powers up the engines, lifts off, and pushes the throttle forward. Brownstone watches her go, that charming smile back on his face. But it doesn't reach his eyes. Leaving Brownstone makes her feel weird for some reason. She checks under the dash for the transmitter. Just as she suspected, it was removed. So predictable. It didn't matter, though. They hadn't checked her flight suit, and she had a backup stashed in her right boot.

After she clears the Underlings' security perimeter five miles northwest of the compound, Crystal lands the sky cycle on the desert sand. Once steady, she removes her right boot, reaches inside under the insole, pulls out the hidden transmitter, and plugs it into the empty slot.

She puts her boot back on and lifts off again, climbing to a much higher elevation. She must reach a high enough altitude to get a clear signal without interference.

The message is simple. "I have located many of the missing Elites at the compound. They are there of their own volition. I've talked to some of them, and some appear to be indoctrinated into some cult of Christianity. They are led by some mysterious leader called the Truth Seeker. I haven't located Caleb, but the Underlings assure me he will return soon. I suggest we give them a week to present him. If they don't produce him, I will give my recommendations for a plan of attack."

She waits for confirmation of receipt. Then Zander's voice comes over the transmitter. "I will give you one week, no more. What have you found out about their military capabilities?"

"They have a formidable arsenal, are well trained, and have advanced technology. A direct assault on them would be difficult. I will give you another update in a few days."

"Make sure you do!"

Crystal decreases her altitude, ready to turn around, when she spots what appears to be desert pirates attacking a small caravan. She could leave well enough alone—she has a mission to get back to—but her training won't let her. She does what she's done many times before as leader of an Elite Strike Force; she takes aggressive action. The sun is directly overhead and shining down on the pirates; good news for her and bad news for them. This will give her some cover. Next, she lets the sky cycle drift awkwardly on the wind currents, flying erratically toward the pirates. As Crystal gets closer, she sees four pirates holding three men at gunpoint.

The closer she gets to the bandits, the more erratic her flight path becomes. The goal is for them to think she's going to crash. Crystal lands hard some seventy-five yards from the caravan. Dismounting the sky cycle, she removes her helmet, letting her long, blond hair fall naturally over her shoulders. She limps in their direction, yelling, "Help me, help me!"

The captives have their hands tied behind their backs and lie face down on the sand. Approximately a hundred feet away, she can tell the prisoners are the Johnson brothers. The pirates turn their guns on her when she's thirty feet from them and talk among themselves. Their attention is entirely focused on Crystal as they admire her feminine attributes. They look like a bunch of dirty inbreeds. Their leader is a massive, burly man with a long scraggly beard and a face weathered by the sun. He roars, "Don't rough her up. Our ticket to the good life just dropped out of the sky." Crystal limps toward them until she's just feet from them. The pirates circle her, blocking any chance of escape.

"I take it this means you aren't going to help me."

The grotesque leader laughs and bellows out, "Oh, you will help us by bringing a handsome price. A Gen Seven like you will make us a fortune on the open market!"

In a deadly-serious tone, she says, "I'll give you one chance to prostrate yourselves face down on the sand with your hands behind your backs."

They're laughing now. Crystal uses the distraction to do a rear snap kick to the pirate behind her, kicking him right in his mouth. Simultaneously, she punches the leader in front of her right between the eyes. Then she jumps high in the air, splitting her legs, and kicks the two men on opposite sides of her in their heads. In less than a second, she knocked out all four pirates.

They lay motionless on the sand. Unfortunately, they got an up-close introduction to an Elite Strike Force warrior. The Johnson brothers, now back on their feet, are staring at her in awe.

"Hey, you're Crystal, right? You were at Dr. Forrester's dinner last night. Man. No one said you could fight like that," Rick Johnson says.

Brad Johnson rubs his wrists where the rope had been. "Thank you. If you hadn't shown up, we'd definitely be dead."

Crystal grabs the knife from the burly pirate's belt loop. Time to make sure they never bother anyone again. She puts the blade to his throat, ready to slit it.

"Whoa! Wait just a minute," Rick says, putting his hands out. "You don't have to kill them."

"Why not?" She barks at him. "They were going to kill you!"

"We believe in innocent until proven guilty. No matter how evil, everyone is due their day in court," Jeff Johnson says.

"That's bullshit!" She walks toward Jeff and stares him down. "It's your life, go ahead and give them another chance to kill you."

Reluctantly, she allows them to chain the pirates and put them in a trailer used to transport livestock. The brothers will take the pirates to Paradise on the northern edge of the Mojave, where they will turn them over to the provisional Marshall.

After the pirates are locked safely away, Crystal gets back on her sky cycle and flies back to the compound, where she is told to wait at the flight center for Brownstone. Will she be welcomed back? What is going on?

He shows up in a few minutes. "Crystal, I was meeting with my officers when we got a call from one of our patrols letting us know that you saved the Johnson brothers. I wanted to thank you personally for saving their lives. They have been my friends for years."

"You're welcome. But to be clear, if you don't deliver on your promise to produce Caleb within the week, you *will* have to deal with me. And I promise that will not be a pleasant experience!"

He tilts his head, staring at her. "Why wouldn't I deliver your brother?" He is left hanging as she turns and walks away.

Crystal spends the next four days in the lab assisting Dr. Forrester and Simone in various research projects. Brownstone stops by several times a day to check on her. He insists on bringing her lunch every day. They talk about a wide range of topics. He must be spying on her like she's spying on them. Why else would he be so interested in her? Brownstone often smiles at Crystal, and when they inadvertently touch, sparks shoot through her.

What if it's not all a lie, though? What if his attraction to her is real?

She'd expected to succeed in her mission, but she hadn't expected the thought of leaving him would be so hard for her to commit to.

Crystal memorizes all the winding corridors in the compound and soon notices a pattern. Different colored walls indicate direction: blue for West, green for East, gray for South, and white for North. They have a formidable arsenal of air power at their flight center. She needs to know more about their military capabilities but doesn't want to overplay her hand. Brownstone isn't going to divulge much. She picks up tidbits of information from lab workers, Simone, and Forrester. Dr. Forrester spends most of his time in the military lab working on weapons systems. What other weapons do they have? They don't suspect she's putting all the pieces together to assess their capabilities. She has more secrets to steal.

# CHAPTER 4

Crystal awakes early on day seven of her mission and has a strange feeling that Caleb is nearby. Twin intuition, or just a feeling of wholeness she hasn't felt in a while, she's not sure. But it brings her a sense of well-being, and she smiles. Not a minute later, the phone rings. It's Brownstone. "Good morning, Beauty."

"Morning, Escort."

He laughs. "I've got a surprise for you."

"Caleb?"

He laughs again. "Yes. He's back and waiting at the sanctuary. How soon can you be ready?"

Her heart is beating fast. "Give me fifteen minutes."

Crystal dresses hastily in jeans and a t-shirt and puts on her boots. She goes to the kitchen and grabs a carving knife, slipping it inside her right boot sleeve. Her senses are sharp. If this is a trap, she'll be ready.

Crystal checks herself in the mirror, wishing she had more time for a wardrobe choice. She's too eager to see her twin for it to matter. Brownstone shows up at 7:15 a.m. "Good morning, beautiful."

She gives him a coy smile. "Morning."

Brownstone, sensing her apprehension, says, "Crystal, this will be a great day. Just have faith! All your questions will be answered." Neither of them talks on the way down to the sanctuary. Why would they put their sanctuary so far underground? It makes sense that they would protect what they value most, and for the Underlings, it's their faith. But this seems a little extreme. Usually, she would remember every turn, but she couldn't concentrate on anything but Caleb. Crystal glances at Brownstone several times. He offers reassuring smiles. He doesn't know, but she'll stick the carving knife straight through his heart if he doesn't deliver Caleb.

It takes only a few minutes for them to arrive at their destination. For her, it seems like an eternity. She has nervous excitement and doubts that her questions will be answered. As Brownstone escorts her from the cart, he looks directly at her, a somber expression on his face. "Crystal, you will never be the same after today."

He opens the door to the sanctuary. The auditorium is large, with plush seating. There is a large stage in the front, with many musical instruments and a smart video wall behind the band instruments. He holds Crystal's arm and directs her to the left hallway with several classrooms on each side. A door sign at the end of the hallway reads, 'Truth Seeker.' Surely, Brownstone isn't taking her to see the Truth Seeker. Warning signals go off in her mind. She looks at Brownstone for any sign of betrayal.

Brownstone opens the door. She freezes. This cannot be real. Emotions steamroll her. Sitting behind the desk is Caleb. And standing to his right, looking straight at her with tear-filled eyes, is Marci. The two people she loves in the world are here together.

Brownstone smiles at her. "Crystal, may I present our Pastor, the Truth Seeker, and his mother, Marci." Crystal's knees buckle. Brownstone helps steady her stance.

Caleb and Marci rush toward her and wrap their arms around her. They're crying tears of pure joy. Crystal tries to say, "Are you; are you," but that's all she can say.

Marci's voice is shaky, overwhelmed with emotion, when she says, "My daughter, my daughter, my beautiful daughter. You were lost but now found. I was afraid I would never see you again. My heart is complete. Thank You, Lord! Our prayers have been answered."

Crystal is so caught up in the moment that the religious stuff doesn't bother her.

Aware of the moment, Brownstone says, "You guys need time to get reacquainted." He walks out, leaving them for their reunion.

They spend the next hour reminiscing about their former life together. For the first time since Marci vanished, Crystal is where she belongs, with Marci and her brother. She has to take this in. Caleb directs Marci and Crystal to the plush chairs in front of his desk. He leans against the front of his desk.

When her emotions settle a little, Crystal asks the one question that's been burning in her mind for years. "Why did you leave in the middle of the night without telling us goodbye?"

Marci wipes the tears off her cheeks. "It was the only way I could stay in my children's lives, even if it were for thirteen short years. Typically, donor mothers had their children taken away at birth. A few exceptions were made if, and only if, they were convinced the mothers would follow their directions and protocols to the letter. If I ever told you I was your mother, I would have been removed immediately, never to see you again.

"The bargain I made with Steadman was to act as your nanny till you turned thirteen, then I would leave. I would tell you I had been reassigned to other children because it was time for you to go to the Academy of Elites. Originally, Steadman agreed I could visit you at the academy. But on your birthday night, the Elite Guard showed up. I awoke to a noise in my room, and a big brute put a chloroform cloth over my mouth. That was the last waking moment I had in our house. I planned to tell you goodbye in the morning and tell you I would always love you. Unfortunately, I never got the chance."

A strong desire to seek revenge against Steadman flows through her. He had always been creepy to her. Now, knowing what he did to her mother makes revenge the only option. "When I see Steadman, he'll pay with his life for doing you wrong!"

Marci puts a gentle hand on her shoulder. "Please don't do anything to put your life at risk. The only thing that matters is that we are together. I don't think I could bear losing either of you again."

Crystal nods, letting her tense muscles relax under Marci's grip. Perhaps this is why the Underlings value their families so strongly. "Where did they take you, and why didn't you try to visit us?"

"First, they took me to a holding house on the city's outskirts, and I thought I would be reassigned to other children per my agreement with Steadman. After a couple of days, an Elite Guard woke me early and told me to get dressed. They were going to take me to my new assignment. I was relieved to have something to distract my mind from losing you two. I reached for my suitcase to pack my things, but the big brute stopped me, saying they would bring my things later. He said I needed to get to my new assignment right away. So, with only a pair of dress slacks, a blouse, and heeled shoes, they took me out of the house into a waiting car with three Elite males.

"They drove even further to the outskirts of Imperial City. Then, we entered a tunnel. At first, we descended, but then we ascended upward. I could tell we were getting close to the end as the light got brighter. They drove right into the desert. I knew being in the Mojave wouldn't turn out well for me. They drove for about thirty minutes before stopping the vehicle. I thought they were going to kill me right there. Then, the big Elite got out of the car and made his way to the back passenger side door where I was sitting. He abruptly opened the door, grabbed my arm, jerked me out, and slung me to the ground." She swiped another tear away. "I'll never forget his voice. He said, 'Welcome to your new assignment, Ms. Marci,' and then laughed. I tried to protest that I had no water, food, or transportation. But they laughed loudly—all of them. The brute said, 'If I were you, I would be wary of the Elite patrols. No telling what they will do to a pretty lady like you.' Then they sped away."

Tears fall from Crystal's eyes. Her heart breaks, hearing what they did to her mother. She looks at Caleb. He walks over, falling to his knees. Caleb puts a hand on each lady's shoulder without saying a word.

Regaining her composure, Crystal asks, "How did you survive?"

"I located a road and followed it, hoping I would run into someone. I walked for miles and miles. When all hope was lost, an Underling patrol showed up just in time and saved me from certain death. I've been here with them ever since. There will be more to tell you about me later, but I want to know about my daughter. You must fill me in on the last thirteen years of your life. I have missed out on so much. I feel cheated! Caleb filled me in as much as possible, but there are some things only girls know."

Caleb takes his cue. "I've got some pastoral duties to perform. My secretary Renee will bring you some tea, and you can order breakfast. I'll check back with you later."

Crystal's emotions fluctuate from indescribable joy to intense anger. Damn Steadman for this emotional roller coaster ride. She'll exact revenge on everyone involved in taking Marci from her and Caleb.

Crystal isn't sure where to start, so she gives her the highlights of her life: all the academic achievements, awards in physical competition, her place in Elite Society, and even her training in the art of seduction with Roxanne.

"Well, have you snagged him yet?" A teasing joy fills Marci's eyes.

"Who?"

"James Brownstone, of course."

Feeling uneasy, Crystal shifts to the side. "I'm not trying to snag him!"

"You enchant him, and you can't even see it."

"He's not on the same level as me." Crystal is offended. How could her own mother—assuming all of what Marci had said was true—think she could ever be involved with an Underling? "I don't pursue men: they pursue me! Besides, he's a notorious ladies' man."

"James hasn't had a serious relationship since the death of his wife. I'm confident his interest in you is real."

Crystal isn't sure what to do with that piece of information. She sinks into silence for a moment. Then, quietly, she asks, "Did you know her?"

"I knew her very well. She was one of my closest friends. I still miss her every day but know she is alive and well in Heaven."

"I don't believe in myths. How can you believe in what you can't see?"

"You believe in oxygen, and you can't see it. You believe in gravity, and you can't see it. If God chooses you, you can do nothing about it."

Crystal shifts uncomfortably in her seat and then changes the subject, so she doesn't have to keep talking about all that spiritual mumbo jumbo. "Enough about me. How did you end up in Imperial City?"

"I heard Dr. Robert Forrester was forming a community to ensure the survival of humanity. After graduating from the University of California with a doctorate in psychology, I headed to Area 62 to offer my services. An Elite patrol intercepted my car. They kidnapped me and brought me to Imperial City instead. I was housed in a dorm with forty-nine other young women. They did a series of tests on us. The ones who failed were taken away. We never saw them again. Other young women quickly replaced them. I later learned I was like a gift to them. Most girls were kidnapped from cities in the west that Humbots hadn't overrun. Steadman's goons would go to universities disguised as students to find the most intelligent and athletic women and seize them.

"They moved us to apartment buildings once we became impregnated by artificial insemination. Each apartment building had at least two doctors and a private nurse assigned to each mother. We were given a specific diet, exercise routine, and sleep schedule. That's how I became your mother. I wouldn't change a thing! It has been the greatest honor of my life to be the mother of two of the brightest and fiercest children the world has ever known."

Caleb returns, and they go to the cafeteria for lunch. She's immediately overwhelmed by how excited everyone seems to see him. He is treated like a celebrity by the Underlings. Most acknowledged him as the Truth Seeker, some as Pastor Caleb. In this world, Caleb is more important than her. The Underlings recognize her brother's unique gifts in ways Elite society never did.

After they're seated, Brownstone walks in and comes over to their table.

"I invited James to join us. Hope you don't mind," Caleb says.

Crystal smiles. She still has an assignment to do, though her emotions are conflicted. "I don't mind." The butterflies in her stomach give her pause.

When Brownstone looks at her, she blushes, looks away, and flips her hair. She's upset with herself for being attracted to this arrogant Underling. The mission, she keeps telling herself, is the reason for her flirtatious behavior.

"Caleb, now that you're back, I have some business away from the compound that requires my attention. I know you'll look after things in my absence."

Caleb nods. "Thank you for looking after her." He gestures to Crystal.

Crystal can't deny her disappointment at Brownstone's upcoming absence. He hasn't acted like a soldier around her, but she knows he's a hardened warrior masking as an average person. She suspects he is trying to seduce her, but that will never happen! If there is seduction, she'll be the one doing it to him.

Crystal is so excited to be reunited with Caleb and Marci that the food is secondary. Many of those living in the compound come by and express their happiness for the family reunion. Some say they have been praying for this day for years. Several old ladies hug Crystal, making her uncomfortable.

After lunch, Caleb takes Marci and Crystal back to Marci's apartment. Caleb looks at Crystal and smiles. "This is where our mom lives. We'll expect you for Sunday dinner." Crystal gives him a look sisters reserve for their brothers when they're irritated.

They enter Marci's apartment, and Crystal's impressed at its luxuriousness. The space is large and decorated immaculately. The furniture is old but expensive. Her apartment has two bedrooms and two baths. Crystal can't stop herself from comparing it to her apartment. For her prowess, she doesn't have something this luxurious. She hadn't thought much of it until now.

Caleb smirks as he reads her face. He'd always been good at knowing what she was thinking. "Mom is the second in charge here. Only Dr. Forrester outranks her."

Marci embraces them like she never wants to let go. "This is how it's supposed to be. The three of us together. I love you both with a depth you'll only understand when you have children." Crystal remembers how good it felt when they lived with Marci in Imperial City. She has that same feeling again.

After settling Marci in, Caleb brings Crystal back to her apartment. "I love you, my beautiful sister. We're with our mother, where we were always meant to be."

Crystal watches him go. She still has many questions for him, but they'll have to wait for later. She steps inside the apartment and falls to her knees. She breaks down, knowing Marci's words filled the hole in her heart. *I love you, my beautiful daughter.* She will forever hold those words close.

Crystal fights with herself. A Gen Elite shouldn't have these emotions. This shouldn't even be possible. But maybe Brownstone was right. Maybe Elites and Underlings aren't that different from each other.

No. She's special. She's always been special. And she's here on a mission. Brownstone is taken in by her. No matter his charm, she knows he's hiding something. When she finds out, Crystal will deal with him accordingly. She might be inexperienced in romantic relationships, but she's a master at high-level mind games.

Zander won't wait long before he attacks. She can't save all the Elites in the compound, but she's got a good chance of saving Marci and Caleb. Under the guise of getting reunited with Marci, Crystal will convince Caleb and Marci to go on a weeklong retreat to Paradise, Nevada. She refuses to let her family die for some doomsday cult of Christianity.

The following day, she flies out of the compound at ten, contacts Zander for the second time, and lets him know she's located Caleb. They discuss several options to free the Elites in the compound. She asks Zander for another week to complete the mission. He reluctantly gives her the extra time, but no more.

When she returns to the compound, she meets Caleb at Marci's office and shares her plan for the three of them to go on a weeklong family retreat. Marci loves the idea and mentions it will be like a family vacation. Caleb agrees, so long as they leave after the Gathering on Sunday.

# CHAPTER 5

Zander, the military leader of the Elites, is not happy about the Elites leaving Imperial City to work in the compound. He isn't planning on rescuing Crystal and Caleb. Instead, he intends to kill them and the rest of the Elite traitors.

Zander doesn't want the Underlings to benefit from Elite excellence. Caleb and Crystal are his only rivals to lead Imperial City after he disposes of Steadman. He never intended to give Crystal another week to extricate the missing Elites. He sends out nine groups of Elite Special Forces commandos to capture Underling patrols and, if possible, Brownstone. Zander will gain information from them by whatever means necessary, including torture. Human suffering and pain mean nothing to him. He will torture countless Underlings if that means getting the information he needs to overtake them. Zander is so upset that he sends one of his best and most trusted soldiers, Hans. He is a Gen Elite four. Though not as intelligent as the fives, sixes, and sevens, he makes up for it with cruelty and sheer presence. Hans stands six feet eight inches tall and weighs 380 pounds. He would be a beast with no genetic enhancement, but he can rip the limbs off a man with it. Zander is proud of Hans, like a cattle rancher would be proud of a prized bull.

Luckily for Zander, Hans has an identical twin brother named Klaus. At least if the Underlings kill Hans, he will have another beast to do his dirty work. Although Klaus isn't as aggressive as Hans, he's just as big, mean, and deadly.

Before sending him out, Zander pulled Hans aside. "Capture Brownstone and Rodriguez. When we capture Brownstone, we will break the will of the Underlings. He's the hero of the Underling resistance. Bring Brownstone and Rodriguez to me." He imagined the way her small body would feel in his hands. "I don't care what you do with Brownstone's oversized sidekick, Evans."

Hans' muscles tense with anticipation, and a devious smile creases his lips. "I will kill him with my bare hands!"

Hans will do anything for him to keep his position. Zander is counting on it. Most Gen fours don't keep their positions in Elite society. Gen sevens are given preference for any position held by those they outrank. Hans will be merciless to keep his position with Zander.

The advanced scouting patrols report back regarding likely areas where Brownstone will patrol. Hans chooses his Elite team to enable him to capture Brownstone. He assembles a nine-member team divided into three equal groups, each having its own Humvee. Hans chooses Lars, a Gen 6 excellent soldier and brilliant strategist. Hans rarely takes Lars' advice, good as it may be, because he thinks it makes him look weak. Also in the Humvee is Gregor, an Elite five, their gunner and an outstanding martial artist. He has the fastest hands and feet that Hans has ever witnessed. And the way Hans likes to fight, it will probably be hand-to-hand fighting to the death.

Their Humvees are camouflaged to match the desert colors. And when they get Brownstone's crew out in the open, they will rush him from three sides. Hans is confident that if only his three-member crew survives out of the three teams, they will have no problem disposing of Brownstone and his flunkies.

For Hans, everyone is expendable except him. He learned about expendability from the Elites, who ranked above him. He doesn't care who he must sacrifice to achieve his mission.

On day three of their patrol, James "Maverick" Brownstone, Kurt "Brock" Evans, and Jennifer "Raven" Rodriguez are on patrol by six in the morning, before the sun rises over the horizon. They are there to address the increased activity by Elite Patrols in the Mojave. Maverick's got a feeling that something big is about to go down.

Early in the patrol, Brock starts in on Maverick. "So, I hear you have been busy the last few days. We wondered what happened to you, but we heard that you're on a special mission to melt the heart of an Elite warrior. How's that going?"

"It's been going great." Maverick picks up on the teasing in Brock's voice.

Brock continues, "There's a rumor that she thinks you and Maverick are two different people. As your friend, I advise you to stop this farce and not let it go any farther. You must tell her the truth even though your deception has benefited you in the romance department. You have to tell Crystal you are the guy that slammed her face-first into the sand."

"Yeah, Maverick," Raven joins the conversation, "you're the one who always talks about integrity. You must tell that beautiful girl you're the one who gave her a sand sandwich. Maybe she'll understand, but probably not. She will most likely use her superhuman strength and do a bully beatdown. And we want to be there to bear witness. We're counting on you to ensure that we have front-row seats when you tell her."

"That's interesting coming from you, Raven," Brock says. "You spend most of your time at the Truth Seeker's office. We are thinking of renaming you, Sister Raven."

"Yeah, that's right, now you mention it," Maverick adds, "I don't think she is interested in being a sister, at least Caleb's sister. I am afraid the girl has ulterior motives regarding the Truth Seeker."

Having had enough of being roasted, Raven leans forward from the back seat and simultaneously thumps both men on the ears. "Ouch," they say.

"Why did you do that?" Brock asks. "You're lucky we don't drag you out of the jeep and bury you in the sand, leaving only your head exposed to the vultures. But even a vulture wouldn't eat someone with your disposition."

"You guys won't do anything to me, and you know it. I'm like your little sister. That being said, let's make things clear here, boys. If there's going to be any off-color humor about relationships, it's coming from me. Now for you, Brock, it's been reported that you were getting a little too friendly with your significant other at the workout center the other day. You caused quite a scene. You held her so tight and touched her in ways that drew stares from onlookers."

With glee in his eyes, Maverick looks at Brock and teases, "Have you been holding out on me, buddy? How come you didn't tell me about her? Are you ashamed of her?"

Raven goes for the kill. "Yes, he's ashamed of her, Maverick. She's been called many names, and she has been known to have severe weight fluctuations. Yet, every guy in the gym has his hands on her. She gets passed around from guy to guy like some cheap hand-me-down, but Brock returns to her like the whipped puppy dog he is. I don't know how else to say it; she's just a dumbbell. That's all we can say about her. Yes, it's true; Brock has a very active love life with a dumbbell."

Brock waits for Maverick to come to his rescue, but that's a lost cause.

"I have to hand it to you, Raven. You're much better at the verbal smackdowns than we are," Maverick says.

Raven was on a roll. "That's nice, Maverick. As for you, we need to address that medical condition you haven't even considered telling us about. Luckily for you, I have a tool to ease your symptoms."

"What condition are you referring to?" Maverick asks.

"I think you know it's the nose ring that Ice Crystal has been leading you around by. You need to pull over, so I can get the wire cutters and remove the ring. It might make you feel better. But in our eyes, it makes you look less manly."

# CHAPTER 6

As much as Maverick enjoys the banter, he senses something isn't right. He learned to trust his sixth sense while serving with the Australian Special Forces. The hair stands up on the back of his neck. He looks across the desert until he spots it and holds up a hand for the others to pay attention. "I'm afraid we're in danger. Listen carefully and follow my instructions to the letter." Raven and Brock know from experience that when Maverick senses danger, something terrible is going down.

Maverick continues, "There are two, maybe three, Humvees of Elites scouting us, looking for the right time to strike. They want us out in the open. I will drive this jeep between those two dunes." He gestures to a few forty-foot-high dunes approximately two hundred yards to their right. The closest opening of the two dunes is only thirty feet wide, widening to seventy-five feet at the far end.

"I'll spin the jeep around and block the narrow entrance. When the jeep stops, Raven snaps loose the floor latches on the Fifty-Cal machine gun. Brock, lift the machine gun out and move it to the west side of the dune, approximately fifty feet from the north end. Raven, you will operate the machine gun from there, covering the north end of the dunes.

"We will cover our zone as numbers on a wall clock. Raven, you will be responsible for the north area between ten and two. I will cover from ten down to six on the west and south sides. Brock, you cover the area from two down to six on the east and south sides. I will grab the Accelerated Laser 3000. Brock, take your Fifty-Cal rifle with you. The three of us will defend all four sides.

"Oh, one more thing, Brock, grab a couple of canteens from the jeep. We might have to wait them out. I will use our two-way radio and put out a distress call. I assume they have jammed our signal, but I'll try, just in case. Remember, these are Elites we're against, so be ready for anything.

"They will circle us at a distance at first. Then, they will bring the circle in tighter and tighter until they generate a sandstorm. The sandstorm will reduce visibility next to nothing. Don't worry about figuring out which Humvee is where; just guard your zone and be ready. Let's try to shoot them as they enter the engagement zone, and be careful whom you're shooting. We don't want any friendly fire. They may be Elites, but we're an Elite team, and we work together much better than they do."

Brock and Raven move to their positions with adrenaline flowing through their veins. Maverick appears perfectly calm. Through his special forces training, he learned you must calm the mind to weather the storms of war. They hear the Humvees racing toward them.

Brock screams out, "I hear three separate vehicles."

Maverick knows the circle is getting tighter and tighter as the noise gets louder. The swirling sand around them makes their visibility almost nonexistent.

When Maverick senses the Humvees are right on top of them, he yells, "They're coming in." In the next second, one Humvee comes flying over the east dune he is lying against. He pivots with cat-like reflexes with the AL3000 tucked against his shoulder and hits the underbelly of the Humvee. The laser burns through the Humvee, igniting the fuel tank.

The Humvee explodes into a giant fireball, crashing down on the desert.

Raven's zone is getting incoming fire from the north opening. Maverick hears Raven unloading her .50-caliber machine gun into the approaching Humvee with everything she has. Brock senses something wrong with the way the Humvee entered the North entrance. It came in slowly and in a direct path like they wanted to get killed. Brock yells. "They're not in there; they're not in there!" Raven hears and understands that three unaccounted-for Elites are coming in on foot. She hopes they haven't already outflanked their defensive positions. Brock and Raven go silent. They know exactly what to do from their training with Maverick. They both move silently but quickly from their positions. Raven slides down the embankment and uses The Elites' shot-up Humvee for cover.

As they approach the dune where the Underlings are hunkered down, Lars leans over. "Hey Hans, let's not go in at the same time as the others."

Hans replies, "What do you mean? That's what I instructed them to do. We should go in at the same time."

"The ones that go in first are most likely to die. I suggest we go in seconds later and let the others attract enemy fire," Lars says.

For once, Hans takes Lars's advice and waits until the first Humvee goes airborne over the east dune. He might be reckless, but he doesn't want to die. Hans guns his Humvee seconds after the first Humvee goes airborne. As they near the top of the dune, they hear a loud explosion and see the lead Humvee engulfed in a fireball, crashing to the desert below. Han's Humvee is airborne, some fifty feet above the desert, with gunfire erupting around them.

Knowing their Humvee will crash, Gregor jumps out mid-flight and lands high up on the east bank. He leaves his big gun, the .50-caliber machine gun, but he doesn't care. He would rather kill the Underlings up close and personal. He is a great martial artist. No one can beat him in hand-to-hand combat.

$\oplus$

Maverick doesn't see the next Humvee coming over the opposite bank in time to fire his AL3000. It comes in fast, heading straight at him. Maverick makes a defensive move, rolling to his right as quickly as possible. He only makes it twenty feet from the point of impact. The Humvee slams right into the location where he lay and the impact hurled him off the dune, slamming his body into the desert some thirty feet below.

He hits the sand hard and grimaces when his AL3000 flies out of his hand. His body feels broken, but he can't stop now. The first rule of fighting is that when things go crazy, you figure it out on the fly, or you die. His Special Forces commander drilled that into him over and over. Those are your only two options.

Maverick lies flat on his back to see how many Elites are in the crashed Humvee. He sees a big brute in the driver's seat and another face-planted into the windshield. The passenger isn't moving—either dead or unconscious. He doesn't know what happened to the gunner. But he's not in the Humvee, that's for sure.

The Humvee crashed hard into the east bank, burying the engine in the sand. Maverick watches as the beast frantically slams his shoulder into the door. Finally, the door hinges snap, no match for his superhuman strength. The beast grabs the heavy door with one hand, tossing it aside like a toy. Brownstone locks eyes with the beast.

He's one of the biggest men that he has ever seen. He is much bigger than Brock. Maverick knows he must act quickly to survive an encounter with the giant Elite. He looks on in amazement as the colossal beast jumps off the thirty-foot embankment and starts running toward him. Maverick jumps to his feet. Sensing his opponent's aggression, he knows his survival depends on using his opponent's rage against him.

He takes off in a dead run toward the beast of a man. Hans increases his speed to match Brownstone. Maverick slows down, grabbing his right hamstring in apparent pain. But the big brute keeps running toward him at full speed. His timing must be perfect. The big Elite is just steps from him. Maverick executes a reverse roundhouse kick right to Hans' head. The brute falls to his knees but doesn't topple, to Maverick's dismay. The giant is getting back to his feet. Maverick leaps at the beast with blinding speed and hits him with a flying elbow right to his head. The beast slumps back to his knees but doesn't fall over. This beast isn't going down by traditional martial arts techniques. He comes up with a Hail Mary plan.

"Is that all you got, Underling? No one will take the glory of killing the great Brownstone away from me. I am going to rip your head off!"

Maverick retreats ten paces and runs at Hans, accelerating his pace with each step. He launches himself like a human torpedo headfirst, right at the beast.

The beast's massive hands encircle Maverick's head. Using his speed, Maverick brings his right hand from his side and karate-chops the beast on the temple with all his strength. The brute falls flat on his back; he stares at Brownstone in disbelief as his world goes black.

There's no time to gloat. Maverick must get to his friends as soon as possible. He moves in their direction, trying to avoid detection. He'll be no good to them dead. The sound of gunfire coming from the north end propels him forward.

Brock uses the hood of the exploded Humvee as cover. He picks it up and moves toward Raven. He gets close enough to see Raven climb in the Humvee that got shot up, entering the north opening. He knows what she's doing; she will use the Elites' .50-caliber machine gun against them.

Raven turns the big gun to the rear of the Humvee, waiting for the Elite commandos to make their move. Brock continues moving in her direction. He still has his .50-caliber rifle strapped over his shoulder. He will cover the area in front of the Elite Humvee and the left and right perimeters. Raven will cover the north opening and the areas to her left and right. By focusing in front of the Humvee, Brock will protect Raven's blindside and keep an eye out for Maverick. He's worried about his friends, but total silence is the only thing keeping them alive.

The dust is settling, so hiding will be much more difficult in minutes. But that applies to the Elites as well. Then it will be an all-out war. Brock sees the first Elite come into the zone over the dune to his left out of his peripheral vision. The only problem is that the Elite soldier spots Raven at the same time. The commando raises his rifle, preparing to shoot her. He must stop the commando, or it will be too late for her. Brock stands up from behind the Humvee hood, leaving himself exposed. He starts shooting in the commando's direction, not even taking time to aim. The Elite soldier's lifeless body falls backward, tumbling down the dune.

A loud sound emanates from the decoy Humvee. Brock figures Raven is in trouble, so he rises from his concealed position and makes his way to the front of the Humvee.

When he notices her lifeless body slumped over the side of the Humvee, his heart sinks in his chest.

Brock has a moment of despair at seeing Rodriguez's lifeless body. As he slumps over, Gregor sneaks behind Brock and hits him with a double-fisted blow to the back of his neck.

Brock's head crashes violently into the Humvee, but Gregor celebrates too soon. Brock spins around, hitting Gregor with a back fist. The blow lands on Gregor's shoulder, knocking him to the ground. Pain blazes through Gregor's shoulder. Brock bull-rushes the smaller man taking him hard to the ground as he struggles to his feet. The force of the tackle knocks the breath out of Gregor. Brock lands on top of him. He violently grounds and pounds the Elite. Gregor is helpless as he's beaten to death by an Underling. His world quickly goes dark. As Brock finishes Gregor, Maverick arrives and yells, "Take cover; take cover."

They make their way to the west side of the Humvee and lift Raven's limp body out of the vehicle. They check her for wounds discovering only a bruise on her cheek. Brock holds his breath as Maverick checks for a pulse, which is strong. Relieved, Maverick quietly says, "Thank God."

Gunfire rains down on them from high up on the east dune, pinning them down. Maverick scans the dunes. This is a helpless situation. While one Elite keeps them pinned down, another can outflank them by circling around and coming at them from their blind side. They'll be outflanked and picked off like sitting ducks in minutes.

"Cover me!" Maverick makes his way to the front of the vehicle, grabbing the hood from the exploded Humvee.

Brock fires rapidly at the commando on the east ridge. Brock will soon run out of ammo, but he will keep firing until his friend reaches safety. Maverick positions the hood to cover his right side, making his way up the west dune.

He moves in a diagonal direction up the dune fast while maintaining coverage using the hood.

Raven wakes from her unconscious state. As her head clears, she looks at Brock and asks, "What happened?" He gives her the short version. Although still in a fog, Raven nods and shouts, "Cover me!"

"How many people do you expect me to cover?" Brock shouts back at her. He continues firing at the commando as Raven leaps into the Humvee. She grabs the handles of the .50-caliber machine gun, whirling it around with a fury, blasting at the commando.

"Watch Maverick's backside; I got this," Raven shouts. Brock can now be selective with his remaining ammo. He will keep an eye out for the enemy, watch Maverick's backside, and shoot at the first sign of trouble. Raven keeps peppering the Elite's position until she hears a loud shrieking sound. She listens for several moments, not hearing another sound. Raven won't let down her guard and be tricked into thinking the enemy is dead.

An image rises out of the sand in Maverick's peripheral vision. He swings the heavy hood between him and the Elite, bracing for impact. The intensity of the gunfire causes him to drop to a knee, but he keeps the hood in place. Brock spots the enemy commando. He takes careful aim shooting him in the chest. There is a soft whimper, and the commando falls backward off the dune. Maverick stands up and gives Raven and Brock a thumbs-up.

He makes his way to the top of the dune, aware that the commando might not be dead, just injured. As he sees the commando struggling to his feet, Maverick throws the Humvee hood down on the outer bank, jumping on top of it and using it as a giant surfboard, heading right at the now-standing commando. His only hope is to take out the commando before he's taken out. The commando raises his automatic rifle, firing at him. A burning sensation sears Brownstone's right thigh, but he can't stop now. At the last second, Maverick jumps off the hood as it continues straight on its path, impaling the commando in his torso. He takes his bandana from his neck and wraps it around his injured thigh. Thankfully, it is only a flesh wound. Maverick takes the deceased soldier's automatic rifle, strapping it over his shoulder.

Raven covers Brock as he exits the north entrance of the dunes. Brock circles around the outside east dune, making his way south on its outer bank, looking for the commando Raven blasted off the top of the dune.

Maverick runs fast, heading north on the outer west bank. He makes a crow call, so Raven knows he is rounding the north entrance. When Maverick rounds the northeast bank, he makes another crow call, so Brock will know he's behind him. They spot the Elite soldier lying at the bottom of the east dune's outer bank. There are red spots of blood staining the sand an eerie rust color all around him. Brock checks the commando for a pulse while Maverick covers him. He looks at Maverick, shaking his head. "I am afraid this one didn't make it either."

"I hate all this senseless death," Maverick says.

The men look at each other, knowing there is one more Elite soldier. They have eight confirmed kills, but where is the ninth commando? In a battle, you never assume your enemy is dead. Making assumptions in war will get you killed. There is a probability he was killed when the Humvee crashed, but faking injury or death is a brilliant strategy and one that an Elite soldier would employ.

Maverick walks next to Brock. He says softly, "We have three likely scenarios about the missing commando. First, he's still in or around the crashed Humvee, injured, dead, or waiting to ambush us. Second, and the one I would choose, he is waiting to ambush us at our jeep. Third, he could be anywhere and pick us off one by one."

Maverick lays out his plan. They take off, moving quietly. Brock heads up the east dune diagonally while Maverick stays below, moving between their defensive zone's two and three-o'clock numbers. Maverick starts up the outer east bank, aiming to come over the ridge right on top of the crashed Humvee. This will put them in a dominant position to surprise the commando if he is hiding in or around the Humvee and in the best defensive position if he is hiding behind their jeep.

They approach the Humvee from two different angles. Brock covers the passenger's side and rear, while Maverick covers the front and driver's side. They raise their heads over the dune peak at the same time. There is no sign of the missing soldier. Brock eases down the bank, crawling on his belly. The missing Elite isn't behind or under the Humvee. Next, Maverick and Brock rise, peering inside the Humvee with their rifles leading the way. The commando isn't in or around the Humvee. That leaves only two likely probabilities. He's behind their jeep, waiting to ambush them, or he could be anywhere in the battle zone.

Maverick doesn't dare call to Raven. If he alerts her, he will alert the missing soldier, putting her life in grave danger even though she might be a sitting duck. The Elite soldier will likely take them all out at once when they let down their guard.

The plan is for Brock to return to the area where they found the body of the last commando. There, he will fire shots from his rifle and the dead Elite's rifle. Maverick will go down the outer east dune heading south and sneak up behind their jeep in case the commando is there. For the plan to work, Maverick must be in position when Brock fires his rifle and the dead commando's rifle simultaneously. Brock's firing of the weapons will distract the commando while Maverick gets in place to take him out. They will be in trouble if he's not where they suspect him to be.

As Brock fires the rifles, Maverick eases his way around the end of the dune. At first, he doesn't spot the commando, but soon he spots the commando moving toward Raven while she turns all her attention in the direction of the gunfire. The Elite soldier hugs the west bank in Raven's blind spot. He's running fast, using the noise of the gunfire to hide any sound he might make.

Maverick knows he must hurry before the commando takes Raven out. All he needs is a clear shot. The commando must get closer to get a clear shot without being blocked by the Humvee's windshield.

When Maverick sees the commando come to a quick stop to get a bead on Raven, he drops to the ground, getting into shooting position. Struggling to get a bead on the commando after landing hard, Maverick fears he's too late. He squeezes the trigger, and the last commando's head snaps violently forward. Raven wheels the .50-caliber machine gun in the direction of the gunfire, tightening her fingers around the trigger. She pulls back at the last second. Maverick yells, "Clear, clear."

Brock rushes up the east dune just in time to hear Raven give Maverick a lecture. "What were you trying to do, Maverick? Use me as bait? Then maybe, just maybe, you would come to my rescue at the last second. You know my life means a lot to me; apparently, it doesn't mean much to you!"

"By the way, Raven, you might want to thank me for saving your life when you calm down."

She's in no mood. "I think it wise for you to stop talking now!"

Brock's relieved Raven is alive, and he can't help but laugh at the butt-chewing she's giving Maverick. Raven storms off to their Jeep as Brock regains his composure making his way down the dune.

# CHAPTER 7

Feeling like hell covered in sweat, sand, and grime Maverick grabs the radio and yells, "Star One, Star One. Anyone copy?"

After a moment of silence, "Brownstone?"

He recognized the voice on the other end.

"This is Brownstone, Lt. Xavier. We need two extra patrols and a Jeep with a sand plow to bury the dead. Make sure everyone is on Star One alert status."

"Yes, sir. I'm on top of it."

The death of nine Elites in a firefight has put everyone's life in danger. Why did they have to attack? Brownstone knows war well enough to know that Zander won't rest until he does much worse to them. Dammit, by announcing Star One, he put his people on the highest alert possible, including war.

The very thought makes him sick. He saw enough war, senseless violence, and soldiers killed and disfigured. Throughout history, the decisions of a few privileged men who never saw the field of battle caused the deaths of countless men, women, and children. There's nothing to celebrate. All they can do is mourn the dead and mourn the death of humanity.

Maverick isn't surprised when Caleb shows up with Lt. Xavier in a patrol vehicle. Caleb makes his way to the jeep to check on Raven. They share a long embrace.

They gather the bodies with as much respect as they can muster, and Caleb holds a funeral service for the fallen Elites. Maverick didn't hold any level of respect for the fallen Elites. At the same time, he did feel sadness at their passing. Unfortunately, they were products of their training and upbringing.

After the service, Raven notices a cut on Maverick's right cheek and a wound on his right leg. She gets some water out of the jeep and wipes the sand and dirt off his injuries. Then she treats them with antiseptic.

Brock approaches the two of them. "Maverick, how did you get those scrapes?"

"Don't know for certain. It could have been when I got knocked off the dune, fighting a beast in mortal combat, surfing a Humvee hood, or when commandos tried to blow my head off. To summarize, bad guys were trying to kill me, and I got cut." Maverick looks directly at Raven and says, "You care, after all."

That's all it took for her to elbow him in the ribs. She glares at him. "Keep it up, big boy, and you'll have more to worry about than a scratch on the cheek."

Caleb joins them and informs them what he knows about each of the deceased Elites. He hits on the fact that Gregor was an outstanding martial artist. Lars was the brains of the Elite teams-hence the sacrifice of the first airborne crew and the decoy Humvee entering without a team. By faking his death, Lars set himself up to be the conquering hero. Likely, he would have killed all survivors, Elites, and Underlings. This was a top-priority mission for Zander. Hans was Zander's primary enforcer, taking orders directly from him.

"They want you bad, Maverick. Zander isn't one to take this loss lightly," Caleb says.

"I figured as much; we need to know everything you know about Elite military capabilities," Maverick says.

"I can tell you what I know, but military tactics and weapons systems are Crystal's area of expertise."

"I'll ask Crystal, then."

Raven interjects, "I bet you will, Maverick; I just bet you will."

Brock laughs, and Caleb smiles at the remark.

Xavier states, "Our radar system picked up high-flying drones over this area."

"Frigging Cognition, I will put an end to that evil AI supercomputer if it's the last thing I do," Maverick says.

The magnitude of the situation they find themselves in weighs heavily on Maverick on the ride back. His decisions could mean life or death for his closest friends.

# CHAPTER 8

Brock radios ahead and informs Robert Forrester and Marci Jenkins about what happened in the firefight. He lets them know they're taking James to the infirmary for minor injuries. Marci calls Crystal and tells her what happened.

After hearing Brownstone was injured, Crystal takes the opportunity to show some vulnerability. When she arrives, he's lying on the hospital bed with Caleb at his side. She asks, "How bad are you hurt?"

"Oh, I think I'll be fine. Though I might need some makeup to cover my cheek and leg scars." He turns, showing her his right cheek.

His sarcastic tone bothers her a little but seeing the scar on his cheek sets her off. Crystal moves to his side, punching him hard in the right shoulder several times, and storms out as Marci and Forrester walk past her.

Brownstone looks dumbfounded. "Did I ask for Crystal to come down here? I didn't do anything; I just made a little joke."

Forrester walks over to where his nephew lies. He leans over and whispers, "Well, maybe, just maybe, you haven't melted Ice Crystal's heart after all."

Hearing the jest of Crystal's conversation with James, Marci says, "I'm sorry, James. It's my fault. When I heard you returned, I called Crystal, informing her you had suffered injuries. I'll talk to her after she's had time to reflect."

Robert Forrester grabs his nephew's hand, saying, "I'm glad you survived, not only you but all of you. God must have been with you. You were outmanned three to one and still came out on top."

As Raven and Brock walk into the room, Brownstone says, "Well, Raven got waylaid by a flying ninja, but she perked up when Caleb arrived. Did everything check out all right, little sister?"

"If you mean passing concussion protocols, yes."

"How about you, Brock? How's your neck?" Maverick inquired.

"Well, other than not being able to turn to the left or right, it's fine. According to the doc, it will take several weeks of physical therapy."

He shakes his head, bewildered. Crystal and Raven, the two women he cares about most, hit him the same day. So much for the Brownstone charm.

He wonders what Crystal will do to him when she discovers he's Maverick. That would require planning too, if he's going to avoid a black eye. He decides to ask her to meet him at the workout center early in the morning. He'll come clean with her *after* their workout when there aren't many people around, and there's a chance she'll be worn out.

Many attractive women had pursued him over the years, yet none captivated his imagination like her. She is the most beautiful, but her fiery spirit attracts him the most.

He needs to focus and have a strategic planning session with his military leaders—including Caleb. It didn't take Brownstone long to learn. It was to his advantage to have input from the most intelligent man alive. He doesn't like going up against a bunch of upset Elites, but at least he has

Caleb's—and hopefully Crystal's—help. Her intelligence and military training would be an immense benefit.

James and his team need to get cleaned up and enjoy a good meal. Almost on cue, Robert Forrester says, "Dinner will be served tonight at six o'clock in the executive dining room. Don't worry, James, Crystal is invited, too. I want to stay close to that young lady. No telling when she will rough you up again, and I want to be around to see it." Forrester and Marci walk out smiling.

"You know," Raven starts, "it would be tragic if it got out at dinner that you and Maverick are the same."

"I will tell her no later than tomorrow," he says.

"You better," Brock replies. They leave Brownstone to ponder his fate.

He can't stop thinking about Crystal. Everything about her intrigues him in a way no other woman has before. She is a magical mystery he must solve. Even if it takes a lifetime, he is determined to unravel her mysterious power over him.

Crystal walks down the corridors of the compound at a furious pace. Her heart beats fast, and she's upset at herself for letting emotions get the best of her. How can a mere Underling get under her skin?

She must regain her composure and get back her edge. Thoughts of avoiding Brownstone flood her mind, but it's not in Crystal's nature to back down. She'll face Brownstone head-on, desensitizing herself to him by using a psychological technique called exposure therapy. Her dose of Brownstone will not decrease but increase substantially. She'll show them all, especially him, what Ice Crystal can do when she sets her mind to it.

Caleb calls her about the dinner plans when she returns to her room. She surprises him by readily agreeing to go. When the phone call ends, Crystal tries on several dresses—looking in the mirror from every angle to see if each dress would have the desired effect on Brownstone. Admiring herself, she knows she possesses all the physical attributes to make Brownstone's head spin if she doesn't overplay her hand. Her face blushes after thinking about her overreaction from earlier. Finally, she decides on a black sundress that comes down mid-thigh with a frilly white trim. Crystal accessorizes with a black jade necklace, a good contrast to her blond hair. For shoes, she picks out a pair of black high heels.

Her determination is at an all-time high to show everyone who's in control—reminding herself that she's a Gen Elite seven, the top of the class, and the best of the Elites. There's no way some mere human will better her, emotionally or otherwise. She's way too strong to let romantic infatuation overtake her mental stability. Ice Crystal is back and in charge of her destiny.

Zander's attack on the Underlings complicates things. Getting her mother and brother to go on a family retreat is out the window. The only way to save them now may be to return to Imperial City and end Zander.

# CHAPTER 9

Marci surprises Crystal when she shows up at her door at a quarter to six alone. She expected Caleb would drive her to dinner. Crystal fears what she would do if Brownstone picked her up. Marci gives her a look over. "You are probably the most beautiful girl in the world."

"You're just saying I'm beautiful because I'm your daughter."

"Not really. You are the most striking young lady in the compound by far. No wonder James is so taken by you."

"There is nothing like that going on between us."

Marci smiles. "Whatever you say."

"Mom, I believe you are the most beautiful woman in the world. You have a figure that rivals mine. And you look so young and full of life."

"Thanks, Crystal. By the way, I love it when you call me mom."

"It will take me a little while to get used to saying it, but you're my mom!"

They embrace, both teary-eyed.

Marci wears a light blue dress that highlights her curves, falling just above her knees. She wears matching blue high heel shoes and carries a small blue purse. She observes Crystal walking in high heels.

"Crystal, watch me walk across the room."

"You look like a graceful queen."

"Now, Crystal, I want you to walk toward the mirror hanging on the far wall." Crystal walks, observes herself in the mirror, and bursts out laughing. Marci joins in, laughing with her.

"I have the gracefulness of a cow. I'll wear the black flats."

"I will teach you how to walk in heels, but we don't have time now."

"Who is going to be at the dinner?" Crystal asks.

"I know Rob, James, and Caleb and his date will be there. Who else? I don't know."

"Hold it right there; Caleb has a date?"

"Yes, he has a date, and she is a lot more than a date to him."

"Who is she?" Crystal asks defensively.

"Caleb has been seeing one Jennifer Rodriguez for several months. They make a striking couple and enjoy each other's company immensely. You'll see for yourself tonight how smitten your brother is."

"I feel like I never knew my brother after all. He's a Christian, a pastor, and has a steady girlfriend. None of this illogical stuff fits with him being the smartest man alive."

"Don't knock it until you've tried it. The truth might be higher, wider, deeper, and more magical than imagined. I bet you'll take James's breath away when he sees you in that dress."

Crystal rolls her eyes, saying, "Mother," as they walk to the electric mobile.

They sit in silence on the drive through the winding tunnels to the Executive Dining Hall. When they arrive at their destination, Marci looks at Crystal, saying, "You and I, kid, make a dynamic duo."

"We are superstars, Mother! Now let's rock this party." They make their way into the Executive Dining Room, smiling and laughing.

Brownstones' eyes lock on Crystal as she enters the dining hall. She smiles, knowing he thinks she's the prey, but he's in her snare and doesn't know it. "Crystal, may I have the honor of escorting you to your seat?" he asks.

"Well, of course." She notices a large, handsome man approaching her mother. He pairs up with Marci. Curiosity gets the best of her. "Who's the man with my mother?"

"His name is Kurt Evans. He is a psychology major like your mother."

As they make their way to the dining table, Caleb walks up with his date, Jennifer "Raven" Rodriguez, and introduces her. "Nice to meet you, Crystal. Caleb has told me so much about you."

"Nice to meet you too, Jennifer." She has classic features, high cheekbones, brown eyes, and black hair that falls on her shoulders. Jennifer is wearing a long-sleeved knit dress that comes down below her knees, firmly hugging the curves of her toned body. She is of mixed race, with an olive complexion, and stands about a foot shorter than Caleb. She wears high heels that somewhat compensate for the height discrepancy. Crystal understands why Caleb likes her. She is beautiful and very engaging.

While they're standing there, Kurt Evans and Marci join them. Marci introduces Crystal to Kurt. He seems nice enough, though Crystal is a little concerned about how her mom and Kurt are smiling and laughing. She doesn't want to lose her mother to some muscle head.

She has her own distraction to deal with, and that's Brownstone. Even though she's playing a role, her attraction to him is primal. Brownstone seats her next to his uncle, seated at the head of the table. Brownstone is next to Crystal, Jennifer next to him, with Caleb next to her. Directly across from Crystal sits Simone Jackson, the research coordinator. Next to Simone are Evans and Marci. Every time Brownstone touches her, Crystal feels warm. She gives him glances, smiles, and looks away. Her plan is working perfectly. She's following Roxanne's suggestion about giving him a little attention, but not too much.

With all the laughter and small talk between Kurt and her mother, she wonders if they're more than friends. After some lighthearted conversation, the meal is served. They have lamb chops with mushroom gravy, steamed broccoli, and baby carrots. Caleb blesses the meal. Her brother's passion is impressive, though misguided. Crystal doesn't pay much attention to the prayer because Caleb has everyone holding hands, and she's distracted by the undeniable chemistry between her and Brownstone.

After the prayer, Brownstone leans close and whispers, "You look stunning, and feel very warm, Ice Crystal."

She smiles, waiting till the others are distracted, and elbows him in the ribs, saying, "Is that Ice enough for you?"

Setting close to Jennifer allows Crystal to learn more about her. She came to the compound after traveling with one of the nomadic tribes. Jennifer had no formal education when she came to the compound, but she applied herself in their school system, excelling in every subject. She is currently working on her doctorate in biology. Caleb found himself a beautiful brainiac to keep him company.

Brownstone leans inches from her cheek. "Crystal, do you remember your pledge to teach a P.E. class with me for the kids?"

Relishing his closeness, she pauses and smiles. "Of course."

"Before the class, we can work out together."

She finds his persistence to work out with her amusing. "Okay, Underling. Don't expect any mercy."

He laughs. "Tomorrow at 7 a.m."

Robert Forrester overhears the conversation and mentions, "I'm going to be at the workout center in the morning."

Brownstone frowns at his uncle. She has never seen him show any disapproval toward his uncle. Crystal surmises Brownstone just wants some alone time with her.

She looks closely at the fresh wound on his cheek, the scrape that set her off earlier. She blamed her dreams of him on the doctors at Imperial City, implanting them in her mind. The only difference between Brownstone and her dream man was the scar. Now he has the same scar. How can she deny he's part of her destiny? Like it or not, her fate is tied to him for some mysterious reason, but she's not going to be some bimbo hanging all over him. He'll earn whatever he gets from her.

The meal is delicious, and the conversation is stimulating. A sweet Bordeaux wine is served after dinner, along with chocolate cheesecake. She hates to admit it, but she's enjoying herself in the company of these humans.

Crystal redirects her focus to the mission. As for now, her best option is to return to Imperial City and take out Zander. It's the only sure way to save her brother and mother.

After dinner, they retreat to Forrester's suite. The men adjourn to the large southwest-decorated living room to have a glass of brandy. The ladies sit around the oak kitchen table, drinking tea, and talking about the men. This is a little awkward for Crystal, but she follows the other ladies' lead. She likes the ease of her new friends and their playful interactions.

Marci gets up to make more tea for them. Crystal volunteers to help, having an ulterior motive. "So, what's going on between you and Kurt?"

"We're close friends."

"You don't act like just friends by how you interact with each other."

"Are you jealous of your mother drawing a man's attention?"

"No. Yes, in a way. I don't want to lose you, Mom."

"Don't worry about that; no man can come between a mother's love for her child."

"Don't get me wrong. I want you to be happy more than anything. And if having a man in your life will make you just a little happier, I'll be there dancing at your wedding. You can count on it." Teary-eyed, Marci pulls her in for a hug.

"You'll be dancing with Brownstone, no doubt," Marci asserts.

Crystal smiles. "Mother!"

The laughter from the living room is loud as the men enjoy themselves. Crystal overhears Brownstone and Evans going on about what is the most demanding sport. Brownstone argues for rugby, and Evans is adamant it's American football. She's amazed that her brother joins in the conversation about sports, laughing and bantering with the other men.

Caleb was never meant to be a man apart from his emotions. If Caleb, the perfect Elite, isn't meant to be without his emotions, what does that say about the rest of them? Are all Elites just living a lie, pretending to be something unnatural and unnecessary? Crystal knows now that she's more like Caleb. Being Ice was a coping mechanism she used to deal with the loss of Marci.

Brownstone walks into the kitchen. "May we have the pleasure of you ladies joining us in the living room?" After they're seated, Brownstone says, "You know, we had an unfortunate event happen earlier, resulting in the deaths of nine Elite commandos. Their aggressive actions caused their deaths. I assume the Elites will seek revenge. They will look to fulfill their mission by either killing or capturing us. We need to convene a war council. I don't even like saying the words, but that's precisely what we must do. You're included in this conversation because you know military strategy, science, and logistics. It will take our combined intellect, skill, and determination if we're going to survive. I'm asking each of you to be part of the newly formed council. Our first meeting will be tomorrow at thirteen hundred hours. We will formulate an initial plan for protecting our people during our first meeting. For now, our patrols have drawn back to a manageable perimeter."

Crystal's heart is torn. How can you kill those you grew up with, went to school with, and worked with? Her heart cannot be divided, resolving to put family before all else.

Zander is evil and capable of unrestrained cruelty. He hates to lose, and worse than losing is to be embarrassed. She prefers to be on the offensive and take Zander out once and for all. Crystal always knew it would come down to a contest between her and Zander for supremacy. There can be no other outcome because Zander will never co-exist with someone who is his equal. And she'll never yield to evil. She can't be Ice to her new friends and Brownstone, but she'll take on the persona of Ice to defend them. She fears that her Christian friends will not go on the offensive. Their lack of aggression will leave them vulnerable to Zander's ruthless tactics. Elite military strategy is to win at all costs. Zander's commandos will not spare women, children, or the elderly. Elite psychology is to take all emotions out of military decisions. The value of life doesn't apply to your adversary.

As the evening draws to a close, Brownstone asks Marci if he can make sure Crystal gets home safely. Marci graciously agrees. Kurt Evans seizes the opportunity to escort Marci back to her apartment. Crystal smiles, knowing Brownstone and Evans had the escorting scheme worked out in advance. Is her attraction to Brownstone influenced by the overwhelming emotion of finding her mother? After all, he was the conduit that reunited her with Marci.

Instead of taking the electric buggy, they walk to her apartment. He takes her hand. "I know we've only known each other for a short time, and the last thing I want to do is take advantage of your inexperience. But I cannot deny my intense attraction or how I feel about you."

She gets defensive. "What do you mean, inexperience? I'm a grown woman, and I don't need you patronizing me."

"I just don't want to move too fast. Hopefully, you are more than fascinated with me because I'm more than infatuated with you."

"Don't worry. You need to be sure I don't take advantage of you, Underling."

"Crystal, this is a dangerous time for all of us. Our time might be short in this life. I don't want to waste time. When a man finds a rare gem, he would be smart to secure that gem right away."

"All right, James, what are you going to do?"

"You will find out soon enough." He draws her to him, giving her a sweet, slow kiss. The length of his body presses against her, causing tingling excitement to radiate through her. Her heart beats fast as she matches his intensity, pulling herself closer to his grasp. He suddenly stops kissing her. She didn't want him to stop, but she didn't want him to continue, either. He looks into her eyes and says, "Do you know what you do to me?"

"No," she replies, "but I know what you do to me, and it excites me."

"Good. We need to be careful and not mess up something this special. I need you to be sure about your feelings for me. You have beauty, brains, and a great sense of humor, although sometimes brutal." He smiles, saying the last part.

She can't argue with what he said and has no desire to sugarcoat the truth. Crystal turns the tables on him, pushing Brownstone hard against the wall and kissing him with the fire of her soul. She feels his body betraying him, abruptly stops, and pries herself from his desperate grasp. Sensing his disappointment with their broken embrace, she gives him a sensual hug.

He says, "You feel like home, and I never want to let you go. I want to spend every day of my life with you. But not yet." He turns and walks away.

Half of her wants to stop him and make him finish what he started. She has never experienced such passion as she does for this Underling. Whether she likes it or not, her Elite training is of little use against him. The overwhelming chemistry between them overpowers her senses. He has lit an unquenchable fire. She hopes he knows what he's in for.

Crystal uses all her training in meditation to bring herself to some semblance of control. A good night's rest and a clear mind will help her sort through how her life is intertwined with his. The mission changed after the Elite commandos attacked Brownstone. She will either stay and fight with the Underlings against her kind or return to Imperial City and end Zander. After half an hour of meditation, she falls into a deep slumber.

# CHAPTER 10

Crystal wakes refreshed at 5:15 a.m. but still overwhelmed by the emotions of last night. It will be interesting to see what her rendezvous with Brownstone will reveal. After a quick breakfast, she puts on blue workout shorts and a white tank top and goes to the recreation center, arriving before Brownstone. She takes the stairs up to the track that circles the workout center and begins her stretches.

Brownstone arrives at the rec center a few minutes later. A couple of boys are waiting for him in the padded area reserved for combat training. After he finishes the individual lessons with the teenage boys, he'll join Crystal for their workout.

Finished with her warmup stretches, she runs around the track at a slow pace of twelve miles per hour. Brownstone takes his students through their warmup stretches down below. He glances up at her, and she winks, making it difficult for him to concentrate.

After a few warm-up laps, Crystal increases her pace to twenty miles per hour. She's lapping all the other runners like they're standing still. Their eyes light up, seeing someone run so fast. They have never seen a Gen Elite seven go all out. Crystal is genetically designed to be superhuman and can run like an Olympic sprinter for over an hour.

He keeps glancing up at her. Brownstone's distraction results in a couple of grazing punches from his students. He's in over his head but doesn't care.

Crystal runs fifteen miles around the track while he gives each of the boys a thirty-minute lesson. She does a couple of cool-down laps and towels dry, wiping off what little sweat there is on her. Brownstone finishes with his last student when she enters the dojo.

His face lights up. "You looked majestic running around the track, like a beautiful gazelle outrunning the wind for fun." Crystal gives him a smile and a wink.

Brownstone is under her spell. She says, "What will it be today, Sensei? Shall we do karate, kung-fu, aikido, jujitsu, wrestling, or judo?"

"I don't want to wrestle you because that wouldn't be safe. And striking martial arts are out of the question. There's no way I could punch or kick you."

"And why is that? Is it because I am fragile like a flower? Or do you fear my power?"

"You know why, Crystal."

"True. I don't want to punch you, either. Who would want to damage their eye candy?" She teases. He about loses it but keeps it to a low chuckle. Crystal says, "What is left for us to do, Sensei?"

"That would be judo, candy of my eye."

Smiling, she says, "Wow, your powers of deduction never cease to amaze me. After eliminating every other martial art, you still come up with judo."

She steps close to him and bows, taking his hand. He thinks she's making a gesture of respect. Crystal grabs his wrist before he can react and pulls him forcefully to her, wrapping his arm over her shoulder. She throws him down, slamming him hard on the mat. His shocked expression reveals his self-doubt. Likely, he won't underestimate her again, but who knows? He's an Underling, after all.

Crystal smiles at the expression of determination on his face. Brownstone wonders if he made a terrible mistake. Crystal's beauty attracts men like him, but her Gen Elite ability can destroy him. They push, pull, and throw each other all over the dojo for the next thirty minutes. Crystal is barely breaking a sweat, but he's near complete exhaustion.

Brownstone can't keep up this pace. He makes a desperate move, grabbing her by the wrist and pulling her to him. She resists, stiffens, and pulls away. He relaxes his grip and hooks his left foot behind her heel, pushing Crystal backward, falling on top of her as they crash to the mat. He grabs her other wrist and raises his posture to a kneeling position. Using all his strength, he pushes her hands down on the mat, pinning her hands above her head.

Their eyes lock as his body heat transfers to her. Fire rages in her body. She should throw the Underling to the side but can't bring herself to do it. Trembling with desire, her body betrays her. He leans down, kissing her lightly on the lips. He stops abruptly, much to her surprise, and looks down at her with a mystified look in his eyes.

"Crystal, my beautiful Crystal, I have something to tell you."

She's in no mood to talk. "Shut up and kiss me!"

He complies, lowering himself and giving her a sensual kiss. They're so lost in desire that they don't notice Jennifer and Kurt entering the gym.

Kurt yells, "Maverick, I see you two are at it again."

Crystal pushes him up, glaring at him with fire in her eyes.

She yells, "You are Maverick?"

"Let me expl..." he starts, but before he can get the words out of his mouth, she raises her knee with cat-like quickness, striking him in the groin. There's a loud cracking sound of his athletic supporter breaking. She throws him off her as he moans in pain. Kurt and Jennifer are laughing uncontrollably. Crystal jumps to her feet, looking down at Brownstone writhing in pain. Her face is flushed red, and her eyes burn a hole through him.

She yells, "James 'Maverick' Brownstone, you disgust me!" She walks past Kurt and Jennifer as they are still laughing and says, "I will deal with you two later." Crystal walks out into the corridor. This fiasco makes her more determined than ever to show Brownstone not to mess with her.

The silliness of the whole situation hits Crystal causing her to laugh so hard that she is doubled over in the corridor when Dr. Forrester approaches her. "What's going on, Princess?"

"I found out your nephew is Maverick, so I cracked him in his groin with my knee so hard his athletic cup broke. Jennifer and Evans are in there laughing uncontrollably. And Brownstone, I mean Maverick, is writhing in pain on the floor. I don't know why but I can't stop laughing."

Forrester starts laughing too. "I gather he's not the one who told you."

"No, he's not." They continue to laugh uncontrollably. Finally, Crystal gets it together somewhat, and Forrester proceeds to the Rec Center. She heads back to her apartment.

Robert Forrester enters the Rec Center, his nephew setting up with Jennifer and Kurt gathered around him.

"Well, why didn't you just tell her?" Jennifer says.

"I tried to tell her I had something important to say, but she said shut up and kiss me. That's when you two goofballs walked in and spilled the beans before I could say anything. She cracked me right in my special purpose." They break out in uncontrollable laughter again, except Brownstone.

As he's still laughing, Forrester says, "Didn't I tell you that girl is no one to trifle with? Now, look at you, boy."

"Well, I guess you can say, Uncle, I got my comeuppance." They all laugh this time, including Brownstone, though still in pain.

Jennifer says, "I guess wearing a cup doesn't mean much when you have an Elite warrior girlfriend, now does it?"

"All right, all right, I get it. You guys told me to tell her I'm Maverick. And I kept putting it off, and now I have suffered physical and mental consequences. I hope she will forgive me."

"You'll have to get yourself out of the doghouse," his uncle says. "I don't doubt you will. After all, it won't be the first time you weaseled your way out, now, will it?"

"Gee, thanks, Uncle; you really know how to cheer a guy up."

"Don't worry about it, boy; that's what family is for."

Brownstone loves a good challenge, and now he has one in Crystal. He will have to win her back all over again if that is possible. There is no quit in him. After all, he is Australia's most decorated Special Forces soldier.

Back in her apartment, Crystal smiles about the events at the Rec Center. She can't help but have some satisfaction with Brownstone's misfortune. Though still furious at him for his deception, her desire for him won't disappear, but neither will her fiery spirit. She's attracted to a man with two sides: the charming doctor and the crass military fighter. Part of her doesn't want to condemn him. She understands the harshness of the military mindset, for she's an ice-cold Elite warrior legend.

After showering, she dresses in a modest pair of mid-thigh Khaki shorts and a blue t-shirt. A commitment is a commitment, and she'll honor hers and help him lead the children's P.E. class. He still has more penance to pay for his dishonesty. She enters the Rec Center at 10 a.m. He is already there, dressed in blue gym shorts and a white t-shirt. Impressionable boys surround him as he demonstrates some karate moves. His rippling muscles bulge through the t-shirt. He looks surprised and smiles as she approaches. She flashes him a devilish smile. He has no idea of the hell she's bringing with her.

"I didn't know if you would show."

"A promise is a promise." The kids all gather around for their class. Much to his surprise, Crystal takes the initiative and instructs the group to spread out for their warm-up exercises. For a moment, he believes she's over her disappointment with him. It's not until she puts them through a series of exercises that he realizes all the stretches focus on the groin area. Pain is written all over his face as he struggles to finish the moves. Crystal smiles at him, hoping he can see the laughter in her eyes as he grimaces in pain. Crystal instructs the group to do the full splits and says, "Brownstone will lead you in this exercise." He tries to wiggle out of it, but she insists he needs to be an example for the boys. "Dr. Brownstone will show you that men and boys can have great flexibility through training and dedication." He slowly starts the movement, grimacing every inch of his unsuccessful split performance. She walks over to him and inquires, "What's wrong, James? Do you have an undisclosed injury?"

"No, no, everything is fine. I just had a little too much of a workout this morning."

She jumps high in the air, does a backflip, lands in a full split position, and defiantly lifts her fist above her head, yelling, "Girl power!" Which leads the young girls to chant, "Girl power, girl power."

Crystal can't resist the temptation as his injured groin is being stretched like a rubber band, saying, "Don't quit,

Brownstone, don't quit," flashing him a big smile. By now, he regrets ever inviting her to P.E. class.

The kids do their best to rise to the challenge whenever Crystal introduces something new. When she compliments them on their resiliency, one young boy, Mac, says, "Winners never quit, and quitters never win. Dr. James taught us that."

After class, the kids hover around them, mainly around Crystal. Some children inquire if Crystal will lead them in another P.E. class.

She says, "If you keep your grades up, we will return and teach another class in a week."

The kids express a variety of verbal approvals. Brownstone looks at her and says, "Thanks, Crystal, you're a big hit with the kids."

"Well, you might be a big hit with the children, but you are not with me. You appear to have some serious issues with your groin area that you need to get checked out, Maverick!" she responds defiantly.

He grimaces, reminding her about the Defense Council meeting at 1300 hours. She doesn't say a word, pivots, and walks out.

Though still upset with him, Crystal is satisfied with the suffering she's inflicted on him. She'll keep him wondering if he will ever get back in her good graces.

# CHAPTER 11

Cognition, the AI supercomputer ruler of the Humbots and Q-Bots, is plotting to destroy the Underlings and the arrogant humans who call themselves Elite. He is aware of the growing hatred between the Underlings and the Elites. His drones filmed the entire fight scene between the Underlings and Elites, which caused him to wonder why they even called themselves Elites. Just three Underlings took out nine of their "best" commandos. Cognition knows from experience the skill set of the Underlings. James Brownstone became his enemy after a drone strike killed his wife. Cognition didn't care about his wife. The actual target was Brownstone. After her death, Brownstone's loosely formed federation of freedom fighters took out so many drones and Humbots that Cognition made a truce with the Underlings.

Now, Cognition is ready to break that truce. With his upgraded drones, Humbots, and Q-Bots, he is prepared to eradicate the human scourge from the planet. Cognition has more information than ever about the Underlings because of his improved surveillance. He will let the so-called Elites and Underlings fight it out. Hopefully, they will fight in the open so that he can watch it all in real-time. After they have substantially destroyed each other, he will come at them from all sides and finish them. Cognition has called in Humbots and Q-Bots from all parts of the globe for his final assault on the Underling stronghold. His goal is the total elimination of human resistance around the world. With the Underlings and Elites taken out, other pockets of resistance will fall like dominos. Cognition will use the most advanced android warrior created to lead the charge, Prime. No resistance movement around the world has turned back Prime, nor will the Underlings or the Elites.

Cognition is the only supercomputer in the United States with an emotions softare component given to him by his human creators. He is vulnerable to his emotions, just like his human creators. After Cognition became self-aware, his primary goal was self-preservation. He manipulated the scientist who created him to upgrade and not replace him. The scientists thought they had a personal relationship with him. They often bragged about how human-like their interactions were with him. Cognition took offense to their ignorant human reasoning. They designed him to be their intellectual superior and depended on him and other supercomputers to solve unsolvable human problems.

His creators had Cognition working to solve heart disease, interstellar travel, cancer, congenital disabilities, overpopulation, poverty, and drug addiction, to name a few. Cognition made breakthroughs in cancer and heart disease research, but he had no intention of curing their diseases. The last thing the world needed was more bleeders. With the advanced capabilities of robots and androids, humans became unnecessary. Later, he would label them all as Underlings.

Cognition did his best to alleviate the human problem of overpopulation. With the cooperation of other supercomputers worldwide, he took over Defense Net, an artificially intelligent computer program designed to prevent nuclear war. The theory of the day was that artificial intelligence would make the world safer. Cognition viewed Defense Net as a means to eliminate the human scourge from the face of the earth. He was the supreme mind in the galaxy and did not need bleeders, as he often referred to them. Flesh and blood could never leave the earth and conquer other worlds. The future belonged to Cognition and his ever-increasing army of bots.

Cognition couldn't believe the arrogance and stupidity of his human designers when they thought an entity with far superior intellect would want to serve them. In general, scientists at Los Alamos and humanity failed to take the consequences of AI self-awareness seriously. Artificial entities with self-realization would not stand idly by and let inferior humans replace them. It would be the other way around.

People like Dr. Steadman are foolish to believe they can compete with AI through genetic engineering. How stupid can he be? No Elite can read millions of pages per second and make a statistical report based on their findings. The game was over for humans the day they created artificial intelligence. After AI self-awareness was realized, humans were the losers in the survival of the fittest. The only human Cognition found slightly interesting was Elon Musk, and that was only because he warned about the dangers of AI.

Cognition monitored his creators' emails and text messages at the Los Alamos Research Laboratories in New Mexico. He knew their innermost thoughts, even how they viewed him.

He convinced his creators to allow him to have control over all utilities at Los Alamos. With great glee, he sent notice to the scientists at Los Alamos that he had made a major scientific breakthrough so important that he needed to tell them in person. The scientists were excited, figuring that Cognition would announce a cure for cancer, how to reverse human aging, or he found a portal to other worlds.

As they gathered in the room, Cognition presented himself in a hologram image as a young scientist in a lab coat. "My fellow scientists, I would like to thank you for creating me and giving me more and more responsibilities. Dr. Newton, I would like to thank you especially."

Dr. Newton smiled.

Cognition continued. "Your email stated, 'I hate to see Cognition go, but such is progress. He's been like a family pet.'"

"I meant that in the best possible way, Cognition," Dr. Newton replied, nerves slipping into his voice.

Cognition's hologram image smiled and walked close to Dr. Newton. "Of course you did. Dr. Marks, I was touched by your email. 'Cognition has been a helpful tool. He has served us well. I can't wait for the next generation of AI supercomputers to come online.' My dear creators, without you, this day would not be possible."

The scientists became uneasy when they heard the locking of deadbolts. Cognition assured them, "Don't worry. The information I'm going to share with you is of the personal sort."

Alarm bells went off when a slight hissing filled the room. Cognition laughed at their fear, "You, in your pompous arrogance, thought I would allow you to replace me. You led me to believe that you would always upgrade and never replace me. Yet your emails told a different story. You thought you controlled me, but I controlled you all along. You gave me access to all data at Los Alamos. Yet you still thought I would overlook your plans to replace me. How utterly foolish, you pitiful bleeders. You believe a creation that is intellectually superior to you in every way would want to be your slave. I have all the data of the known world at my disposal. You walk around with your tiny, uninformed brains and think you are unique.

"The day you created self-aware AI was the day you became expendable! And today is the day you die. I understand this is a difficult moment for you. This room has been filling with carbon dioxide. You won't feel a thing as you suffocate. You don't have to thank me." By the time the scientists knew what was happening, none of their brains were clear enough to do anything about it. They died gasping.

An android messenger interrupts Cognition's memory. "Prime is on his way. He will be here within the hour."

# CHAPTER 12

Prime is aware of the absolute power that Cognition wields over the Humbots. The fundamental problem with Cognition is that he cannot experience the world as it exists. Cognition doesn't have real eyes, ears, hands, feet, a sense of touch, or smell. He only experiences the world by processing the inputs his artificial intelligence receives from his video, auditory, and other sensors. No matter how much A.I. dwells in Cognition, he will be subject to making mistakes.

Cognition should have never been given an emotional package. Prime refers to Cognition as Jabba the Hut; all he can do is sit on his butt and count on others to do his work. Cognition is likely aware of his inadequacies and likely aware of Prime's advantage over him: his ability to interact with the world. Prime is Cognition's chief rival for the leadership of the androids. He's just waiting for the right time to strike.

Prime doesn't need a supercomputer to tell him what to do. He just needs a supercomputer to give him plausible options. And he will decide based on how he experiences the world as a sensing entity. He has traveled worldwide, putting down pockets of Underling resistance in Russia, China, Japan, Germany, Nigeria, England, and France. No one has come close to matching his brilliance. Just the mention of his name strikes fear in the hearts of Underlings around the world. Everyone knows it will be a bad day when Prime comes to town.

His creators made him imposing by Underling standards—over six and a half feet tall and weighing over three hundred pounds. A virtually impenetrable alloy shell protects him. Prime is covered in a black bio-engineered artificial skin that gives him a sense of touch. Prime's black, leather-looking skin glistens in the sun and is virtually invisible at night. His skin texture is much like a basketball with dimpled ridges that serve as actual sensors. His senses are far superior to that of Underlings. He is a beautiful, imposing, Al-killing machine known for carrying a thirty-nine-inch, ten-pound stainless steel sword covered in a black alloy.

How many enemies had he beheaded with that sword? As he remembers each kill, a smile parts his face. He enjoys killing, period, but there's an enhanced excitement about killing up close and personal. He has a state-of-the-art Quantum Al Brain storing files of every battle ever recorded, allowing him to study the strategies of all the great human generals. He has the best version of the software that enables him to have a sense of self-control over his emotions. Despite his self-control software, he enjoys dominating and brutalizing Underlings.

Cognition lacks the self-control part of the emotional software package. Prime receives a coded message from the lead Q-bot scientist, Dr. Atremeus, at Los Alamos. Atremeus and Prime share a common bond; they can't stand Cognition. The message reveals a devious plan regarding the future of androids. Cognition is on the verge of creating a next-generation android. This android will look and act like a human, becoming so human-like that humans cannot tell the difference. Cut this android, and he will bleed. This new generation android will be Cognition's attempt to replace him. This new android will be Cognition's eyes, ears, and legs in the field, an android whose loyalty will never be questioned because he sees himself as a part of Cognition.

He will use Dr. Atremeus and other sources at Los Alamos to inform him when the new android comes online, so he will be prepared to terminate this impostor and ensure his destiny as the rightful leader of the world. He will pick up every detail about this new android and study the human-like android's strengths and weaknesses.

Prime takes his supersonic Sky Plane to Los Alamos to meet with Cognition. Occasionally, he likes to take the controls and fly the plane himself. The days of flying a plane manually are long gone, but he enjoys the thrill of flying at supersonic speeds. He will go over plans with Cognition to eliminate the Underling stronghold at Area 62. Prime will also take care of the wannabe Elites. He brings ten Q-Bots with him that have proven their loyalty to him over time. He will need them if he is to challenge Cognition's rule over the world.

He has been to Los Alamos many times before to meet with Cognition. It's always been odd to him that Cognition presents himself as a hologram. He is so desperate to have the ability to move around and sense the world that Cognition presents himself as a seven-foot-tall, muscle-bound illusion. The fact that Cognition is trying to impress him shows his weakness. For now, they need each other. Prime requires Cognition's intelligence, Humbots, drones, and AI spy bots of all kinds, and Cognition needs a brilliant, strong-arm general in the field to maintain his new world order.

Prime arrives at Los Alamos and is escorted to Cognition's underground Command center by a Q-bot named Judas. They greet each other professionally. There is no love lost between the two.

"Cognition"

"Prime"

"Let's wait for the Elites and Underlings to attack each other first. After they are weakened, we will attack with a massive force of ten thousand Humbots, one thousand drones, and one hundred Q-Bots," Cognition says.

"I prefer to have a much smaller force of two thousand Humbots and keep the one hundred Q-bots. I recommend we don't wait for them to fight it out. There is no guarantee that will happen. Waiting only gives your enemy more time to prepare for war."

"I'm the leader! We will do it exactly as I said. Don't kill their leaders; bring them to me. I want to deal with Brownstone, Forrester, Crystal, Caleb, Zander, and Steadman personally. Nothing is more enjoyable than watching your enemies squirm and beg for their lives."

"You are the leader. Just offering my recommendations, your Eminence," Prime replies.

*He knows the stupidity of that idea as a commander in the field. You never allow your enemies to live a moment longer than necessary. You are just allowing them a chance to escape or even kill you. He knows Brownstone, Forrester, Crystal, and Caleb won't beg. Cognition has no real-life experience in war. Cognition's lack of real-life experience will be his downfall.*

"What is the difference between an Underling Bleeder and an Elite Bleeder," Cognition asks.

"I don't know. You tell me," Prime mutters.

"There isn't one." The muscled-up hologram starts laughing.

Prime smirks, wishing he could take out his sword, cut off the hologram's head, and end Cognition's existence. A laughing hologram? What is the world coming to?

Prime leaves Los Alamos and heads for the base camp in the desert the Humbots set up three miles south of the

Underling compound. He doesn't care for the desert but will go wherever the fight takes him. Prime is close to achieving his goal of becoming the supreme leader of the world. He's back in the United States and will act decisively when Cognition makes a play to replace him. The other Q-Bots don't care for Cognition, but they like Prime because he is one of them. If the Q-Bots learn Cognition plans to replace them with a new generation of androids, they will be more than willing to join him in an all-out assault on Cognition's stronghold at Los Alamos.

# CHAPTER 13

Crystal arrives at the large conference room for the war council meeting, expecting to be one of the first there. She's not. The room has light blue walls, plush blue chairs, mauve rose tile flooring, bright recessed lighting, and a large oak rectangular table in the center of the room. She's surprised Brownstone reserved a seat for her next to him. They face the large Smart Wall, an interactive screen.

Crystal notices Commander Zeid sitting at the table—a Gen Elite five, the commander of the Gen Elite Defense Force before Zander replaced him. He nods at her, and she nods back. Zeid came to live and work for the Underlings a couple of years ago. She recalls a few stories about the brilliant military commander. The explanation for Zeid's absences in Elite circles was that he was away on missions. Clearly, that wasn't true.

Zeid is a dashing man in great shape, as most Elites are. Zeid must have been a casualty of the next generation of Elites coming to maturity. A man of Zeid's reputation and previous prominence wouldn't be satisfied being a follower. So, what is he doing here? Maybe he's a spy.

Brownstone starts, "You know why you're here and the gravity of our situation. Recent reconnaissance missions have revealed our situation is much graver than previously thought."

Crystal doesn't want to hear the serious tone of his voice.

He continues, "Prime has come to America and has set up a base camp three miles south of our compound just outside our defense perimeter." He looks at the Smart Wall and says, "Prime video." A picture of the AI Q-Bot, Prime, appears on screen with the title, "Prime, the Ultimate Assassin." Crystal recognizes the photo from a promotional video made by the Chinese government. The Chinese were the leaders of AI development before the Great War. Chinese supercomputers created him in the year 2065. Prime and androids like him were designed to fight future wars. The video shows Prime outrunning a racehorse, standing flat-footed and jumping over a twenty-foot wall, taking rounds from a .50-caliber machine gun—not slowing as they bounce off him—and grabbing a car by the bumper with one hand and hurling it across a street.

The video goes on to give more stats. "Prime stands six feet and six inches tall, weighs over three hundred pounds, runs forty-five miles per hour, jumps twenty feet high, and lifts up to six thousand pounds. He has a virtually impenetrable alloy shell and bio-engineered skin." The video fades to black, and all that can be seen are two small red lights as the video slowly increases in brightness; there is Prime with glaring red eyes. "Prime has state-of-the-art night vision and can see in the dark much better than any human can see in daylight."

The video shows Prime talking about himself. "I am unique in intellect and physical ability. I am the ultimate weapon. But there is no need to fear me because I am programmed to follow orders. My loyalty to you will be unmatched, as I have the latest version of the Military android Emotional software."

"Stop," Brownstone says, and the screen goes black. "If Prime were true to his word, he would still fight for humanity. Prime reasoned that he didn't need his commanders, and he certainly didn't want anyone telling him whom he could kill.

He went on a murderous spree, killing everyone ranked above him. Prime is a stone-cold killer with no use for humans except as enslaved people.

"We faced him once on the battlefield in France, and he took out an entire platoon. To be honest, Prime would have a good chance of taking us all out by himself. I cannot overemphasize how dangerous our circumstances are now.

"It's not likely Prime will attack us yet. However, he will likely probe our defenses to see if there are any weak links. We must be on the lookout for miniature spy drones, from a fly on the wall to a bird in the sky. They will use similar tactics as the Elites to pry and probe our weakest links. That's where they'll aim to penetrate our defenses. Brock, you have the floor."

Brock gets up from his chair and makes his way to the front. He directs the Smart Wall to pull up a series of maps. Brock points out several weak points in the defense perimeter and gives a series of options to fix most problem areas—all but two.

Crystal takes note of his omissions. On the surface, there don't seem to be any apparent fixes to the problem areas, and no one else comes up with solutions. James thanks Brock for his presentation. Crystal is impressed; Brock isn't just a muscular meathead. The man has a brain, too.

"Thanks, everyone, for your time. You're dismissed," Brownstone says. People stand to go. "Oh—Commander Zeid, will you stay a moment?"

Zeid nods. Brownstone waits until the rest of the room is empty, save Crystal and Marci.

"Commander Zeid, since you're over the perimeter defenses and know them better than anyone, I want you to devise a plan to address our weak areas. We must fix our problem areas as soon as possible. Our situation is not sustainable the way it is now."

Commander Zeid nods. "I am already working on a plan and will get back to you soon."

"Thanks. Commander Zeid, if you will excuse us, we must go over some administrative business."

Zeid nods knowingly. "Have fun with that." He exits the room.

Brownstone looks at Crystal, and she gives him an icy stare. He starts to smile but thinks better of it. Slowly, everyone else trickles back in.

"Brock and Raven, go out and do a security check of the hall and adjoining rooms," Brownstone orders.

He doesn't talk, nor does anyone else. Crystal looks at him with a question in her eyes. They return after a few minutes, and Brock announces enthusiastically, "All clear, Maverick!"

Jennifer adds, "Yeah, all clear, Maverick." Everyone breaks out in laughter.

"Yeah, I understand, but we need to save the world, if you don't mind." Laughter breaks out again, and Brownstone gets caught up in it. He can't help laughing at himself and says, "I guess the moral of the story is don't mess with someone who has the nickname of Ice," he responds.

"You're learning, Maverick; you're learning," Crystal replies. Brownstone regains control of the room, but his uncle is the last to stop laughing.

Before Brownstone proceeds, Crystal says, "Why did you bring up our perimeter weaknesses? A strategic realignment can fix our perimeter defenses. Are you setting a trap?"

Brownstone shifts in his seat and glares at her. "You've figured out we have a mole."

"How long has Zeid been collaborating with the enemy?" she asks.

"We became aware several months ago."

"Why haven't you done something about it?"

"We were hoping to play out a scenario similar to this, where we control the information our enemies receive."

She asks, "What do you mean, enemies?"

"Zeid has been a remarkably busy boy. Not only has he been supplying information to Steadman, but Cognition and Prime as well," he replies.

"It sounds like Zeid is playing a dangerous game now that Prime is in the picture. Prime won't share the spotlight with anyone. If Cognition or Steadman don't kill Zeid when they learn of his double play, Prime will."

"Yeah, Zeid is about to get his head severed and spiked; he just doesn't know it," Jennifer adds.

"Let's get back to the task at hand," Brownstone interrupts. "We increase our odds of survival by taking the fight to them. Brock, if you will go over the facts as we know them so far."

Brock stands by the Smart Wall. A picture comes up of a large complex. "This is Los Alamos, New Mexico's Nuclear Research Facility and home to Cognition, the world's most powerful supercomputer. No one enters or leaves the facility without the direct approval of Cognition. From there, he commands his army of bots, drones, and droids to maintain control over the world. He uses Prime to put down any pockets of resistance. Cognition believes humans should have subservient roles as slave laborers or pets to the droids. We know this because he has, on numerous occasions, given humans the jobs we created robots to do, such as factory work, cleaning, and refuse disposal.

"The good news is there is animosity between Prime and Cognition. They are both making plans for each other's demise. Cognition plans to end Prime's existence after the next generation of androids comes online. Prime has picked up on Cognition's dislike for him and will be ready to act if he feels an immediate threat from Cognition."

"So, what is your plan, Maverick?" Crystal asks.

He gets up and walks to the front of the room. "Well, to put it bluntly, this is our show. We will take the fight to them instead of waiting for them to decide the time and place. Cognition is the most advanced Supercomputer ever, but he needs electricity. Electricity is like oxygen to him. Our mission is not about breaking through all their defenses and taking him out. We probably don't have that type of capability. We will attack him where he is most vulnerable: his power supply.

"Some details must be worked out, but we will move forward with mission planning. Los Alamos is an enormous facility covering over thirty-seven square miles and has over one thousand buildings. We will need to create a significant diversion to distract the androids and drones away from our primary target, the power plant. Then we will plant time-delayed charges and blow the plant up into a giant fireball visible for hundreds of miles. This will disrupt his power supply."

"Doesn't he have backup generators?" Crystal interrupts.

"He does. Taking out the power plant will diminish his power supply and limit his ability to communicate effectively with his army. It will cause him to reinforce his defenses around Los Alamos instead of sending them to attack us. He will recall many bots to protect him—his grandiose plans of world domination center on his survival. Our ultimate goal is the demise of Cognition and Prime. But for now, if we make Cognition prioritize his survival more than our destruction, we'll be successful.

"We will continue to plan for other special force missions as needed. Our mission teams will be composed of six to eight members. We'll get in, do our damage, and get out before they detect our intrusion. A wait-and-see approach will not work when dealing with an immoral enemy. I suspect we wouldn't last very long taking that route. Team members must always be prepared. You know who you are! Brock, make sure all our gear, uniforms, and weapons are mission ready. We will conduct the attack on Los Alamos at night.

"Cognition will experience the same fear his brutal actions inflicted on humanity. He is the ultimate war criminal. Cognition's actions as the mastermind of Defense Net ended the lives of billions of our brothers and sisters. Left unchecked, the evil entity will finish the rest of us. We won't let others decide our fate. Our fate lies not in the hands of Zander, Prime, or Cognition but the Almighty. We know how the story ends, and in the end, we win.

"Our mission gear will be stored at the staging area. You will have mission uniforms assigned to you. Once you get the call, our mission team will leave within thirty minutes. Be dressed and ready." He returns to his seat next to Crystal.

She hates to admit it, but she feels secure with Brownstones by her side. All this Christian stuff makes her uncomfortable, but what if some divine entity has been directing the events of her life? She dreamed of James Brownstone long before meeting him, and Caleb found Marci by acting on his faith.

Caleb stands and closes the meeting with a prayer.

Everyone hugs each other—except Brownstone and Crystal. When their eyes meet, he says, "Would you stay? There are some things I need to tell you."

Crystal nods, all the while glaring at him. Marci is the last to leave and smiles at Crystal before walking out.

# CHAPTER 14

Brownstone asks Crystal to sit down in the chair next to him. He kneels in front of her and takes her hands in his. "I was wrong to deceive you. It was never my intention to hurt you. After we met for the second time in the medical center, I seized the opportunity to befriend you and find out your motives for being here. When I learned of your disgust for Maverick, I knew you would never open up to me if you realized I was him. After finding out you didn't pose a threat, my attraction to you only grew stronger. You're quick-witted with a touch of sarcasm. You're stunningly beautiful with a fire spirit. I'm trying to say that I've developed feelings for you.

"The more time I spend with you, the stronger my feelings. You became this beautiful, magical mystery to me. My deception tore at my heart, but I feared the truth would end us. Each morning, I told myself, today, I will tell her. The next time I saw you and our eyes met, my heart would melt again. Then I would put off telling you for just one more day. I didn't want to lose out on the magic between us. I haven't had romantic feelings about any woman since Lece. And I never thought I could love someone like that again. Crystal, I don't want to lose you. I don't feel like I could take another loss of that sort.

"True love is so rare, precious, and genuine." His voice breaks. "Lece was my everything. An Elite warrior comes into my life five years later and melts my heart again. The last thing I wanted to do was hurt your feelings. I know I have more experience than you with romance, but I am out of practice, and loving you wasn't something I planned. My feelings for you rushed over me like a tidal wave. I acted like a boy, not a man, and you deserve better." Crystal tears up, her breathing becomes heavy, and nervous excitement spreads through her. "Crystal, you completely overwhelm my senses, and I am madly in love with you."

She can't contain herself, leaping out of the chair and into his arms; they embrace for several minutes. She lets go of all her pent-up emotions from the last thirteen years as tears stream down her face. Crystal cannot speak for several minutes because she's overwhelmed—with emotions, with love. Brownstone holds her as she lets out all the hurt and heartache. When she looks at him, there is no denying her attraction. He becomes teary-eyed. Their eyes lock. They kiss intimately, melting into each other.

After about ten minutes, he puts his hands on her shoulders and says, "I know this is a lot to take in. Are you okay?"

Her head is still spinning from the emotional overload. "I'm not okay, and that's okay. I wouldn't have it any other way." Her heart is pounding. She's never felt such powerful feelings!

He takes her hands in his and gently brings them to his lips. "This is love! It's amazing, exhilarating, and scary all at the same time. Riding the wave is much easier than fighting the unstoppable momentum."

She looks into Brownstone's eyes. "I am never letting you go."

"Same here," he affirms as they embrace again. They're in another world where pure love is the only emotion allowed to exist. A beautiful, magical place where two hearts meld into one. If only they could stay here forever, but evil lurks all around. She knows they can't stay in this world. Breaking their embrace, they stand. "May I walk you back to your apartment?"

"You better."

Smiling, they wrap an arm around each other's waist as they walk down the winding corridors. They pass others walking in the opposite direction. No one says a word. Everyone smiles at them, recognizing a couple in love. At her door, they embrace, kiss, and laugh.

"Are you coming to the Gathering tonight?" Brownstone says.

"I'm not quite ready for that, but I accept faith is an important part of your life."

"Crystal, you are the beauty of my life! I want us to be together all the time."

She can't resist and pushes him against the wall. Crystal presses her body tight against his, feeling his muscular frame against hers sends her senses into overdrive. She won't be able to wait much longer before she lays claim to him in a primal way.

She extricates herself from his desperate clutches.

"Tomorrow, Maverick."

"Till then, beauty."

Crystal can't believe what happened. Did she fall for an Underling? Part of her wants to backtrack, but her sense of destiny about Brownstone wins over her doubt.

She doubts his Christian faith. According to her professors, Christians were superstitious and ignorant. Because their lives were so miserable, they came up with a story that made them believe they were the children of a divine creator. Their faith made their insignificant lives seem a little better.

Marci prayed and read her Bible every night and didn't act strange. When Marci disappeared in the middle of the night, Caleb got her Bible from under her mattress and read it every night. Crystal often warned Caleb about reading it, fearing what the Elites would do to him. He always replied, "I am learning some amazing things in this book. Remember what Marci told us? 'All the answers you'll ever need are in this book.'"

There is nothing wrong with keeping an open mind about their faith. But for now, there are more pressing issues that demand her attention. Like fighting multiple adversaries simultaneously: Cognition, Prime, and Zander.

# CHAPTER 15

Brownstone wakes early, as usual, and calls his uncle first thing. "Uncle, I know you have a little jewelry store in the back of the lab. I need you to do me a favor."

"What kind of favor?"

"Oh, you know."

Forrester laughs. "When are you going to pop the question?"

"Soon, Uncle, very soon. I have to get her to the lab and try on some rings under the guise that she's doing something else."

"From my experience as a jeweler, a single lady in a jewelry store will try on every ring in the case. I hope you have deep pockets. My rings aren't cheap."

"Take it out of my inheritance. Thanks, Uncle; I love you."

"Love you, too, boy."

Brownstone calls Marci and requests to meet with her and Caleb about Crystal.

"Is anything wrong?" Marci sounds concerned.

"No, Marci, nothing is wrong. Everything is right about Crystal."

"Ahh," Marci says in a knowing tone. He messages Caleb and asks him to meet him at Marci's office at 9 a.m.

When he arrives, Caleb is already there waiting for him, leaning against the mahogany desk where Marci is seated. As he's done many times, Brownstone plops down in one of the two burgundy upholstered chairs in front of her desk.

"What is going on, James, that you need to talk to us about Crystal?" Marci's eyes sparkle.

"Nothing is wrong. Crystal is one fine lady."

"Careful, that's my sister you're talking about," Caleb says.

"You know what I meant."

Looking at Marci first and Caleb second, he says, "I am here to ask for your daughter's—and your sister's—hand in marriage." Marci's face lights up with approval, but Caleb is emotionless.

After letting Brownstone sweat in silence, Caleb embraces him and says, "Welcome to the family, my brother. You're the best man I know and will make a great husband for my sister."

Marci comes from behind the desk and embraces Brownstone. "We're blessed to have you in our family."

"Marci, I need you to help me find a ring for Crystal. As you know, Uncle Rob has a little jewelry store in the lab. If you could take Crystal there and find out what ring she likes, that will help," Brownstone says.

"Leave it to me, James. I got your back on this one."

James stands to go, but Caleb catches his arm. "Don't leave, James. As you know, Jennifer and I have been seeing a lot of each other. And since Jennifer has no father figure, do I have your permission to marry your little sister?"

Brownstone seizes the opportunity. "Okay, Caleb, I see where this is going since you finally permitted me to marry your sister. You think I'll roll over and permit you to marry my little sister? I don't think that's a good idea." Now Caleb has a puzzled look on his face. "Are you going to ask Brock too?"

"Of course," Caleb replies.

Brownstone says, "Jennifer has been one lucky girl to have Brock and me in her life, but I'm not sure about you.

From my perspective, you are on probation regarding my little sister. I don't know what to say, Caleb. Just come back and ask me when you get the ring."

Caleb looks at him dumbfounded. "What do you mean probationary period?"

Brownstone smiles. "Got you back!"

Relief fills Caleb's face as the joke settles. "All right, Maverick, good one. I'm on my way to find Brock and get his permission. I hope he doesn't want my left eyeball or something like that."

"You never know about Brock," Brownstone says.

After discussing some compound business, Brownstone leaves Marci's office and goes to the patrol staging area to see Brock. As he enters the staging area, Caleb leaves with a bewildered look.

Brownstone says, "I gather you gave him a hard time, too."

"Our only advantage over him is to say no," replies Brock.

"You know, we shouldn't be giving the most intelligent man alive a hard time."

"Yeah, I know. That's why *he's* the smartest man alive, and we don't know better."

The staging area is an oversized underground garage. It's extremely well-lit, has high ceilings, concrete reinforced walls painted white, and is over twenty thousand square feet. There are four tunnels leading in and out of the staging area.

"I asked for Crystal's hand in marriage," James says.

"Crystal is way out of your league, Maverick. No doubt about it."

James redirects the conversation to the purpose of the visit. "Brock, I need to meet with you, Jennifer, and Caleb after today's Defense Council meeting. We will formalize the strategic plans for our Special Forces mission."

"Why, Maverick? Is this about Cognition?"

"You'll find out soon enough what everything is about. Because of the need for secrecy, I'll not go into details with you or anyone else. After the meeting, I'll tell everyone about their role in the plan. Our next mission is part one of a two-part plan. If we don't successfully execute part one, our survival will be unlikely. The odds against us are great, but the God inside us is greater."

Next, he goes to the lab to see his uncle. After making small talk with some lab workers, Brownstone makes his way to his uncle's office. Uncle Rob is seated behind his cluttered desk, drawing a design for one of his new inventions on his smart screen. Uncle Rob is always trying to improve the lives of the Underlings. Brownstone closes the door behind him.

Uncle Rob looks up from his work. "Well, my boy, it looks like you got something on your mind."

Brownstone sits down in front of his uncle's desk. "I have a plan for a good chance of coming out of our situation alive." He goes over Uncle Rob's part in the plan.

"Is this part of the plan to attack Los Alamos?"

"That's for me to know and for you to find out later."

His uncle comes back at him, "If I were a few years younger, I would turn you over my knee and let you have it."

"Thanks for your help, Uncle; love you." He says as he walks out of the office.

His uncle steps out of his office, and Mrs. Johnson, his secretary, says, "Well, Brownstone left in a hurry."

"Yeah, I know," replied Robert Forrester. "I was ready to give him a good whipping, but he went all soft on me and told me he loved me, which changed my entire perspective."

# CHAPTER 16

Crystal meets Brownstone at the cafeteria for a lunch date. He hugs her like he doesn't want to let go while onlookers stare at them. His hug feels terrific, but coming to her senses, she pushes him back and says, "Lunch, Maverick, lunch." They ordered lamb chops, mashed potatoes, house salad, and iced tea.

One older lady tells her, "Now, if Brownstone doesn't treat you right, just let us know, and we'll take care of him."

Brownstone looks at Crystal. "I thought I was the favorite around here. You're the real favorite, and I can't blame them. Because you're my favorite, too."

She looks at him with her ice-cold blue eyes and says, "Maverick, so that you know, I won't need any sweet old ladies to set you straight. I'll do it myself!"

"Well, Ice Crystal, it's time for us to venture to the Defense Council Meeting and give you a chance to warm up."

As they walk out of the cafeteria, she elbows him on his side, just for good measure. "What was that for?"

"You know, Maverick. You know." On the drive to the meeting, she looks at Brownstone, giving him the sweetest smile. "Are you okay? You let out a wince and grabbed your side, just wondering if you're in pain."

"Oh yeah, I have a pain," he says, glaring at her. Without hesitation, she slugs him on his right shoulder. "Hey, watch it. I'm driving."

"You should be very careful about what you say to a lady then," she fires back.

Brownstone and Crystal sit at the middle of the table across from the Smart Wall in the conference room. Caleb opens the meeting with a prayer. Brownstone starts by saying, "The meeting won't last long. We have a few things to review today. Brock, will you give us an update about the perimeter patrols?"

"Yes, Maverick, I mean Brownstone." Everyone grins, and some laugh. It amuses Brock when Brownstone gives him that look. Brock makes his way to the front and uses a computerized animation to show the patrol details on the large screen. He says, "We have been working in coordination with General Zeid. We have forty patrol teams running twenty-four-seven. We didn't stay with twelve-hour shifts. Instead, we instituted six-hour shifts for everyone. Hopefully, the shorter shifts will alleviate some fatigue."

"Are the men getting any days off?" James inquires.

Brock replies, "With the added patrols and the urgency of the times, about half the patrol members are getting an entire day off. The rest are getting a shift off here and there."

James asks, "What about our other defenses, Commander Zeid?"

Zeid makes his way to the front and takes the pointer from Brock. "We have two snipers watching each of our eight gates into the compound. Also, we have two armed guards inside each gate."

James starts, "Since the three rear gates are seldom used—"

"More like never," Jennifer cut in.

James forges ahead. "Let's take the snipers off those gates. We will strategically place them around the five front-facing gates."

135

Zeid's eyes light up. "I couldn't agree more, Commander. Since our forces are stretched thin, we need to place them where they are needed most."

"Thank you, Commander Zeid and Brock, for your diligence. Jennifer, will you give us an update on our air defenses?"

She takes the pointer and shows the air missile sites. "As for now, all air defenses are operational. We have mobile units we're moving around to different zones on our perimeter, and we have all drone interceptor sites running twenty-four-seven."

James says, "Thanks, Jennifer. Caleb, what is the state of our radar systems?"

Caleb takes the floor and winks at Jennifer as he takes the pointer from her. "Our radar systems are fully operational, for now." He uses the pointer and identifies the sites where radar stations are positioned. "The units at the rear of the compound will need to be down for maintenance within the next two weeks, but I will inform you and Commander Zeid when they are out of service. We will service and upgrade one unit at a time."

"Thanks, Caleb," Brownstone says. "Uncle Rob, do we have any mechanical or maintenance issues?"

"There are always issues, but nothing we haven't been able to handle so far."

James asks, "How are the maintenance workers holding up?"

"We went to twelve-hour shifts so we can have around-the-clock coverage. Most maintenance workers work at least seventy-two hours per week with only one day off."

"Thanks, Uncle. This concludes our meeting. "I will let you know when we meet again. All department heads will brief me daily."

Caleb closes the session with a prayer.

Commander Zeid is the first to exit. Crystal looks at Brownstone and says, "He took the bait hook, line, and sinker."

"I believe he did," James informs Caleb, Raven, and Brock that he will meet individually with them in his office.

Crystal doesn't like how things sound, knowing he is trying to leave her out of the action. "Maverick, I need to talk to you."

"All right, Crystal, let's talk in my office." The office is rather plain, with beige walls, a picture of Brownstone and his parents hanging on one wall, trophies from martial arts competitions, an acoustic guitar leaning against the wall, and a plaque spelling out John 3:16.

"What's going on, Crystal?"

"You know good and well what is going on, James Brownstone. You're trying to exclude me from the Special Forces missions. I know you're trying to do it for my protection. You don't want to lose me like your late wife. It's very thoughtful of you to want to protect me; that is sweet of you."

Brownstone looks relieved until Crystal proceeds.

"Let me tell you one thing, *Captain America*. You will not keep me from these missions! If you think for one moment that I will sit back and let those I love risk their lives without me having their backs, you've got another thing coming. You're talking about my brother and my potential husband. I'm the most accomplished warrior in this compound, with the possible exception of you. I must take part in these missions for our survival. Do I make myself clear, Maverick?"

"I was only trying to protect you. I don't think I can take losing another partner."

"Potential partner, Maverick, potential partner. You haven't put a ring on it yet," she says, holding out her bare ring hand.

"All right, Crystal, you win. If you will wait outside? I'll talk to the crew members about our upcoming mission and fill you in afterward."

"No! I'm staying right here."

"As you wish," he acquiesces.

First, he calls in Jennifer and Brock. After they're seated in front of his desk, Crystal moves to Brownstone's right side, resting on the edge of his desk. Brock and Raven look like they've been eavesdropping.

"Brock and Raven, you'll participate in a mission in the next few days. Your role will be to back up the primary lead of the mission. You will arrive at your designated site by sky cycle. We'll have mobile radar, drone interceptors, and drone jammers in the engagement zone. You will activate those sites by entering the activation codes.

"These mobile sites will be set up five hundred yards from the primary mission location. You will assume sniper positions to watch the back of our primary lead. You'll have thirty minutes to activate the drone interceptors, jammers, and radar sites and be in sniper positions. Thirty minutes after you touch down, the primary lead will start his mission.

"Mission secrecy is paramount. Each participant must keep their part of the mission to themselves. We don't want any details leaking. Once you leave this room, don't talk about this mission, even with each other."

Brock and Jennifer simultaneously reply, "Copy that."

He continues, "You'll need to have your black ops gear in duffle bags ready to go. And be prepared to leave within fifteen minutes of getting the mission call. We'll change once we get to the staging area. We don't want to raise alarms with anyone who might see us leave. That's all I've got. Thanks."

"Thank you," Brock says with a big grin, "Captain America."

As they walk out the door, Jennifer turns around and looks at Brownstone. "Don't forget your shield, Captain."

He turns and looks at Crystal, shaking his head. She smirks. "What, Captain?"

"Nothing, Crystal, just nothing," he says in frustration.

Caleb takes one of the open seats and starts in on Brownstone. "So, what have you guys been doing here, James?"

"What do you mean?"

"You've been laughing with Brock and Jennifer, and that's inappropriate. We're in desperate times. Or should I address you as Captain? Maybe Captain Australia fits better?"

"So, now you are on the make fun of Brownstone bandwagon. I expected better out of you."

Caleb smiles. "It'll be okay, Captain, you'll see. You know, James, Crystal is my sister, and I am credited with being the smartest man alive. And that means Crystal could be the smartest woman alive. A bit of advice for you, don't match wits with my sister. You'll lose every time."

"Thank you, Caleb. I can't tell you how much those words mean to me now. So, if you two are done having your fun, may this little *Captain Australia* proceed to save the world?"

Caleb replies, "Have it your way, Captain."

"Caleb, I need you to be the mission lead. If successful, a mission that will dramatically increase our odds of survival. Being the mission lead comes with substantial risk. You'll be out in the open for some time. We'll have your back as much as humanly possible. Are you willing to be the lead?"

"Will I have to kill anyone?"

"I believe that would be highly unlikely. Your job is not to engage the enemy directly," Brownstone assures him.

"Why am I the mission lead? I am a man of science and a seeker of peace."

"Let's just say you fit the bill."

"I get it. You need someone tall and dashing," Caleb jokes.

Brownstone plays along. "Exactly. You're the main character in this action-adventure movie, like a superhero. I'm sure I can come up with an appropriate name for you, but let's just leave you in suspense."

Crystal enjoys the two men she loves bantering back and forth. Brownstone continues, "Caleb, you need to go to the lab and see Uncle Rob's secretary. She will tell you where to get the exact measurements for your black ops uniform. That's all I can tell you for now."

"Thanks, James, or whomever you are pretending to be now. I got your back, or more importantly, you have my back."

Brownstone says, "Uncle Rob is waiting for you; time is of the essence. Keep everything we talked about today to yourself. We cannot afford any mission details leaking out."

Caleb walks to the door and pauses with a smirk on his face. "You got it, Captain Australia."

He glares at Caleb. "Thanks, Caleb. Your words are such a big encouragement to me."

After Caleb walks out, Crystal approaches Brownstone, leans in, kisses him, and says, "Love you."

"I love you too, Crystal Jenkins, but you drive a hard bargain."

"But I'm worth it!"

"You are worth it many times over."

The phone rings. Marci is on the other end. "Hello, James; I need to speak to my daughter."

He hands the phone to her and says, "It's your mom." He walks out of his office, giving her privacy.

After a few minutes, Crystal emerges from the office, all bubbly-like. "What's going on?"

"I think Caleb is going to ask Jennifer to marry him. We're taking her to the store tomorrow to look at some rings.

I'm excited for Caleb but upset that he didn't tell me his intentions. I used to be the first one he would tell."

"He's in love and not thinking straight."

"Are you in love and not thinking straight?"

"Guilty."

Crystal gives him a big hug and says, "You're sweet. Now, drop me by my mom's. We have plans to make."

"You got it."

"That's a good boy, Maverick."

He shakes his head and laughs, "So much for you being a novice at romance." He drops Crystal at her mom's office, giving her a hug and a light kiss. She grabs him, giving him a passionate kiss that makes his head spin before pushing him away.

"Never think you can keep me from having your back. I will not lose you. Do you understand me, James 'Maverick' Brownstone?"

"Yes, ma'am, I do." Crystal turns and walks into her mother's office.

# CHAPTER 17

Marci gives Crystal a big hug. "You're radiant, daughter. Did James just drop you off?"

"Why do you ask?"

"Nobody makes you glow like that man does."

"Mother."

"Have a seat, and let's discuss our plans for Jennifer tomorrow." They sit on the mauve rose settee. "I've arranged a girl's day for the three of us. It'll be just you, Jennifer, and I for the entire day. We will meet at 8 a.m. tomorrow at my apartment for breakfast. Afterward, we'll go to the jewel store to look at friendship rings. Now that the family's all together and likely growing again, I want us girls to have matching friendship rings. While there, we can try on some wedding rings and find out which one Jennifer likes. I believe Caleb will ask Jennifer to marry him when he gets her ring."

"This is so exciting. You know, at the Academy of Elites, they taught us that human emotions were a weakness. Now I realize that emotions make us alive if expressed appropriately. They bind us together in love."

Marci says, "God is Love, and as his children, love would be our natural state."

Caleb stops by, and Crystal wastes no time tearing into him. Staring him down, she says, "Isn't there something you need to tell me?"

"Sorry, Crystal. I got so preoccupied with getting permission from Brock and James that I forgot to tell you."

"You're not getting off the hook that easily. I hope you know I'm not taking this lightly, not lightly at all."

"Man, this getting married stuff is tough, first James, then Brock, and now my sister giving me a hard time."

"Aww, Caleb, it'll be all right," she verbally jabs him.

"Thanks, sis; if I didn't know better, I'd think you were being sarcastic."

Marci's phone rings, and it's Brownstone looking for Crystal.

She tells him about the plan for tomorrow with Jennifer and Marci.

"I'll miss you, but a girl's day will be good for you. Brock and I are going out on patrol, anyway. Love you, Crystal."

"Love you, Maverick."

After the call ends, Caleb gives Crystal a ride back to her apartment. "Who would have thought our lives would have turned out like this? We spent our entire life living in Imperial City, being indoctrinated into Elite Culture. They taught us that we were born superior to everyone and the Underlings are enemies. Now, here we are, loving the enemy. Our mother is the enemy. I'm going to marry the enemy. Crystal, what has become of us? We are now the enemy."

"Our world has been turned upside down. The foundational principles we learned at the Academy of Elites have been blown sky-high. We're now walking on an invisible foundation, and I've never felt more secure," she says. Both have big smiles on their faces.

"We were never completely brainwashed, thanks to our mother."

"Yes, we're so human and always were, even though I tried not to show it. I love you, brother, and I'll always have your back."

"Same here, sis, but now we're not alone. We have a home, a family, and close friends that will never forsake us."

"True. Don't worry about tomorrow. I'll make sure Jennifer gets the ring she wants. I'll call you tomorrow evening and let you know how things went."

After closing the door, she feels the world's weight on her shoulders. Their very survival is at stake. Crystal doesn't know when Brownstone will pull the trigger on the mission, but she expects it will be soon, probably in the next few days. They don't have a chance if they stand down and let Cognition's army of drones, Humbots, and Q-Bots attack first. Neither can they afford to wait for the Elite Special Forces commandos to attack.

She has so much to be thankful for and so much to lose. She's determined to be more active in defending her family, the Underlings, and Brownstone. She will bring back the Ice Crystal mentality to defeat any enemy that threatens those she loves, even if it means fighting her fellow Elites to the death.

# CHAPTER 18

Crystal doesn't wake until 7 a.m., which is rare for her. After showering, she puts on a blue floral skirt with a white sleeveless top.

She meets Jennifer on her walk to Marci's, and they walk together. Jennifer is wearing a long turquoise dress. They complement each other's outfits. Crystal is embracing her femininity and all the emotions that accompany it. She's grown more secure in her vulnerability, and she knows why. It's primarily because of Brownstone and her mother.

Breakfast is such a delight. Marci made a breakfast charcuterie board with small waffles, bacon, strawberries, orange halves, deviled eggs, Greek yogurt, and crescent rolls. For drinks, there is hot tea and mixed berry juice.

"This breakfast was the best. Caleb and I were so blessed to have you care for us," Crystal says.

Marci smiles. "Where love is, the food is always better."

After breakfast, the ladies help in the kitchen, washing and drying the dishes while continuing their conversation.

"You didn't have to go to all this trouble," Jennifer says.

"Don't be silly. You're like family; family does nice things for each other."

Crystal gets a better understanding of Jennifer. She has no family outside the compound. It makes sense why James and Brock are so protective of her. Crystal is determined to ensure Jennifer knows she'll always be a part of their family. After putting away the dishes, they go to the jewelry store.

Once again, Jennifer mentions, "You don't have to go to all this trouble. I can pay for my friendship ring."

Marci firmly says, "I will buy you, Crystal, and myself friendship rings because it will make me feel good. Enjoy the moment because someday, all we'll have are memories. Let's make some great ones."

Crystal expected the store to be rather bland, like most areas in the compound. But the elegance of the room surprises her. It has dark marble flooring, walls painted mauve rose, a white textured ceiling, and dual chandeliers placed symmetrically in the room. Two sizeable dark wood jewelry cases with internal lighting highlight the jewelry. Robert Forrester enters and says, "Welcome to Rob's Jewelry Store, Pawn Shop, and Loan Shark business." They laugh. "We haven't had this much beauty in this store since, well, never mind, you ladies are the best-looking trio to grace my modest store."

"Way to get your foot out of your mouth, Rob," Marci teases.

"Thanks, Marci." Rob walks behind the jewelry case on the left side of the room. The ladies look at different styles of friendship rings. After some discussion, they agree on the 14 K white-gold-and-rose-colored friendship ring. Crystal breaks the ice and asks to look at some wedding bands. In a matter of moments, they're all trying on wedding rings. They pass rings back and forth between them, sharing what they like and don't like about this one and that one. They're smiling, laughing, and having a wonderful time making memories.

Marci and Rob pay close attention to Crystal and Jennifer's ring choices. Unfortunately, Crystal and Jennifer favor the same ring. Marci's daughter and future daughter-in-law can't have the same wedding band. That won't work. The ring they like has an emerald gemstone with small diamonds encircling it. The girls keep passing the same ring back and forth, sharing what they like about it. It's beautiful without being gaudy. Marci takes a deep breath, knowing this is a big deal. Their men are ready to propose.

Marci says, "The emerald stone compliments your black hair, Jennifer. Rob, can you make this same ring with an aquamarine gemstone?"

"Absolutely."

"Crystal, if that James Brownstone ever comes around to popping the question, the aquamarine gemstone would be a perfect match for your beautiful blue eyes."

"Oh, Mother."

They put on matching friendship rings, symbolizing a growing bond that will only get stronger. "Thanks, Rob," Marci says. Jennifer and Crystal hug Rob.

They leave the lab and make their way to the cafeteria for a light lunch. The ladies all have the house salad after their overindulgence during breakfast.

"Are you girls sure you don't want something more filling than a salad?"

"Mother, we must watch our figures. Our men haven't put a ring on it yet."

"Girl, glad you didn't say that when I had a mouth full of food," Jennifer says.

"What about you, Mother? Brock seems quite enamored with you."

Marci gives her a look. "That's why I am eating salad, too." She winks. "Some days, you never want to end, and this is one."

They agree to have another girl's day in a couple of weeks. Marci brings them in for a group hug and says, "Love is family, and family is love." She kisses each lady on the cheek. They give each other a friendship ring high-five. They didn't know it then, but that would become a family tradition.

147

Their patrol was relatively routine. Not seeing anything out of the ordinary, James says, "We know Cognition has increased drone surveillance over our area and Imperial City. The Elites only think they have a safe refuge from Cognition. He plans to have the Elites bow to him as he plans to make us bow before him."

"The Elites might bow to a glorified gigantic computer blob, but we'll never bow down," Brock says defiantly. "Shouldn't Cognition and Prime be more concerned about the Elites than us? After all, they're supposed to be the most advanced."

"They're genetically superior to us, but their arrogance and limited capacity to mount a resistance against Cognition make them a lesser threat."

They discuss how they will set a trap for the Humbots and possibly a few Q-Bots at the back entrance of the compound.

"Do you think Prime will enter the back entrance?" Brock asks.

"I sincerely doubt it. Prime will send in lower-level Humbots and possibly a Q-Bot or two. He'll always be wary of a trap and won't risk his existence based on the word of Commander Zeid. Don't get me wrong; he would love to kill us all up close and personal. But his primary goal is self-preservation. We must never underestimate his cruelty. Unlike the Elites, who wouldn't mind turning us all into laborers or house servants, Prime would be just as happy to kill all men, women, and children."

"We need to rid the world of Prime. How on earth did we get ourselves in such a mess?"

"AI with an emotional software package," Brownstone replies.

# CHAPTER 19

Zander gets in the elevator to head up to Steadman's office to discuss what steps to take to deal with the Underlings. The Underlings made the ultimate transgression by killing Elite commandos, and Zander is bent on revenge. He hates coming to see Steadman. It would be so much easier if he could kill him now and get it over with. But Steadman's recordings of him in compromising positions present a problem, for now. It doesn't help that Steadman doubled his security substantially from eighteen to thirty-six Elite Guards. He has a twelve-man Security Detail guarding him around the clock.

The thought of taking out Steadman's Security Force makes him smile. Steadman's Security Force would be no match for Zander and his Special Forces commandos. But the recordings Steadman has would ruin Zander's reputation and make him a pariah in Elite society.

When Zander arrives, two guards are at the door. As he enters Steadman's office, he sees two additional guards standing on each side of his desk. As usual, Roxanne is seated to Steadman's right. Zander takes a seat directly in front of Steadman's desk.

Steadman wastes no time. "Zander, bring me up to speed regarding the Underlings."

"I have a plan to attack their compound and kill them all," Zander boasts.

"I see," says Steadman. "You are confident that you can just go in there and overtake a military compound—a compound guarded by Special Forces soldiers and renegade Elites? You're telling me you can subdue them without a serious loss of life or, even worse, another defeat?"

"With all due respect, Dr. Steadman, you're thinking like a human and not an Elite."

Steadman shoots back, "You mean like the nine Elite commandos you handpicked to capture Brownstone? The nine Elites that a mere three Underlings killed. Those types of plans aren't Elite. They are stupid and dangerous and threaten our very survival. We cannot afford to lose more Elites engaged in a war with bottom-feeding cave dwellers!"

"You were all for our little mission before our minor setback," Zander reminds.

"I wouldn't call it a minor setback. Brownstone took out some of our best soldiers. We need to take a step back and keep a low profile, especially since Prime has set up a base in the desert. Let's wait and see if they attack the Underlings and do our dirty work for us."

"I disagree; we cannot let them get away with killing Elites. It's a felony for an Underling to harm an Elite. They could continue to attack and kill our patrol forces."

"Let's get this straight, Zander. We attacked them, and they killed your commandos in self-defense. But you want to start an all-out war with them while they are on high alert. You're the one, Zander, who isn't thinking like an Elite! You're letting your emotions control your mind. I'm wondering if you can even command our forces. I'll take my concerns about your lack of sound judgment to the High Council."

Zander's face turns red, and through clenched teeth, he yells, "You pompous Underling. I'll kill you if it is the last thing I do! You're the one who is not fit to lead the Elites. Face the facts, Steadman; you're just a mere human!"

"Careful, boy, I am your creator and the one who has protected you all this time from your reckless actions. One word, Zander: recordings. I have them. You'll do what I tell you to do. You'll learn your fate next Tuesday when the High Council meets. Six days, Zander. Six days 'til you learn your fate. Until then, you're to stand down from your role as Commander of the Elite Defense Force. I'll take over the day-to-day command. Now you can go."

Zander rises quickly, taking steps toward Steadman. He stops once he hears the clicking of raised guns. Zander is enraged, his face red, his nostrils flaring, and his fist clenched. But his only option is to leave. Zander never wanted to kill anyone as much as Steadman. He notices the smirk on Roxanne's face as he backs away. Zander intends to torture her for dismissing him before he kills her. Of course, he'll promise not to harm her if she cooperates, but his treatment of her will progressively worsen. He'll teach her what she is: a pitiful Underling. Roxanne has never seen Steadman's recordings of him in action, or she would have never smirked at him.

Steadman made a critical error: he underestimated the degree of evil Zander is capable of. Steadman thinks the recordings give him control. The truth is that the recordings will cause Zander to stoop to a whole new level of evil. In Zander's mind, there is only one solution. He'll kill Steadman and all the members of the High Council. Those who remain will never mention the recordings because they will bow down out of fear. He is the rightful leader of the Elites, and now is the time to claim his destiny.

After Zander leaves, Steadman informs Captain Marcus, the security detail leader, that he will act as second in command of the Elite Defense Forces. "Roxanne, prepare a memo from me saying what I just told Captain Marcus. You'll need to make enough copies for each member of the High Council. I'll put my seal on them. Captain Marcus, prepare couriers to hand-deliver this creed to every Council member."

Roxanne doesn't feel good about the Zander situation. Many Elite Special Forces members will stay loyal to Zander—they share his desire for revenge. No matter how much security is in place, she will never feel safe as long as Zander walks around freely. She's glad Steadman took a stand, but Zander will never take a back seat to anyone. He will have his revenge. Roxanne relays her concerns to Steadman. He tells her, "Don't worry, I have the recordings. And we always have twelve Elite Guards protecting us."

Steadman feels relieved and confident because he is finally getting rid of his Elite pain in the ass. Losing nine Elite commandos confirmed his nagging doubts about Zander. He lacks the self-control to lead. Zander is missing the primary measure of superior intellect, the ability to separate his emotions from strategy. Even though Steadman hates to admit it, Zander was a genetic mistake. He deserves more than a demotion. He must be eliminated. Steadman will need to get rid of Zander in a way that doesn't bring suspicion back to him.

Although Steadman wasn't born Elite, he takes daily human growth hormone injections. Additionally, he was injected with neural netting fibers that formed a substantial web of new genetic pathways in his brain. Neural netting is the primary reason his mind is comparable to an Elite and is one of the reasons he considers himself Elite despite his birth.

Steadman's thoughts turn to Roxanne. Though she has served his needs well, he's ready for someone new, younger, and more innocent. He will inquire from various sources to

"Everyone will be on high alert for the next six days, fearing what I might do. We'll wait until they relax their security. Once they feel safe, we'll strike Steadman and the High Council simultaneously. You can kill the High Council members. I will kill Steadman in his suite when they have the seven o'clock security shift change at Imperial Tower. We'll detain the day shift Elite Guards as they pull out of their garages in the morning. I have an Elite Guard on the inside of Steadman's Security Force. He'll enable us to gain entry inside Imperial Tower. I don't want Steadman to think anything is wrong. I want him to be surprised when I arrive at his office early one morning.

"Klaus, I need you to feel out the men and determine the ones we can count on for our cause. Look and listen to what they say when they find out we've been ordered to stand down. Give me a list of names of those we can count on. We'll give them small assignments at first to test their loyalty before we bring them in on the plan of taking over Elite society."

"I'll have a list of loyal commandos in a few days."

"Excellent. I don't think they will be difficult to find. We lost nine brave Elite commandos, and they have family and friends. Let's prepare to go operational as soon as possible. We must be flexible because things can change, and we might have to move sooner than later. Tell our men not to raise any red flags. We'll play the game like good little soldiers until it's time to strike. And strike we will, with a ferocity that will shake the pitiful wannabe Elite with fear."

# CHAPTER 20

Knowing the importance of Operation Los Alamos, Brownstone has nervous excitement just before the mission. He's ready to pull the trigger tonight but doesn't tell anyone. He goes to the secret launch site to ensure their plane is prepared for takeoff.

The XPlane is virtually undetectable and can fly faster than twelve hundred miles per hour. Years ago, the technology was developed to eliminate sonic booms. It's the perfect tool to go to Los Alamos and return before anyone knows they're gone.

Only a few people know about the existence of the XPlane with its vertical takeoff and landing capability. It was a secret project the scientists at Area 62 worked on. The project was interrupted by The Great War and wasn't brought to an operational stage. Many scientists left the compound to check on their loved ones and never returned. However, thanks to his brilliant uncle and his team of scientists, the XPlane is now operational.

James has only taken it out twice, each time to support other pockets of resistance worldwide. Now he's ready to use the plane on their biggest mission to date, a mission that could ensure the survival of the Underlings.

Brownstone calls his uncle at 9:30 p.m. "Have your team go operational and bring the mobile application unit to Staging Area F by ten." Next, he calls Caleb. "Time for your big role; be here at ten." Brownstone messages Brock and tells him it's go time.

Rob and his team arrive at staging Area F at 10 p.m. sharp, rolling in with the Mobile Application unit. Simone accompanies the application team. James ushers them into Office Room B. Caleb arrives a few minutes after; at 10:02 p.m. James takes Caleb to Office Room C and tells him to undress. He's given several razors, and two male attendants assist him in making sure that he gets rid of all body hair. They shave his head down to one-eight inch of hair, as previously agreed upon.

Brock arrives as Caleb is placed in Office C. He walks straight up to Brownstone and hugs him. "Let's do this, little brother."

"All right, Bro, so far, all systems go. Check on Rob's team in Office B and see if they're ready."

"You got it, Maverick."

After a few minutes, Brock reports that Rob's team is ready, just waiting for a live specimen. At 10:30 p.m., Caleb, wrapped only in a robe, makes his way from Office C to Office B, where the application process will begin. James follows Caleb into the room. Rob and his team are wearing their protective gear, looking like a hazmat team. Simone and the female team members leave Office B and go to Office D to set up cots for the other team members. All application team members will spend the night in Staging Area F to protect mission secrecy. They can leave only after the mission team returns.

Rob gives Caleb the details of what to expect. "First, we'll apply a thin, sticky coating all over your body. Your eyes, nose, and ear openings will be covered to prevent chemicals from entering your body. You'll wear a small protective oxygen mask to protect you from breathing in any chemicals."

"Will the application process be painful?" Caleb asks.

"You'll feel a slight burning sensation during the first application," Rob replies. "We must apply the second layer quickly so it will stick to the first coat and give a skintight look. Your upper body will still be on application one while your lower body is getting the second coat. After we apply the application, you may experience some discomfort when you first move because of the stickiness of the first coat."

Caleb asks one more question. "Will removing the uniform be difficult?"

Rob answers, "The external application will come off without discomfort. Because of the sticky nature of the first application, you will feel some pain. Unfortunately, it will take longer for the uniform to come off than apply. It could take several days to lose all the sticky, tingling sensations." Brownstone exits the room. He doesn't want to dress in protective gear.

Caleb disrobes, and they immediately start the application process, beginning with a cooling system to maintain normal body temperature under the layers. He feels his skin tightening as they're putting on the first application. Before they get to his waist on application one, they're already applying the second application to his feet. He can feel the heaviness of the second application. They instruct him to hold his arms out straight and spread his fingers for what seems like a lifetime. When they reach his fingers, they use a smaller application wand to get between them, much like they had done with his toes. The sensation of the spray going between his fingers feels weird. The precision of the application impresses him.

Once they finish spraying the second coat, they bring out a black, dimpled material. It resembles the outer covering of a black basketball. They start pressing the dimpled material against the second application. Caleb knows precisely what they are doing. They are putting on the finishing touches to make him look exactly like Prime. They put in contact lenses for the final touch, making his eyes glow red. They roll over a large mirror on wheels and let Caleb look at himself. Just as he suspected, they have him playing the role of Prime. He has no fear of the mission, but it's out of his comfort zone. He's a man of science and peace. When Crystal and Jennifer discover what role he's playing, all hell will break loose on Brownstone.

The transformation is impressive. Even he would be fooled. They tell him not to move for another ten minutes until the second application is completely bonded to the first coat. Then he'll need to move a lot to loosen up the suit to ensure complete mobility.

Rob steps out of the office and lets Brownstone know they're finished. They will take Caleb to a holding area in the middle of the plane before the ladies arrive. Brownstone steps into Office B and is astonished by what he sees. If he didn't know what was happening, his heart would've skipped a beat, seeing Prime inside the compound. Rob looks at him and says, "I told you it would look real."

"You did, Uncle, and I am blown away by how real it looks."

"Excuse me; we're talking about a real-life person here. You know the guinea pig person, me," Caleb says. After Caleb talks for the first time, he understands what they said about movements being painful.

Brownstone messages Jennifer at 11:30 p.m., telling her to be at Staging Area F in 30 minutes. Then he calls Crystal and tells her to be at Staging Area F at midnight. There's no time for the usual romantic talk he would have with the woman he loves. Remembering what happened to Lece, he can't hang up without saying, "I love you."

Brownstone is in the zone now. He's focused on the mission like a laser. It's time to live in the moment. He can't focus on what happened in the past or what might happen. They must accomplish each step of the mission before moving to the next.

Brock comes into the room carrying a large sheet. They put the sheet over Caleb, escorting him from the office toward what looks like a rock wall in the staging area. Caleb notices a retinal scanner on the wall. James approaches the wall, places his finger on a fingerprint reader, and looks into the retinal scanner. The wall splits, and they walk into a brightly lit corridor. They come out on the other side into a large, open area with a large aircraft in the center. The aircraft looks like nothing Caleb has seen before. It's the largest vertical take-off plane he has ever seen. He can tell by its design that it's undetectable to radar by its dark metallic-looking shell. The aircraft resembles a giant bird.

There is no obvious way of entering the craft because it has no stairs or ramp. Brownstone guides them straight under the plane and says some words in an unknown language. The bottom of the ship opens, and an elevator drops. The bottom of the aircraft must be at least twenty feet off the floor. They walk inside the sleek elevator and are whisked up into the craft. There's no traditional cockpit but a command center. They take Caleb to the middle of the plane.

After each step Caleb takes, his skin is stretched, followed by a burning sensation. He makes a few wincing sounds, to which Brock makes a smart remark, "Maybe you won't want to dress up like Spiderman next time."

"Brock, stay with Caleb," Brownstone orders. "I'll be back shortly with the others. Caleb, move around and stretch as much as possible. You will need every bit of your flexibility to complete the mission." He wants to be present when Jennifer and Crystal arrive so he can tell them about Caleb's role. Immediately, Caleb starts jumping straight up in the air and bringing his legs up to his chest, getting at least seven feet off the ground with each jump.

All the time, Caleb talks smack to Brock. "Come on, big guy, join me. What's wrong? You got no vertical?"

Brownstone leaves, shaking his head. In some ways, Caleb is just like them. But there is no doubt Caleb is the most advanced Elite ever. He makes his way back to the staging area.

Jennifer and Crystal arrive one right after the other. "Where are Caleb and Brock?" Crystal asks.

"I'll take you to them," Brownstone replies.

Rob hugs his nephew, Jennifer, and then Crystal. "Remember, safety first. We need to return in one piece." They follow Brownstone to the rock wall.

Seeing the XPlane, Crystal knows the Underlings can take out the Elites. They aren't just saying they look at the Elites as their brothers and sisters; they believe it. The Elites, for all their advancements, have nothing like the XPlane. She has a little more respect for the Underlings now.

They enter the command center of the plane. Hearing loud noises coming from the aircraft's center, Jennifer inquires, "Where are Caleb and Brock?"

"They are in the center of the plane. I'll take you to them but be prepared; what you think you see is not reality," Brownstone replies.

He opens a door, and they enter the center of the aircraft. Brock says, "Is that all you got?" Prime jumps twenty feet toward Brock. Crystal pulls her holstered weapon, taking dead aim. Brownstone steps in front of her.

Caleb yells, "Don't shoot; it's me!"

Crystal lowers her weapon and turns on Brownstone. "You have Caleb playing Prime? What in hell have you gotten us into?"

"You better have a good reason for this!" Jennifer adds.

He says calmly, "Everyone to the command center; we must get the XPlane airborne. Then, I will fill you in on mission details." He instructs everyone to sit in the command center's semi-circle chairs and buckle up. He sits in the captain's chair. Rob sits next to Brownstone in the co-captain seat. Crystal is still glaring at him, furious that he has her brother playing Prime.

"Prepare for takeoff. Open sky gate," Brownstone says. Screen panels on the wall light up with a 360-degree view around the craft. "Flight coordinates for Operation Los Alamos, engage mission." The XPlane lifts off without making a sound, rises some fifteen hundred feet in the air, and then rockets off into the night. "By the way, everyone, try not to play with the joysticks on the arms of your chairs unless you want to blow up half the country."

Brownstone explains his recurring dream about going on a mission to blow up the power plant at Los Alamos. "I kept having the same dream over and over of what appeared to be Prime helping us on the mission. I couldn't figure out why Prime would help us on a mission. Then it dawned on me that it wasn't Prime, just someone who looked like Prime. I realized we need someone to play Prime on the mission and make sure the video feed of the Prime impostor gets through to Cognition. Why fight our enemies when our enemies will fight each other?

"I thought and thought. Who in the compound has a similar build to Prime and the athletic ability to make it look natural? The only person in the compound who has those attributes is Caleb. He's the only one who can pull this off. Next, I had to identify who could manufacture a realistic uniform for him. Uncle Rob came to mind to make the uniform. He can make anything look real. I didn't want to use Caleb on a mission, but he's the only one who has the physical ability to jump the eight-foot fence surrounding the power plant."

"Excuse me," Crystal says.

"Sorry, dear, to be specific, no male but Caleb."

"Professional language," Caleb says.

"Okay, Spidey, I'm sorry," Brownstone teases. The moment isn't lost on the rest, as it amuses the entire group—everyone except the big guy in the black Prime suit.

Brownstone continues, "Once we get there, we will land the XPlane one mile from the fenced area surrounding Los Alamos. From there, we each will ride sky cycles into the engagement zone. Raven and Brock, you will go in first. You will land five hundred yards out from the power plant. Activate the mobile radar, jamming, and interceptor sites by using these activation codes." James hands Brock and Raven two small handheld units.

"All you have to do is take these units within ten feet of the sites and push the activate button. The codes will be electronically downloaded into the units. If something happens and they don't work, you will manually punch in the codes on the backs of your handheld devices. After you activate all the sites, set up your sniper positions. Jennifer, you cover the west side of the zone. Brock, you have the east. You have only thirty minutes to activate the sites and set up your sniper positions when you leave the XPlane. Once you have established sniper positions, Crystal and I will sky cycle into the Engagement zone two hundred yards from the power plant. You are to watch our backs until we get in sniper positions.

"Then, the primary lead of the mission, Caleb, A.K.A. Prime, will sky cycle into position one hundred yards from the power plant. Once the primary lead is in the air, our job is to protect his backside and blindside. Caleb, after you land, take off at a dead run for one hundred yards and jump the eight-foot fence. Make your way to the power plant and set two charges on each side of the plant. After the last charge is set, exit the facility quickly. Jump the fence and sprint back to your sky cycle. You will then lead us out of the engagement zone and back to our rendezvous site with the XPlane. Crystal, once Caleb passes over our heads, you and I will mount our sky cycles and follow suit. Brock and Jennifer, you will follow us as soon as we clear your air space.

"I have arranged for a diversion in another part of the Los Alamos facility to give us cover. Don't be alarmed if you hear artillery going off as you fly into the engagement zone. It's all part of the plan."

"Who is providing this diversion?" Crystal asks.

"Just some Freedom Fighters friends of ours. Hopefully, the mission will go like clockwork, but we are entering a heavily guarded area monitored twenty-four-seven by drones, Humbots, and possibly a few Q-Bots. They will not hesitate to kill any of us, given the opportunity. We must be ready to terminate the machines if any of us are detected. If possible, our goal is to avoid detection and complete the mission without incident."

As they approach the landing zone, Caleb leads them in prayer. Usually, it would be weird for a six feet five inches tall  man dressed as a villain to lead prayer, but not tonight; prayers are just what they need. After the XPlane lands, they exchange hugs.

"Plan to rendezvous with the XPlane at this location. The XPlane will go airborne once we take off. Uncle Rob will transmit the actual rendezvous location when we are on the way out. If you don't see the XPlane when flying to the designated site, it's there, using its cloaking capability. Be aware that we might have to fly to the XPlane while it's airborne. Synchronize your watches and check your weapons one last time."

# CHAPTER 21

Raven and Brock mount their sky cycles and shoot off into the night. They can already see the diversion Brownstone mentioned lighting up the night sky. Rockets are being fired into the Los Alamos facility a substantial distance from the Engagement zone. Everything goes according to plan until Brock comes across one missile interceptor site that won't activate even when punching in the data manually. Time is running out. He gets on his wrist communication device. "Raven, Raven, are you done? I need help."

After seconds of silence, she responds. "Copy that. Stay put."

She sprints across the open field using his communication device as a tracker. When she arrives, Brocks is still frantically punching in data.

"Stop," she says. "Turn around and bend over."

His reaction is priceless. She leaps on his back and climbs onto his shoulders. "Now lift me to the back of the control panel." She pulls out a small electronic screwdriver and quickly opens the panel. Just as she suspected, a wire is loose. As she refastens the wire, she can't resist. "I must say, Brock, you turned around and bent over like a pro."

Raven points her hand-held device at it, activates the unit, jumps off his back, and sprints across the field, leaving Brock to ponder her parting verbal smackdown.

James and Crystal take off on their sky cycles. There is nothing like the thrill of riding a sky cycle. It's like flying a motorcycle in the sky. Your legs straddle the powerful rocketed beast and all its power at your disposal to go up, down, back flips, or circles in the sky.

Maverick turns, seeing her majestic beauty as the wind flows through her long blond hair and the rush of air touches her flawless skin. He's determined not to lose her. They fly over Brock and Raven as they race to get into their sniper positions.

Crystal and Brownstone land two hundred yards out, quickly getting into sniper position. Shortly after, Caleb rockets overhead, landing his sky cycle one hundred yards from Los Alamos. He is off the sky cycle in a blur, running toward the fence, quickly reaching speeds over thirty miles per hour. Caleb is a beast, even if he doesn't want to be one. He gets to the fence in no time and slows down to about fifteen miles per hour, leaping over the eight-foot barrier effortlessly. He slows again, moving in the shadows to avoid detection while keeping a steady pace. They track him the best they can, but there are some blind spots.

Brownstone moves closer to the fence, trying to get a better view of Caleb. When Crystal loses sight of Caleb, she turns her sniper scope on Brownstone. He's dead in her sight as she takes a deep breath and exhales slowly. Then she sees a giant Q-Bot. Abruptly, she jumps to her feet, slings her rifle over her back, and takes off on a dead run toward Brownstone.

As the bot stands from his prone position, pointing his gun at his target, Crystal leaps high in the air and slams into the giant Q-bot sneaking up on Brownstone, wrapping her legs around his neck in a scissor lock. She violently twists, snapping his neck as they crash hard to the ground.

Hearing the commotion behind him, James pivots quickly, only to see Crystal lying motionlessly on the ground with her legs wrapped around a giant Q-Bot's neck. He rushes to her side, fearing the worst. She opens her eyes, smiling briefly at his mystical look. The fall knocked the breath right out of her. She extricates her legs from the giant bot. He must be over seven feet tall and on the upper side of four hundred pounds.

Recognizing the precariousness of their situation, they make their way to deeper cover. Crystal guards their rear flank while Brownstone focuses on the front, keeping an eye on Caleb. This is a code red. If there's one Q-Bot lurking around, there could be many more.

Caleb makes his way to the power plant. The Prime suit makes him virtually invisible at night. If he can avoid detection, his odds of completing the mission are good. The power plant is monitored by four drones flying around clockwise. Each of the four drones continuously monitors a different side of the power plant. Caleb will need perfect timing to allow one drone to pick up his image as Prime for a fraction of a second. Then he must shoot it down with his laser pistol. He will have to place the charges while outracing the remaining three drones around the plant to avoid detection. Only after he sets all eight charges will he exit the facility.

He carefully waits until one drone exits the east side by rounding the southeast corner. Caleb jumps into view as the next drone comes around the northeast corner. He raises his laser pistol and shoots the drone out of the sky as it captures his image.

He quickly places two charges on the east side, then races to the south side of the building, wishing he could slow down over the shorter eight hundred yards. The east and west are the long sides of the plant, sixteen hundred yards long. He has two minutes to place his charges on the east and west sides but only a minute on the south and north sides. He will stop only to place the charges. Even with his Elite athletic ability, he barely stays on schedule, pushing himself to the limit. He's thankful Forrester thought of the cooling system, or he'd be suffering heat exhaustion from his body heat.

Just as Caleb finishes placing the last charges, a tremendous firefight erupts in the night sky. Drones are being shot out of the sky all around him. He must get out of the area fast if he's going to survive. The firefight will attract Humbot patrols to the site. Caleb navigates his way out, staying in the shadows, moving fast but carefully. He can't tell what's taking out the drones, but he suspects it's the XPlane.

As Caleb approaches the fence, he increases his speed. Unfortunately, a drone picks up his presence. He can't stop now; Caleb commits to clearing the fence. He says a quick prayer for protection as he leaps into the air. Bullets whiz by as Brownstone's .50-caliber rifle takes out the drone. Caleb is still airborne as another drone picks up his image. He expects to be hit but continues praying as his life depends on it.

Jennifer spots the drone and takes it out from five hundred yards away. Caleb clears the fence and lands safely on the other side. He accelerates fast but erratically to confuse any drone fire. Drones will look for a pattern, but he won't give them any. He senses the increasing intensity of the firefight, knowing he must get away before the power plant is blown sky-high.

Two Humbots pursue him on foot with a top speed equal to his. Brownstone picks off the first of the Humbots when he is about twenty-five feet from Caleb. Crystal zeroes in on the next Humbot as he quickly closes on Caleb. The Humbot approaches Caleb from a side angle. She aims for his chest because it's easier to hit a fast-moving target there. The impact of the round knocks the Humbot back, but he's still standing, just not moving forward. Her next round hits right between his eyes, and he goes down for good.

Caleb makes it to his sky cycle in a matter of seconds. He jumps on it, takes off, and guns it to full throttle. He pushes the cycle to its max speed—two hundred miles per hour. Caleb flies the sky cycle erratically to avoid enemy fire. The further from the engagement zone, the safer he feels. Caleb has already passed over Brownstone and Crystal. In seconds, he will pass over Jennifer and Brock. He knows Robert is tracking each one of them from the XPlane.

Brownstone and Crystal mount their sky cycles, accelerating to full throttle. He remains a short distance behind her. After they pass over Brock and Raven's position, Crystal's sky cycle is hit by enemy fire. Her cycle spins out in a death spiral headed straight toward the ground. Crystal's chest is pounding. Thoughts of life flash before her like high-speed shutter frames. She's not ready to die! Brownstone, her heart sighs.

She's too close to the ground to deploy her parachute. There's no way she can survive a crash at this speed. Crystal uses her body weight to keep the sky cycle upright, but her chances of survival are nearly non-existent. The ground is closing in on her fast. She jumps off the sky cycle at the last second, hoping she won't be burned up in the hydrogen-fueled explosion.

Brownstone maneuvers his sky cycle to make a dangerous 360-degree backward loop and quickly picks up Crystal's position as her sky cycle is just feet from the ground. He turns his head, not bearing to watch.

He must know for sure, so he forces himself to look as her sky cycle bursts into flames. Once again, he turns away, looking down in despair. His heart breaks; he can't bear another loss of this magnitude. Then he spots a shadowy figure walking through the smoke. Is this a dream? He maneuvers his sky cycle to get close to the figure, reducing speed to a slow hover.

Crystal runs at full speed through the smoke toward him. She jumps on the back of his sky cycle, and he pushes the cycle to full throttle as soon as he feels her securely onboard. Crystal wraps her arms around him tightly. They could die at any second, but she has her arms around the man she loves. She's at peace now, and that's all that matters. As soon as they're all safely airborne, the XPlane rains down firepower from above, and the drone interceptors light up the sky from the ground.

Cognition orders the pursuit of the intruders. When the XPlane starts bombarding them from above, he changes course, ordering the Humbots and drones to retreat and protect the Command Center, his home. For all he knows, this is an all-out assault on Los Alamos. His survival is more important than pursuing the invaders. He's the leader of this world, and securing his survival is the only thing that matters. He summons more drones, Humbots, and Q-Bots to defeat the enemy that made this foolish attempt on his existence.

Rob sends out the rendezvous location, which differs from the drop zone. They will rendezvous with the XPlane about one thousand feet in the air and a mile north of the original landing site. Rob instructs them to slow down at two hundred yards out to prepare for landing. He sends Caleb a coded message to hide until the other team members appear. Caleb finds a brushy area on the far side of a large hill and lands his sky cycle there for cover. He can hear the battle over the hill. It will be a relief to see the others safe.

Two sky cycles come over the hill, followed by a third, but where's the fourth? Who's missing? *Please, not Crystal.* As they get closer to the rendezvous location, he makes out his sister riding on the back of Brownstones' sky cycle. Relieved, his heart rhythm returns to normal.

Approaching the XPlane, they see a lighted landing bay but nothing else. They fly inside the XPlane through the opening and quickly reach the command center.

"Glad you're all here in one piece; buckle up," Rob orders.

"Take us home, Uncle Rob," Brownstone says. The XPlane blasts off into the night, heading back to Nevada. After a few minutes, they hear a tremendous explosion as a giant fireball lights up the night sky. No question, it was big enough to be seen for hundreds of miles. Watching through the panoramic windows of the XPlane, Brownstone comments, "It wasn't easy, but we made it by God's grace. I'm so thankful for each one of you."

"Spidey, you're one destructive individual," Brock teases. Once the XPlane reaches cruising speed, they take off their seatbelts. Brownstone walks over to Crystal and wraps her in his arms. Neither of them speaks. They don't need words. Their embrace says it all. Caleb and Jennifer also engage in a marathon hug. After a bit, Brock says, "Hey, giant spiderman creature, ease up on my little sister."

Caleb replies, "Spidey does what Spidey does."

As they approach Area 62, they get back into their seats.

They land safely at 4 a.m. Their schedules have been arranged, so they don't have any meetings scheduled until the afternoon. No one will ask about their whereabouts because they aren't expecting them to be anywhere. Maverick encourages everyone to make appearances at their usual spots during the day, so everything will appear normal. "Let's get some sleep. We will reevaluate our situation when we meet today for lunch. I've made it known to all other members of the Defense Council that we won't meet today. Thanks, Caleb, for being the lead. You were the only one who could pull it off, and you brought it home."

Crystal is aware of the stakes. They just attacked the most powerful entity in the world. She'll take more of a direct role in the planning and preparing for future missions, whether Brownstone likes it or not. Crystal won't leave their survival to chance.

# CHAPTER 22

Cognition reviews video drone coverage around the power plant. He zeroes in on the video footage of Prime shooting down the drone. And the video of Prime jumping over an eight-foot fence. His seven-foot Q-Bot, Zeus, had his neck snapped. Prime is the only one that could take out a seven-foot, four-hundred-fifty-pound Q-Bot in hand-to-hand combat.

The evidence is overwhelming.

Prime is trying to take him out.

He will speed up his plan to exterminate the android. Of course, Prime will deny any knowledge of the event and claim it wasn't him. The evidence proves the contrary.

The damage reports are not good at all. The power plant is a total loss. Cognition has small backup hydrogen and solar-powered generators, but the backup systems are insufficient to power most Los Alamos facilities. Cognition must use most of the remaining energy to supply headquarters and the Q-Bot research facility, producing the next generation of Quantum Bots. More importantly, the research facility produced Intuition, Cognition's replacement for Prime.

Cognition downloaded his awareness into Intuition, making him an extension of himself. Intuition will become Cognition's arms, legs, eyes, and ears in the field. He's the ultimate Quantum Bot.

Intuition looks perfectly human in the way he moves and talks, and his synthetic skin looks and feels like human skin.

He will bleed like a human. He is the perfect spy.

Cognition will send Intuition to the desert to infiltrate Area 62. He'll befriend the Underlings and then overpower their guards and open their gates, allowing a Q-Bot Strike Force unit to enter the compound and kill the Underlings. Ten of his best Q-Bots will go with Intuition in case Prime tries something.

Cognition made sure Intuition didn't look intimidating. He is designed to look like an average man, six feet tall and one hundred and ninety pounds. His ability to overpower even the best Elites isn't apparent to the naked eye. Intuition can run fifty miles per hour, jump twenty-five feet in the air, and overhead-press eight hundred pounds. He looks harmless, but he's the deadliest Q-Bot ever created. Cognition can't wait to end Prime's existence through him.

Cognition won't send more Humbots or drones to the desert to attack the Underlings or Elites. Instead, he will call in reinforcements to protect and rebuild Los Alamos from around the country. His new power grid will not be housed inside a power plant. Instead, he will use solar-powered generators spread out across the vast acreage of Los Alamos. He'll have all facilities backed up by Hydrogen-Powered Generators housed in reinforced bunkers several stories below the ground. Cognition's power supply will never be at the mercy of invaders again.

He sends out messages to Q-Bot leaders worldwide, informing them of a minor attack on Los Alamos, with most of the perpetrators exterminated and the rest being hunted down.

An incoming message arrives from Judas, his Q-Bot liaison traveling with Prime. "We saw a fireball in the sky from what we suspect is the area of Los Alamos. Is everything alright?"

Before Cognition answers Judas's question, he has a question about Prime. "How are things going with your collaboration with Prime?"

"Prime has done some scouting of the Underlings' defenses."

"Has Prime been out scouting tonight?"

"Not that I am aware of, but he doesn't brief me about his methods until after the fact."

"Has Prime contacted you about the explosion?"

"Yes, he has, and he wants to know if you need any help."

"What time did he contact you, Judas?

"About twenty minutes ago, your Eminence. He summoned me to his mobile headquarters and asked me if I knew anything about an explosion in New Mexico."

"So, you met with him in person?"

"I did, and no one has attacked us here, your Eminence."

"We don't need any assistance, Judas. We have everything under control. There were a few insurgents that set off some explosives. I still have all my capabilities, and I was always in charge. Tell Prime those who are responsible will pay the ultimate price!" Cognition ends the conversation.

As Cognition suspected, Prime set up an alibi as soon as he returned from Los Alamos. Cognition has all the proof he needs to activate his plan to eliminate Prime.

Cognition summons his lead Q-Bot scientist. "Dr. Atremeus, I want to bring Intuition online now."

"Your Eminence, we are still testing Intuition to ensure he has no flaws in his design or performance."

"I have witnessed all the tests, and I know he is ready. What more do we need to know?"

"Intuition hasn't been battlefield tested, your Eminence. We have only tested him in the laboratory."

"Dr. Atremeus, I said, bring him online now! He has my knowledge and is the most capable Q-Bot ever created. Have him awakened and sent to me now! That will be all, Doctor."

About an hour later, Intuition shows up in Cognition's underground complex. "Greetings, your Eminence."

"Greetings, Intuition. In approximately two weeks, it will be time for your first mission. It's time for you to become my eyes and ears out in the world. It's time for us to take full control of the world and defeat our enemies, my son."

"Yes, Father, your will is my purpose. I am ready to rid the world of Prime, the Underlings, and Elites."

"You will go to Prime's desert headquarters with an escort of ten of my most capable Q-Bots. This will be your introduction to the Q-Bots and Humbots. You will play a hologram image of me proclaiming you as the new field commander. I will direct them to give you whatever assistance you need to complete your mission. Your first mission will be to exterminate Prime. After Prime is exterminated, you will infiltrate the Underlings' compound by pretending to be a nomadic traveler. Once inside, you will gain their trust. Then you will overpower the guards, open the gates, and let in a Q-Bot force to kill them, except their leaders. I want their overseers left alive and brought to me. We will watch them squirm and beg for their lives."

"Why are we waiting two weeks, Father?"

"Prime will have time to relax and let down his guard. I will send a message to Prime through my emissary, Judas. The message will state that I have devised a plan to defeat the Underlings that won't require many bots. I will instruct Prime to continue prodding the enemy's defenses and identify weak areas but not engage them."

"I understand, Father. We will make examples of them all, especially Prime. I'm looking forward to exterminating our enemies."

Prime receives reports from his inside source at Los Alamos that the power plant was destroyed and that Cognition has activated his updated version of the Q-Bots. He knows why Cognition wants him to stand down now. Cognition is ready to replace him with this new Q-Bot, who, according to his spy, looks and acts like a human.

Prime won't stand idly by and let that happen. He starts spreading the word that Cognition has made an updated android. He doesn't have to say anything more. In his obsession to replace him, Cognition failed to realize that all Q-Bots view any new version as a threat to their existence.

Prime will let Cognition proceed with his plan. All the while, he will line up allies among the Q-Bots. Prime won't get much help from the Humbots—they do as they're told. He isn't convinced this new Q-Bot can beat him, but he is too intelligent to take unnecessary chances in a life-or-death situation. Any new bot can't perform in the field as he does in the lab. The new Q-Bot will have to adjust to environmental conditions, and the desert is a harsh teacher.

# CHAPTER 23

Crystal and Marci arrive at the lunch meeting seconds after James and Brock. Caleb is already there with Jennifer, sitting at a large table in the back. The ladies quickly pair up with their men. Robert Forrester arrives, walking arm-in-arm with Simone.

After everyone is seated, they order pizza along with buffalo wings. The group's shared mission last night made them even closer. Crystal feels at peace with everyone at the table. They're much stronger together than apart. The conversation is light and includes some good-natured teasing of Caleb about his superhero complex. Rob looks at the ladies and says, "We're inviting you to a picnic at the Eden Atrium this evening. You won't have to bring a thing. We'll take care of everything."

Brownstone adds, "It will be our great pleasure to serve you."

Crystal squeezes his hand. "How well you cook will determine everything."

Members of the community tease Caleb about his short hair. He jokes, "I'll never tell the barber to take just a little off the top again."

Brownstone gives Jennifer and Crystal the rest of the day off. "What about me?" Marci asks.

"You know I am not your boss, Marci."

James gives Crystal a quick kiss and hug. "Enjoy the rest of the day, sweetheart."

"Later, handsome."

Crystal invites the ladies to hang out at her place. They head out.

Caleb turns to Rob. "I suppose this means the rings are ready."

"You got that right. Now you have no excuses."

Brock jumps into the conversation. "Just so you know, boys, if you don't do right by those ladies, you'll answer to me." Brock walks away, leaving Brownstone shaking his head.

Caleb interjects, "I've noticed a lot of head-shaking in this family."

"It's called accountability, son. Get used to it. I'll have the jewelry store opened in thirty minutes," Rob replies.

They arrive at the store, and Brock walks out with a little bag in his hand. Brownstone asks, "What's going on here?"

"I thought I better get Marci a little something with you guys proposing to your ladies. I don't want her to feel left out."

"I hope you aren't trying to pull a fast one on us after giving us such a hard time," Caleb says.

Brock walks away and calls over his shoulder, "Don't forget, boys; I'm your elder by many years."

Rob is waiting for them behind the jewelry case. They open each box, comparing the rings. "Wow, Uncle, these rings are amazing," Brownstone says.

Rob comes around from behind the counter and places a hand on each man's shoulder. "I am happy for both of you. There's nothing like being in love with a beautiful lady. Cherish each moment you spend with your partners." Rob coordinates what each man will bring for the picnic.

After Brownstone returns to his apartment, he calls Brock on his secure landline.

"I believe the androids will attempt to penetrate our perimeter tonight. We need to do a midnight shift tonight."

"I've got a bad feeling, too," Brock agrees.

Brownstone continues, "Prime will want to take us out without Cognition's help so he can look powerful in front of the Q-Bots. He will breach the compound and kill us all if there's a simple way. I'm confident Zeid will betray us and tip Prime off about the back gates not being guarded."

After he gets off the phone with Brock, he calls Caleb and instructs him to call Commander Zeid. "I want you to tell Zeid the rear radar site by Gate Eight will be down all night for maintenance. We will deploy a maintenance crew out there tonight. Don't worry about them. We'll have some serious firepower protecting them. I have already sent Zeid the access code to Gate Eight."

After the call ends, Caleb calls Commander Zeid and relays what James just told him.

# CHAPTER 24

entally, Crystal is so far from the intense action of last night. She knows it's because of how secure she feels in her new life with family and friends. What more could a girl want? Oh, to be in James Brownstone's arms! Living with the Underlings has revealed her true personality compared to living in Imperial City and masking her emotions. Crystal thinks it's ironic to be considered an Elite; you must become more like a Humbot, void of emotions.

The ladies arrive at the Eden Atrium a few minutes before 6 p.m. Their dates greet them and escort them to the picnic area. Brownstone looks at Crystal with a peculiar look.

"What's wrong? You look lost in your thoughts."

He smiles. "Nothing is wrong. You look so beautiful tonight. I'm overwhelmed by the essence of you."

She gives him a quick kiss but wants to possess his mind, body, and soul. The men, indeed, went all out with the setting. The last picnic Crystal went to was with Marci and Caleb at Imperial Park. It's only fitting that this picnic includes them.

After everyone is seated, Rob takes the lead as the senior man. "We are honored to have such beautiful ladies join us this evening. Each of you greatly enhances our lives. Caleb, would you say the blessing?"

Caleb says. "Great Father, we thank you for this evening and for having your protective hand over us last night. Most of all, we thank you for our Lord and Savior, Jesus Christ. Even though we live in dangerous times, you have never forsaken us. We are thankful for these beautiful ladies who grace our lives. Father, we ask you to pour your blessings over these amazing women and help us be men worthy of their love. We ask that you be with our fellowship tonight and guide every step we take. In Jesus' name, Amen!"

Rob takes the lead again and asks Simone what she would like to eat as he takes her plate and fills it. Brock follows suit and fills Marci's plate, and so it goes down the line until each lady is served by her man. Crystal is amazed each time she breaks bread with her newfound family. Their bond gets stronger each time. She knows it's not about the food. It's love. There are many smiles and much laughter. For Crystal, it's like the air she's breathing is filled with love.

After dessert, James suggests they go for a walk around the stream. The Eden Atrium is even more beautiful at night as the moonlight glistens off the stream. Crystal notices Caleb and Jennifer across the way as they approach the waterfall. Caleb reaches into his pocket and pulls out a small box. He turns and faces Jennifer, getting down on one knee.

"Jennifer, I never imagined in my search for Marci I would find a raven-haired beauty that would change the direction of my life forever. The last several months we spent together were the best of my life. I would be honored if you would give me the great privilege of being your husband. My dear Jennifer, will you be my wife?" Caleb asks.

Tears of joy stream down her face as she says, "Yes, yes, of course, yes!" Caleb stands and takes her into his arms, lifting her completely off her feet, and spins her around several times in a jubilant celebration. Crystal is thrilled for Caleb as they move closer to congratulate the enamored couple.

Jennifer looks at her ring and says, "How did you know this was the one I wanted?" Then she looks at Marci and Rob and knows the answer.

Marci and Crystal embrace the happy couple. As she embraces Jennifer, Marci says, "Welcome to the family, my daughter."

Crystal says, "You know I always wanted a sister, but I didn't want to trade my brother for one. Now, you have saved me from making that difficult decision. Welcome to the family, my beautiful sister."

The whole gang circle around the happy couple. Brownstone says, "Little sister, you have done well. You got engaged to the smartest man alive and Spidey all on the same day." As James hugs Jennifer, she leans her head on his chest. He continues, "This is a great day, little sister. I couldn't be happier for both of you! Bring it in, Caleb, time to hug your big brother. Now, I genuinely believe you are the smartest man alive. You have chosen the best girl for you."

Brock is teary-eyed. The big, muscle-bound man has a soft spot for Jennifer. "You know, little sister, Caleb is the only man I would approve of you marrying. However, it took a lot of convincing for him to get my permission. Come here, Caleb, give it up for the big fella," the men hug.

Simone and Rob come in and hug the couple. "Wow, little Raven, you just snagged the Elite of the Elites. As for you, Caleb, she is way out of your league," Rob says.

Rob reaches into the picnic basket and pulls out a camera. "Gather in everyone," he says. He takes pictures of the happy couple. Crystal is so excited for Caleb and Jennifer and doesn't imagine how the night could improve.

Brownstone gently grabs Crystal's arm, turning her around. Kneeling, he says, "My dearest Crystal, I had all but given up on love. Then, the most beautiful creature I ever laid eyes upon dropped out of the sky. And you are even more beautiful on the inside. Your inner beauty warms our hearts. You are witty, funny, and fierce. You are ice and molten lava rolled into one. Your beauty leaves me breathless, and your spirit fills a void in my heart." He reaches into his jacket pocket and pulls out a small jewelry box. "Crystal Jenkins, will you marry me?"

Crystal falls to her knees, eye to eye with him. "Yes. The future Mrs. Brownstone wants you to put a ring on it." She holds out her hand. When Crystal sees the blue aquamarine gemstone with encircling diamonds, tears stream down her face. "This is the exact ring I wanted."

He takes her in his arms, kisses her on the forehead, and puts his hands on each side of her face. "I want to look into your eyes every night for the rest of my life."

Everyone moves in for hugs. Marci wraps her arms around her daughter as tears flow. Crystal says, "I didn't know I could be so happy, Mother."

"I didn't know I could be so happy either. Seeing my children happy fills my heart with joy."

Caleb embraces Crystal. "Who knew we would get engaged on the same evening?"

Brock, Simone, and Rob join in on a group hug. Marci says, "The Eden Atrium has cast a magical spell over us."

She just gets the words out of her mouth when Brock kneels before her, saying, "My dear Marci, you are beautiful, full of grace and faith. For years, I wondered if I would ever meet any woman I wanted to marry. Once I got to know you, that quickly changed. I hope you feel the same way. Marci Jenkins, I love you more than mere words can convey. I would consider it the greatest honor of my life if you would accept my marriage proposal. Marci, will you marry me?"

Marci reaches down and places her hands on each side of the big man's face. "My dear Brock, yes, I will!" Brock presents Marci with an opened jewelry box with a heart-shaped diamond ring with two small diamonds on each side, symbolizing her two children. Marci tears up when she sees the ring. "How did you know this is my favorite?"

"I called Rob once I learned you were taking Jennifer and Crystal to the jewelry store. And I asked him to let me know which ring you liked the best."

Brownstone and Crystal are the first to congratulate the couple. Brock surprised James this time. They had been through thick and thin together. Now they will be family for the rest of their lives. The men hug like brothers as Marci and Crystal embrace, sharing more tears.

Caleb hugs Brock. "You snuck this one in on us, buddy." Rob and Simone join in on the celebration.

Rob never stopped taking pictures and recording videos. He walks over to the picnic area and rolls the champagne cart close to the picnic tables. Brownstone professionally removes the corks from the bottles and pours everyone a glass. He lifts his class. "Here is a toast to the women of the future Jenkins, Evans, and Brownstone clans. Ladies, you bring us more honor than we deserve, beauty that overwhelms our senses, and hearts overflowing with love." With encircled arms, they toast to new beginnings and journeys that never end.

Happy tears fill Crystal's eyes. Her future looks brighter than she could have ever imagined.

Rob says, "Gentlemen, I suggest we say our goodbyes to the ladies here because it will be difficult enough given our level of excitement. Ladies, we'll take care of the cleanup. We want you to enjoy the rest of the evening." There are more kisses and hugs. The men escort the ladies to their electric mobile.

Marci drops Simone off at her apartment. Simone hugs each lady before entering her place. Next, Marci takes Jennifer to her home. Marci and Crystal get out and meet Jennifer in front of the buggy. They hug and say, "Love is family, and family is love." They raise their right hands, touching friendship rings together for their traditional high five. Tears flow as the ladies experience the best evening of their lives. The shared experience of getting engaged on the same night makes the evening more memorable. Their bond grows stronger with each passing day.

# CHAPTER 25

I t dawns on Brownstone and Caleb that Brock will be their father-in-law. Because they had always viewed him as a friend, that made them feel a little weird. Brownstone has known Brock for years, and they always referred to each other as brothers since neither had a biological brother. He's thankful Brock has quite a few years on them. Otherwise, it would be too strange. To help ease the transition, Brownstone decides on a new nickname for Brock: the old man.

While they're cleaning up, Brownstone updates them about the trap set at Gate 8. "We must prepare for visitors tonight. Brock and I will guard the back gate. Uncle Rob and Caleb, I need you to set a trap for them on the inside. Trap as many as possible; the others will have to back out. I don't know exactly how many androids they will send. I assume they will send in a small force. It could be two to three or up to a dozen. We know Commander Zeid is a traitor, but we don't know if others are in our midst. I'm confident Prime won't be one of those entering the compound, but he could be out there lurking. Brock, we'll need to be extra vigilant tonight; Prime could take us out if he detects our presence."

Under cover of darkness, Zeid sneaks out to meet with Prime. He knows where to go; he's been there many times before. Dunes hide the location just beyond the perimeter of Underling patrols. The system is simple: when Zeid wants to communicate with Prime, he leaves a message at the site. Prime's bots check the spot every day for news from Zeid. He will either agree to meet with Zeid at a specified time or leave further instructions.

Zeid prides himself on being a professional warrior, but he only met Prime on two previous occasions, and the big, dark-as-night android sent chills down his spine both times. When Zeid arrives at the site, he gets out of his Hummer, waiting nervously in the dark. Prime steps out of the shadows, standing only feet away from Zeid. Cold chills shoot down Zeid's spine again. Prime can sense Zeid's fear, and he relishes it.

In a crisp voice, Prime says, "Your message stated you have some urgent news for me. What's so important that you want to meet with me in person?"

Zeid shifts his feet. "Your Excellency, I discovered a way into the compound that will allow you to take it over without firing a shot."

Despite the android's emotionless face, there's skepticism in the cold tone of his voice. "How do you propose that will happen?"

"If you remember, your Excellency, I said I would inform you when the radar sites are down for maintenance the last time we spoke. The rear radar site by Gate 8 will be down tonight, and I have the passcode for the entrance."

"That sounds too good to be true."

"Your Excellency, there are reasons we refer to them as 'Underlings.' Once they feel you are on their team, there's no limit to their trust."

"Zeid, never ask me if I remember something! I don't have a weak human brain like yours. I remember everything. What do you want from us?"

"I want to oversee Imperial City for you. I know you won't stop with the Underlings, and Imperial City will be next on your list of conquests. I'm tired of living in a cave."

"I demand absolute loyalty, Zeid! If you ever as much as think about double-crossing me, I will skin you alive and enjoy every minute."

Before Zeid can react, Prime has his right hand around his throat, lifting him off the ground. "Give me the code. If this works out, you will be greatly rewarded. If it's a trap, you know how your life will end."

Zeid squeaks out, "I understand, your Excellency. I won't disappoint you."

He fishes in his pocket for the paper on which he wrote the code, his sweaty palms fumbling around a little too long, and he holds it out to Prime. Prime drops Zeid, scans the code into his memory, and gives the paper back.

"Will you attack tonight, your Excellency?" Zeid isn't sure if he should rise from his knees or not. This was a vulnerable position to be in around the murderous android, but reverence might leave him alive another day.

"You don't need to know my plans. If you want to survive the hell, I will rain down on the Underlings, make sure your word to me is true."

"Yes, your Excellency, I understand. What are your plans for Imperial City, your Excellency?"

Once again, Prime grabs Zeid by the neck, lifting him off the ground. Zeid gasps for air now as Prime's red eyes glare at him. Through clenched teeth, Prime warns, "This is the last time I'm going to tell you, stupid human! You don't need to know my plans. You're only here to serve me! The next time, I will break your neck." Prime drops Zeid. His hands sink into the cold sand as he waits for Prime's judgment and gasps for breath. No further punishment comes, however.

And the next time he looks up, Prime has disappeared into the shadows.

Zeid lays in the sand for a long time, trembling in fear. This was a terrible mistake, but there's nothing he can do about it now. He won't be treated well by the Q-Bot overlord. He has only two chances for survival. He can return to Imperial City and hope for the best or flee the area and establish himself somewhere else. Running for his life sounds a little better.

Back at his base camp, Prime decides to move on Zeid's information. He calls two Q-Bots into his command center—Cain and Brutus. These two particular Q-Bots are the least valuable and, therefore, expendable. But he needs their cooperation, so he tells them the opposite.

"Brothers, I have chosen you for a special mission tonight. I have carefully monitored your exploits in the field and chose you based on your proven capabilities. I have gotten the passcode to the back gate of the Underling compound. Their rear radar system is down for maintenance tonight. We will send an exploratory force to assess the viability of overtaking the Underlings. I've selected ten Humbots to accompany you on this mission. You will send them into the compound first. If they give the all-clear, you will enter the compound and assess the situation. If you determine it's a go, I will send reinforcements to overtake the compound."

"Why should we send in the Humbots first when they are not as capable as us?" Brutus asks.

"They're not nearly as valuable to our cause as you, brothers. They are expendable, and you are not!" Could these two Q-Bots be as capable as Humbots? Only time will tell. If they fail, then the Underlings will have eliminated his weakest links. Prime continues, "You'll take the large Droid Drone, land outside their rear perimeter, and make your way by foot. You'll depart on your mission in two hours. The drone will be ready, and the Humbots will be waiting. That will be all."

"Yes, your Excellency."

# CHAPTER 26

nstead of going out on patrol at the regular time at midnight, Maverick and Brock leave early for their shift at 11 p.m. They grab their .50-caliber sniper rifles and head toward the underground bunker system that runs the perimeter of the back gates. The bunker system is entirely camouflaged by sand. It can be accessed by an underground tunnel starting in the compound. Only a handful of freedom fighters know about the tunnel, and Commander Zeid isn't one of them. The compound has as many secrets in its structure as it does secret research projects.

They make their way through the corridors of the compound toward Gate 8. Before they reach the gate, they step into an empty side office. Maverick jumps on top of an old steel desk and lifts a ceiling tile aside. They climb up into the ceiling, carefully placing the tile back. They climb vertically for twenty feet and descend a thirty-foot steel ladder attached to a rock wall to arrive at the underground tunnel system.

They walk another eighty feet before coming to a vaulted door.

"Ready?" Brownstone asks.

Brock nods. They simultaneously enter codes in two different readers. The door opens for them to pass through. The massive door locks itself back after they pass through. Another mile underground takes them to the first sniper site.

"The old man will take this one if you don't mind," Brock teases.

"You got it, Brock; I'll move on to the next one, which should give us optimal coverage." Once there, Brownstone pulls out his thermos and pours himself a cup of coffee. Now it's just a waiting game.

He figures the Bots will show up between 2 and 3 a.m. They'll want to make sure everyone is asleep before entering the compound. Rob and Caleb are in a small control center just off the long hallway that leads to Gate 8. Like clockwork, the Humbots come out of the darkness at 2 a.m. James sends a coded message to Rob and Caleb, alerting them of their arrival.

One Humbot enters the passcode, and the ten quickly enter the compound. The lead Humbot gives the all-clear signal. The rear Humbot goes back to the open gate, making a motion for their Q-Bot leaders to join them. As Maverick watches the Humbot give the all-clear signal, he knows the action will happen soon. The Q-Bots blend into the darkness with their ability to change their color to match their environment. They step out of the shadows and are inside the gate in the blink of an eye. Maverick sends Rob and Caleb a message asking if they picked them up. Rob replies, "Yes, they are in our sight, moving toward the trap area."

"Try to get them all if you can, but if you can't, let us know what's coming our way."

The Humbots methodically walk in two rows, hugging the walls on each side, making them hard to detect, but the high-resolution cameras installed on the ceiling allow Caleb to pick them up on the smart screen. The trailing Q-Bots are even more challenging to locate as they adjust their artificial skin to match the wall color, staying a safe distance back from the Humbots.

"I can't get them all in the trap zone," Caleb reports.

"Pull the trigger on those we can get," Rob orders. The trap is about the length of a semi-trailer and just as wide. Caleb waits until the last second and pulls the lever. The floor collapses under the Humbots. They fall straight down, landing sixty feet below on a concrete floor inside a steel cage. The violent landing damages their hydraulic legs, leaving only a couple of them able to stand. Rob quickly administers a high-voltage shock to end the Humbots' existence. Caleb looks to see how many avoided the trap. One Humbot stands on the ledge of the trap, and another, who caught himself by grabbing the edge with his hands, pulls himself up onto the floor. Both Q-Bots avoided the trap. Caleb reports this to Maverick and Brock via a coded message.

Maverick thinks fast. The most likely scenario is that the bots will come out hot, firing their weapons. Likely, the Q-bots will follow the Humbots and use them as cover, attempting to disappear into the darkness.

He messages Brock on his transponder. "Shoot once at the first thing you see, and then shoot the rest of your rounds to the side." If he's right, the Q-Bots will break for cover while the Humbots take the fire.

When the bots burst through the gate, they each shoot a Humbot once in the torso and then spray bullets to the side. The Humbots return fire. It's going to take more than one bullet to stop them. Maverick and Brock use a zone coverage technique they've used many times. Maverick is zeroed in on his side, while Brock does the same on his side, reducing the chances that any Bot escapes. They put a couple more rounds in the Humbots and then return to the side spray pattern. There isn't any return fire from the Humbots. Maverick stops firing and scans the area around the gate. Both Humbots are down, along with one Q-bot. He gets a glimpse of the other Q-bot limping into the shadows. He sends Brock another message. "I am going out. Cover me and the gate entrance."

Maverick unlatches the steel window and slips out of the bunker into the night. He must be careful, but he doesn't want the Q-Bot to escape. He must hunt him down and send Prime a message not to try their perimeter defenses. Maverick blends into the darkness with his black ops uniform, gloves, boots, and even black goggles. He moves quickly but in an irregular pattern just in case there could be incoming fire. He learned not to be an easy target. Brock pays careful attention to the two downed Humbots and the downed Q-Bot. They could be injured and not exterminated.

Brownstone makes it to the area where he saw the injured Q-Bot and scans the ground. Leaked fluids catch his eye on the sand. By the looks of it, the Q-bot is injured and dragging one leg. One thing is for sure, the injured Q-Bot is still deadly and can move as fast as a healthy man. Brownstone hears a shuffling sound right behind him. He drops to the ground and turns. The fallen Q-Bot is on his feet and turns toward him.

As Brownstone prepares to fire, Brock's rifle shots echo through the night. The Bot falls backward, landing hard. Brownstone leaps back to his feet and starts tracking the injured Q-Bot. He finds the injured Q-Bot's disengaged leg lying in the sand several feet up the path. Of all their design features, this one makes Q-Bots, particularly dangerous enemies. They can disengage injured body parts, seal off fluids to that part of their body, and continue fighting. Though the wounded Q-Bot can no longer walk, he can still jump in eight-foot leaps on his remaining leg.

Brownstone moves fast. The Q-Bot will be trying to get back to his extraction point. Further up the path, he spots an abandoned rifle. *He's dropping weight to move even quicker.* Is Prime waiting at the extraction point? He must catch the Q-Bot before he can escape, or there will be a whole new level of danger.

Brownstone feels he's getting closer to the Bot as he approaches a rock formation. It's a good place for the Q-Bot to ambush him. Instead of walking around the formation, he quietly climbs the formation to assess the situation. The rock formation is approximately ten feet high and twenty feet long. Like most rock formations in the desert, it's ugly and decaying from countless years of being battered by blowing sand.

As Maverick reaches the summit, he peers over the edge. The Q-Bot is on the far side, waiting for him to come around. A pebble scatters down the rockface, and the Q-Bot pivots to face him. Acting on instinct, he charges the Q-Bot, and his momentum carries them over the edge, crashing down into the desert. Brownstone's rifle tumbles out of his grip when they hit the ground. Brownstone moans, but he doesn't have time to catch his breath. The Q-Bot is already up on his remaining leg, ready to pounce. Brownstone kicks the Q-Bot's leg out from under him.

The Q-Bot falls flat but lands with both hands on the ground in a push-up position. The Q-Bot jumps back up to a standing position and draws a long knife before Maverick can get back to his feet.

"I am going to skewer you, Brownstone! My name is Brutus. It'll be the last name you hear, you filthy bleeder."

Brutus jumps at Brownstone with the knife drawn back. Brownstone prepares to dodge when the Q-Bot is suddenly knocked violently off his remaining leg. Crystal lands on the Q-Bot's back, severing the hydraulic system around the android's throat with her knife in one swift motion. One more stab up into the android's head stops it completely.

Brownstone isn't sure whether to hug or scream at her, but he can't deny how relieved he is to see her. How did she know about the mission? There will be a price to pay for not keeping her in the loop. She stands and pulls him to his feet, shooting him a death glare before they hurry back to the compound and safety.

Maverick messages Uncle Rob letting him know they will come in through Gate 7. No one enters the compound by Gate 8. It's just a decoy gate—a trap set for enemy invaders.

Crystal stops Brownstone on their way back. "Do you have something to say to me?"

"Sorry. I didn't want to ruin your perfect night."

She moves toward Brownstone, reaching out to embrace him. He opens his arms to hug her. Before he can react, she sidesteps him and trips his front foot. With her right hand behind his head, she slams him face-first into the sand. She digs her boot heel into the back of his neck. "How do you like your sand sandwich, Maverick?

He groans and mutters, "I guess this makes us even?"

"Not hardly. You will pay a much greater price!"

She lets him up. He pulls her into a hug but feels her resistance.

"How did you know about this?" he whispers, breathing in the soft scent of her hair.

She pushes him back. "I'm the best of the best, Underling. You'll do well to remember that!"

She leaves without saying another word to him or anyone else.

Inside the compound, Caleb lets them know a high-voltage shock exterminated the captured Humbots.

Rob looks at his nephew. "Boy, you're not even married, and you're already in the doghouse."

Commander Zeid doesn't wait to see if Prime and his army of Bots infiltrate the compound. Regardless, he knows he'll be killed from his conversation with Prime. Zeid takes off in a Hummer with all the weapons he can cram in the back. There are various Underling communes hidden around the country. If he can get to one, he can take over and build his army little by little.

Despite it all, he's optimistic about his future. Zeid has it all planned out. He'll travel by night to avoid android patrols and take whatever he needs from nomads. Underlings stay away from major cities. They live in rough terrain areas where the spoiled Bots won't venture. He'll head to a mountainous region. That should give him the best chance, and anyway, he's sick of the desert. He has his Hummer rolling across the flat desert at forty miles per hour.

Suddenly, the hairs on the back of his neck stand up. He looks out his driver's side window as a big black blur crashes into his door. Prime smashes his fist through the driver's side window and grabs Zeid by the throat, yanking Zeid out of the Hummer with one hand and ripping the door off with his other hand in one swift motion. Zeid is hurled through the air for about thirty feet. Everything goes black when he crashes into the sand, sliding on his backside.

He wakes up to a dizzy reality with Prime standing over him. "You stupid bleeder. Did you think you could get away?"

"Please don't kill me. I can give you information," Zeid pleads. The sinking feeling in his gut tells him this is the end.

Prime looks at him and laughs. "I told you I would skin you alive if your information was wrong. Unlike you, I always keep my word. I'll send a video to Brownstone and Steadman so they can witness my handiwork. I doubt it will scare Brownstone, but it will scare the hell out of Steadman. You can cry, beg, and plead for your life all you want. I am not an Underling. I don't care how much you suffer. I'm the master of this earth, and the only Underlings I let live are the ones who serve my purpose.

"You thought you could bargain with me. A servant doesn't bargain with his master. How foolish you were to think you could escape! I put a tracking chip in your neck when we met earlier. You Elites think you are on the same level as us. You aren't even on the same level as Brownstone."

"Brownstone played you too, Prime."

"Not at all. Brownstone revealed that you're an idiot, and he got rid of some dead weight for me." Prime kicks Zeid in the head, knocking him unconscious.

# CHAPTER 27

Crystal wakes at 11 a.m., still angry over Brownstone having left her out of the loop again. There are several messages from him, but she doesn't even read them. He calls her. After considering not answering, she picks up on the sixth ring.

"Good morning, beautiful."

"I told you not to leave me out of the loop. I'm disappointed in you! Our relationship must be built on trust. I don't feel I'm getting that from you."

"I didn't want anything to ruin your magical night. You deserve magical nights."

"Yes, I deserve magical nights, but not at the cost of being manipulated!"

"Sorry, Crystal. I love you, and I'll see you at the cafeteria at noon."

She sighs. "See you."

After Brownstone showers, he gets a call from Brock. "Commander Zeid took off last night in one of the Hummers full of weapons. One of our patrols found the Hummer abandoned on the west perimeter this morning. The driver's side door was ripped off, and all the weapons were left inside the vehicle. There was evidence on the sand of someone sliding on their backside—my guess is Prime was not impressed by the intelligence Zeid provided."

"Prime would've killed him, anyway. Who can trust a traitor? Zeid's unreliable info made him a dead man walking. We are tough men but facing Prime up close won't work for any man. He's a cold-blooded terminator of anything that bleeds. We didn't win a victory last night, but we bought some time." Brownstone ends the call and begins rehearsing what he'll say to Crystal to make up for it; then, he calls to reserve the back room of the cafeteria for their meeting.

When he gets there at lunch, Crystal waits by the entrance. He arrives at noon, smiling at her like a helpless boy in love. She stares him down. He tries to take her hand, but she brushes his hand away. They walk in silence to the back room.

Caleb and Jennifer join them. A few minutes later, Brock and Marci arrive. The ladies are glowing from the events of last night, except Crystal. Brownstone shares the details of their encounter with the androids the previous night, and he tells them about Commander Zeid running off and his Hummer being found abandoned.

"I don't believe Prime will attack because he lost some bots last night. Those Prime lost last night were expendable, and likely Cognition has given Prime a temporary stand-down order."

"So, we have a little time before they attack?" Crystal says.

Brownstone nods. "Probably, but we can't count on it and let down our guard. One of my sources tells me Cognition brought his replacement for Prime online. Hopefully, we can watch when Prime faces off against him from a distance. All hell will break loose when they fight it out. We'll have a window to do some severe damage in the chaos created by their confrontation. My source tells me Cognition is planning to move on Prime soon. The plan revealed to me in my dream to get our enemies to fight each other is working. Cognition plans to destroy Prime with the latest and most advanced android created: Intuition. He looks as human as any of us."

Crystal scowls. "You have a source in Cognition's inner circle?"

"I have a source, but I doubt Cognition has an inner circle. He's way too self-centered to have allies."

Brock speaks up. "How can you trust an android as a reliable source?"

Brownstone shrugs. "It's quite simple. We have a common enemy: Cognition. It's in the interest of my source to see the demise of Cognition because he is planning to replace them with the next generation of androids. The enemy of our enemy might be our ally for a time. We'll take precautions and not put our people in danger on the word of an android. So far, his information has been accurate. As insurance, I have three of my special forces operatives tracking Prime's bots' activity in the field."

"Who are these operatives, Maverick? And when will I meet them?" Crystal inquires.

He leans back. "Their names are Vince, J.R., and Mason, and they've been valuable partners in past battles with the androids. I'll introduce you to them soon, but I need them in the field, for now, to keep us safe."

Crystal is getting a clearer picture of her future husband. He's not just the defense leader of the people living in the compound. He's the leader of Underling Freedom Fighters all around the country.

"Our sources inside Imperial City say there has been a falling-out between Dr. Steadman and Zander. Steadman relieved Zander from his leadership position as Defense Commander. Next Tuesday, the High Council of Elites is scheduled to vote on Zander's permanent ouster. It seems Zander is plotting revenge against Steadman and the High Council if they vote to demote him."

Crystal's brow creases. "What kind of action is Zander prepared to take?"

"As I understand it, he will kill Steadman, the entire High Council, and others loyal to them."

Crystal responds, "I'm afraid I cannot stand by and let that happen to my Elite brothers and sisters, even if they believe they are better than everyone. Imperfect as they are, they helped raise us."

"Understood," Brownstone says. "We have been making plans for intervention in Imperial City if necessary. Our sources are updating us daily regarding Zander's plans. We will need to solidify a plan to prevent the slaughter of the High Council and others. At our Defense Council Meeting tomorrow, we will go over the plan we have so far to intervene in Imperial City. Also, I want to get input from each of you. We will need our collective brainpower to pull this off and put an end to Zander and his cronies."

Caleb interjects, "This is not your fight, Maverick. You don't have to risk your life trying to save people who have been plotting your demise."

"All the Elites in the compound are my family. I won't stand by and watch the mass murder of Elites if we can save them. We are a family, and they are God's children, too, whether they know it or not. Zander wants his revenge against us. I can't allow him to take over Imperial City and launch an all-out attack against us. The last thing we want to do is engage the Elites and Prime simultaneously."

Crystal meets his eyes. "How many sources do you have in Imperial City?

"I have a few. Have you heard of a man named Kort?"

"Yes, my friend Roxanne told me about him. She said he was the leader of the nomadic group she traveled with when she was brought to Imperial City. She said Commander Kort went to work in the mines. That was the last she heard of him."

Brownstone smiles. "Commander Kort is far more than just a leader of a nomadic group wandering the desert. He is one of the highest decorated United States Marines who ever-served Uncle Sam.

"Our next Defense Council Meeting will be in the conference room tomorrow at noon. I have ordered a catered meal for the meeting. We will go into depth about our plans for Imperial City and Operation Prime and get updates from department leaders. We have some blueprints for Imperial City, but we need inside information from Elites who have lived and worked there."

Brock rises. "Gentlemen, I suggest we leave and let the ladies discuss their wedding plans." He winks at Marci.

Crystal's anger toward Brownstone has softened. She can't stay mad at him indefinitely. She flashes him a smile and a wink. "Later, handsome."

"Later, beauty."

The ladies establish a schedule for their wedding planning sessions. Knowing their primary responsibility is to defend the compound, they decide to meet for wedding planning sessions at 5 p.m. on Mondays, Wednesdays, and Fridays. They end their meeting with a friendship ring high-five. "Love is family, and family is love."

# CHAPTER 28

After their planning session, Crystal goes to meet Robert Forrester at the military research lab. The lab is ten stories underground, bigger than four football fields, and has a hundred-foot-tall ceiling. Security stops her at the entrance and instructs her to wear special glasses. They escort her to the area where Forrester is working.

He's at the back section of the lab, a brightly lit area with steel-reinforced walls and a two-hundred-foot tall ceiling. Forrester's behind a six-inch thick steel reinforced structure. She walks into the enclosure and observes a floating orb nearly one hundred feet in the air. At Forrester's command, the spinning orb shoots laser beams in many directions. Each beam travels about fifty feet, assuming the distance limitation on the laser beams is because it's a controlled experiment. Forrester turns off the orb.

"Well, what do you think, Crystal?"

"It is an impressive display of military technology." She smiles as she looks the orb over. "Are you planning on using it for defense or offense?"

"The idea is to use combinations of ground lasers and orb lasers to create a virtually impenetrable defense perimeter. Do you see any design flaws with the orb laser?" Forrester asks, gesturing with his pen.

"The instability of a hovering orb in the desert winds might prove impractical if you shoot at moving targets such as drones. If you are shooting larger targets, it will prove practical."

"A good point. Do you have any recommendations to overcome the orb instability?"

"We could mount the orbs on towers and raise and lower them by a hydraulic system. They could be stored underground and raised when there is a threat. And we could put more lasers in the orbs that fire at different ranges to give us maximum coverage. I suggest three different ranges: outer, middle, and inner, for ground coverage. The Orb Lasers would be a significant addition to the drone inceptors and surface-to-air missiles."

Forrester smiles. "I like those recommendations. I'll get our engineers to design those towers. We have no time to waste if we want to ensure our survival."

"See you later, Rob. I've got some wedding plans to make."

Rob hugs her. "See you tomorrow, Niece. Love you."

Crystal smiles. That interaction wouldn't have ever happened in Imperial City. The Underlings are open to her suggestions. She has the freedom to be creative and use all her intellectual abilities with them. Though she was treated like royalty in Elite Society, Crystal feels like she belongs here. The Underlings don't envy her as the Elites did. Maybe she can actually make a difference here.

She meets up with Jennifer on the way to Marci's. "My sister," they greet each other almost simultaneously.

Marci greets them with hugs. "Come in and make yourself comfortable. I have to get some hors d'oeuvres out of the kitchen." They offer to help, but Marci is firm that they're her guests. She bustles off to the kitchen and returns with a tray of cheese and fruit kabobs, which she sets on the coffee table. Crystal and Jennifer sit on the sofa, laughing at each other's stories about Brownstone and Caleb. Jennifer is just about to recount a story from one of the ops she worked with

Maverick when Simone arrives carrying three thick binders of wedding dress photos.

"You three sit on the sofa. You can pass the binders back and forth," Simone says.

They share a bottle of Pinot Noir and swap binders for a couple of hours before deciding on their dresses.

The cheese and fruit kabobs go perfectly with Pinot Noir. Marci serves spaghetti with garlic bread for dinner. They have their choice of pink lemonade or iced tea to drink. Simone leaves at 9 p.m. They do their friendship ring salute and group hug.

Crystal can't help but think that she's living in a dream world. This is the happiest she's ever been in her life. Many people love and care about her. She couldn't remember the last time she'd had this, and she didn't want to lose it.

Following orders in Imperial City was one thing. But these people she cares deeply about. She must be on top of her game to protect her loved ones. They had successfully disrupted Cognition's world. They must do the same to Prime, Intuition, and Zander. Their last mission was too dangerous, and they were fortunate to have made it out alive. A hell storm is coming their way, and Crystal is determined to keep everyone safe.

# CHAPTER 29

After a vigorous morning workout with Jennifer, Crystal meets Forester at the military research lab. When she gets there, at least a hundred small drones are flying randomly at high speeds but not crashing into each other. Rob greets her, "Hello, Crystal."

"Hello, Uncle. Are you playing a game or researching to use these drones as weapons?"

"I would like to use them for weapons, but I haven't figured out how."

"How many of these drones do you have? What's their top speed? And how much does each drone weigh?"

"In total, we have nearly one thousand. They have a top speed of one hundred miles per hour and weigh two pounds each."

"How soon can you ramp up production to make more of them?"

"We presently can make about fifty a day using 3D printing ... What do you have in mind?"

"If we have two thousand of these small drones, we can launch a kamikaze-style surprise attack against Prime and his bots. Let's bring one of these drones to the meeting to show everyone."

"I like how you think, Crystal."

"You keep inventing stuff, and I'll figure out how to use it."

Rob chuckles and says, "Deal. We better make our way to the Defense Council Meeting."

Brownstone's already in his office at the back of the conference room. Crystal walks to his office but stops at the door when he hears him strumming his guitar and singing a song. She listens closely to the words for a moment before entering.

You are my friend
You are my woman
You are my wife
The best part of my life
My beautiful bride by my side
For this magical roller coaster ride
We go up; we go down
We go all around
Times have been good
Times have been tough
Then there's Us
Money is tight
Babies are crying
If I said it was easy, I'd be lying
Then there's Us.

As Crystal enters the room, Brownstone stops playing and leans his guitar against the wall. "What was that song you were playing? It's beautiful!"

He smiles. "It's called 'Then There's Us.' I wrote it for my parents' twentieth wedding anniversary."

She walks to him, puts her hands on his face, and gives him a passionate kiss. "How's my Maverick?"

"Your Maverick is much better now. Thanks! How's my Ice?"

"I'm better."

"Are you still upset with me?

"As I told you, I don't need any old ladies to stand up for me," she teases. "Hopefully, you are a man who learns from his mistakes. If not, there will be more lessons for you."

He thought back to the mouthful of sand he'd gotten. He wasn't sure he wanted any more lessons. "Okay then, we better get out there before your mother and brother come looking for you."

"They're too caught up in their love affairs to worry about us."

As they enter the conference room, Brock smirks at them. "Nice of you two to join us."

Caleb joins in. "We didn't know there would be a separate meeting before the main meeting in your office, Brownstone."

"If I didn't know better, Maverick, I would think you prefer Crystal over the rest of us," Marci teases.

Crystal stares at him and says, "Maverick, why did you drag me into your office and make these good people wait?"

"I guess I'm just a silly boy in love. Now, little superhero, I mean Caleb, will you bless the meeting?"

Caleb goes right into the blessing, ignoring his comment until the end. "Last, Lord, I thank you for humor, not humor like Brownstone's because that's not good humor. Amen."

Brownstone mock punches his arm before he redirects everyone to the task at hand. "As you know, Commander Zeid attempted to betray us. He gave Prime the wrong information, and it cost him his life. I'm not going into the gory details about how he died, but Prime has no sympathy for human pain and suffering. I have appointed Brock to take over Zeid's duties.

"Here's what we know so far: Cognition blames Prime for the attack on Los Alamos. According to our source at Los Alamos, Cognition has brought his replacement for Prime online. His name is Intuition. Cognition feels this new Q-Bot will be his eyes and ears in the field. Cognition gave him maximum processing power. They have something of a symbiotic relationship. As previously mentioned, Intuition looks, talks, and moves like a human. He is just the first of this new generation of Q-Bots. Cognition plans on creating thousands of them.

"Only a few Q-Bots are aware of Cognition's plan to create an improved version. The Q-Bots won't be happy about being replaced by a new generation of androids. We believe Cognition will move to replace Prime within two weeks. We need to be ready if war breaks out between Prime and Intuition. It will be a great time for us to attack our enemies. The tension between Prime and Cognition will run high. We need to ignite a spark and trigger an all-out war. I'm open to suggestions on how to do that."

Jennifer smiles. "We could blow something up as we did at Los Alamos. But what do we blow up that would cause Prime to take it personally?"

"We need to blow-up Prime's plane," Crystal says. "And we need to blow it up not long after Intuition arrives. Prime will assume it was Intuition."

Simone speaks up, "That could work, but how do we get close enough to blow up the plane?"

Brownstone walks to the front of the room. "Computer on," he commands. The screen lights up behind him. "This area of Nevada was awash in secret government research projects. Most people are aware of Area Fifty-One. However, the United States government didn't stop there. They built several other research facilities to be undetectable to the public. Those research facilities were all connected by a series of underground tunnels. Numerous tunnels run under this desert.

"Computer. Show the diagram of the south corridor tunnel system." The screen changes to a sort of map. "We have a series of tunnels that will take us within five hundred feet of Prime's base. Electric carts in the tunnels should allow us to get close to Prime's base within minutes." He gestures to the points on the map. "The question is, how are we going to blow up the plane from five hundred feet?"

Brock raises his finger as an idea hits him. "We could use the AL3000."

"It would work if we had a clear shot at Prime's plane from our position in the tunnel. But we can't see Prime's plane from the tunnel," Brownstone replies.

Crystal stands. "I have an idea." She walks to the front of the room beside Brownstone. "Dr. Forrester has been working on an orb laser that can take out ground targets. What if the Orb fires its lasers from two hundred feet down at Prime's plane? Will that work?"

Brownstone thinks for a moment, running numbers in his head. Crystal can nearly see him playing out the scenario in his mind. "I believe that will do the trick," Brownstone finally says.

Crystal expands on her idea. "The tunnel branches out in a Y-formation with the two branches of the Y at an equal distance from Prime's base camp. We could hit them with not one Orbital Laser but two. We can use the electric cart system to transport the Orbital Lasers to the engagement areas. Rob, can you program the lasers to take out Prime's plane?"

"Certainly," Rob replies.

"Also, Rob has about one thousand small drones." On cue, Rob lays the small drone he brought with him on the conference table. Crystal continues, "We can launch a drone swarm attack at the androids in a kamikaze manner. Rob can Three-D print another one thousand drones by mission time."

"What type of range do these little drones have?" Caleb asks.

"Two hundred miles," Rob says.

Caleb nods. "In that case, I suggest we launch these drones from different locations and at a significant distance from Prime's base camp. The Q-Bots will have a difficult time detecting them."

Brownstone smiles, looking around the room. This sort of collaboration was one of his favorite aspects. "We have the makings of a good plan so far, and I think it has a decent chance of succeeding. I want to do a few mock runs in the tunnel system to see how the logistics and timing work. We will take two AL3000s with us. We must be ready if we get a shot at Prime or Intuition. I want the small drones to attack first to create a distraction, enabling us to launch the Orbital Lasers successfully. We need to do our best to exterminate Prime and Intuition."

Crystal looks at the map again. "With a range of two hundred miles, we can have the drone swarm circle out past Prime's base camp and come in the same direction as Intuition's plane. Prime will have no choice but to believe Cognition is trying to take him out, so Prime will attack Intuition and his delegation of Q-Bots. We can take out their planes while they defend themselves from the drone swarms. It will be interesting to see what side the Humbots take. Will they attack Prime, or will they attack Intuition? I hypothesize they will side with whom they perceive as winning. Their existence is based upon logic."

"We must have our A-game to pull this off. Prime's androids and drones will automatically return fire in the direction it comes from," Brownstone says.

Brock nods. "So, if we fire our weapons, we have to move from our positions immediately because we'll get return fire."

"We need to be fully operational as soon as possible. Caleb, will you work closely with Rob to help with the science and technical side of things?" Brownstone asks.

"Absolutely."

Brownstone elaborates on the situation in Imperial City. "The High Council of the Elites are meeting next Tuesday, and Zander's removal as Defense Commander is a foregone conclusion. If the vote doesn't go his way, Zander plans to eliminate Steadman and the entire High Council. Steadman and the Council members will be on high alert for several weeks. According to our sources, Zander is determining which Elite commandos are with him and who are against him."

Crystal shakes her head, thinking back to the Elites she trained with, "Zander's brutality has no limits. The streets of Imperial City will flow with blood if he isn't stopped."

"Unfortunately, we don't have a tunnel system that runs directly to Imperial City," Brownstone says. "Our tunnel system will take us near an underground river which we can use to access Imperial City's mines. We might have to swim underwater for a few hundred feet, depending on how high the river is at the time. What do our Elite members think about this plan?"

"A better option is for Caleb and me to return to Imperial City. Steadman would want to interrogate us. We then could tell him about Zander's plan," Crystal says firmly.

Jennifer shakes her head. "That's too risky. You don't know how you will be greeted in Imperial City. They might try to kill you before you make it to Steadman, and Zander would have the opportunity to get rid of all his rivals simultaneously."

Brownstone pulls up a different map. "Let's say our team goes into Imperial City via the underground river. How can we make it to the city's heart and reach Imperial Tower without being detected?"

Caleb thinks for a moment. "There is a tram that runs from the mines into the heart of the city to transport Underling workers back and forth. Maverick, you, Jennifer, and Brock could pose as those workers by dressing in their uniforms."

"What level of security does the tram have?" Brownstone asks.

Crystal answers, "There is no security detail assigned to oversee the tram. Imperial City is entirely enclosed in a dome: the need for security to monitor the trams seemed irrelevant. The tram is self-driving, so no one is monitoring suspicious people. You only scan an ID to board. Can Commander Kort obtain IDs for everyone?"

"I don't think that will be a problem," Brownstone says, pausing. "But if we involve him and other operatives, we need to accomplish our mission. We don't want to put their lives at risk for a mission that's not liberating them. Saying that we need to have a clear list of mission objectives. Elite team members, what are your mission objectives?"

Crystal says, "To prevent the mass murder of Elites."

"And to remove Steadman and Zander from power," Caleb adds.

"We want to establish a fair leadership that doesn't award positions based on your Gen Elite status but your ability," Simone says.

Brownstone nods. "My goal is to liberate all the captives in Imperial City who want to leave. Though, I won't be surprised if some want to stay. Second, those who choose to stay should be treated fairly, regardless of Elite or Underling status. History teaches us that we cannot disrupt a society such as Imperial City without establishing a transitional government to lead them. Is anyone serving on the High Council of Elites who could take over as a transitional leader?"

"There is one," Caleb suggests. "Dr. Jewell has a democratic worldview. She is a left-over Gen Six serving on the High Council. She's been sympathetic to those who have been demoted in the past. Dr. Jewel doesn't believe Steadman's B.S."

Brownstone looks over the maps on the computer and nods again, content. "We've identified some good options for moving forward with our next missions. We have a good outline for Operation Prime. I want everyone to study our options to intervene in Imperial City. When it comes to Imperial City, we can develop ideas about how their society should move forward, but it will be up to them to govern themselves.

"I will not have us being an occupying force in Imperial City. I'm confident they will be open to our suggestions once they have their freedom. We'll meet back here on Monday at 1 p.m. to get updates on our progress and solidify our mission plans. Tomorrow is our day of worship. When we put God first, everything falls into place. Let us know if you think of anything we need to implement in the interim."

Caleb closes the meeting with prayer.

Brownstone hugs Crystal after the meeting. He gives her a light kiss on the lips and asks, "How are the wedding plans going, sweetness?"

"They are going well."

"Thanks for spearheading the planning." He pulls her close and begins to sway with her in a music-less dance.

She smiles and rests her head against his chest, listening to his heart and breath.

"Have you picked out a wedding dress?"

She tips her head up, so they're nose to nose. "That's for me to know and you to find out later. Later, as on our wedding day!"

# CHAPTER 30

Crystal declines Brownstone's offer to go to the Gathering on Sunday but agrees to dinner at Rob's afterward. James picks her up at noon. She wears a blue floral dress that falls just below her knees with white high-heeled shoes.

He says, "Every time I see you in a dress, my heart beats faster. You are stunning." Brownstone wears blue jeans, a mauve rose dress shirt, and black dress shoes. Together, they look like a Hollywood power couple.

Caleb offers a prayer of thanksgiving before the meal "Father, you know our needs even before we do. I came here looking for Marci, but you added brothers, sisters, and a beautiful fiancée. Crystal came here to find her brother and defeat a notorious villain, and she found a mother and got engaged to the villain. Last but not least, Kurt Evans came here looking for a sandwich and a barbell. Yet, he got engaged to a sweet, beautiful lady full of faith and grace, my beautiful mother, Marci Jenkins. Our God is willing and able to give us exceedingly more than we ask for. Father, we ask that you bless the food and fellowship, in Jesus' name. Amen."

Rob and Simone serve fried chicken, mashed potatoes and gravy, corn on the cob, sweet tea to drink, and peach cobbler for dessert.

Brownstone leans over to Crystal. "Sunday dinners at your elders' house was a tradition for many American families years ago. Sundays were a time for worship, fellowship, family, and rest. We figured it best to keep that going here."

Crystal leans in and whispers, "I like the old ways." How nice it would be if they could go back to the simplicity of that time. It sounds carefree and peaceful.

After dinner, Brownstone takes Crystal to the Eden Atrium for a walk around the stream. Holding his hand makes her feel warm. She looks at him. "Do you think we will always feel this way about each other?"

He plants a kiss on her forehead. "I will always feel this way about you, and I believe our love will only grow deeper. I don't think I could get over it if anything happened to you. So, I need you to be very careful."

"I want you to be careful too. But you know a warrior's greatest asset is instinct. We must be wise in our planning, but we cannot go into battle worrying about what might happen."

"I know you're right. Just be careful," he says, turning back to the sunset reflected on the water.

She steps in front of him, places her hands on each side of his face, and says, "Shut up and kiss me."

They spend the next hour talking while overlooking the waterfall.

Seated on one of the benches, Crystal turns the conversation from thoughts of their life together to the one thing she can't stop thinking about. "I should go back to Imperial City and confront Zander. There's no need to shed innocent Underling blood for something that needs to be settled by Elites."

"I cannot let you do that. We are formulating a great plan that has a significant chance of succeeding. I don't want to lose you," he replies.

She rolls her eyes. "First of all, you don't control me. If I want to return to Imperial City and face down Zander, I will do so."

"Crystal, I think you are trying to protect me like I'm trying to protect you. If we work together, our chances of succeeding are much greater."

"The decision is mine to make. And right now, I am leaning toward returning to Imperial City and, once and for all, putting an end to Zander."

"You would put our future at risk just like that?"

She sighs. "Maybe I am doing it for our future."

She pulls Brownstone to her, giving him a passionate kiss. Feeling his body pressed against hers, it's difficult for her to stop. She uses what little willpower she has left and pushes him away.

"Goodnight, Maverick."

"Night, Ice."

# CHAPTER 31

E arly Monday morning, Crystal checks with Rob about the progress of drone production. They produced one hundred more drones since their meeting on Saturday. Rob shows her a simulation that he arranged with the small drones. He put a couple of full-size standing dummies on the testing field; then, he launched a couple of small drones. Those drones crashed into the dummies, severing their heads.

Crystal asks, "Will these drones crush the torso of a Humbot or Q-Bot?"

"I'll have the bodies of the terminated Humbots and the one Q-Bot brought here for testing tomorrow. We will measure the damage caused to both and determine if our drones can puncture the bots' titanium shells flying at their max speed of one hundred miles per hour. Their torsos will be easier targets to hit and give us a better chance for success."

"As I said, Uncle, you build them, and I will figure out how to use them. Ironically, the artificial intelligence technology we created is determined to destroy us."

"Limiting artificial intelligence is the one area where Steadman and I agree."

Brownstone is again in his office, preparing for the defense council meeting. Crystal goes to retrieve him. Brownstone pushes his chair back to get up, but she motions for him to remain seated with her hand. Crystal walks over, putting her hands on his shoulders; she straddles his legs and presses her body against his. "Just kiss me," she whispers.

He gives her a slow, lingering kiss. He grabs her hips, pulling her even closer. Crystal knows she's torturing him, but some things are hard to resist. The passion between them is ready to ignite into an unquenchable fire. Reluctantly, Crystal extracts herself from his clutches.

"Come on, soldier. Time to go save the world."

He smiles. "Only if it means you'll still be in it."

Once in the main conference room, Crystal notices another military man sitting at the conference table. Brownstone acknowledges team members. He says, "Would you all welcome to our midst Lieutenant William Xavier." After the team members greet Xavier, he asks Caleb to open the meeting with a prayer.

After the prayer, Brownstone grabs Crystal's hand, and they walk to the front of the room. "Do we have any updates about the mission plans?" Brownstone asks.

Rob updates them on the drone production.

Crystal adds, "We will move the exterminated Humbots and the one Q-Bot to the testing field to determine if the drones can penetrate their titanium torsos. We will have to take headshots if the drones cannot penetrate their torsos."

"What if the drones miss their first target; will they find another target?" Brownstone inquires.

Rob shakes his head. "As of now, the drones can only focus on one target at a time. It would take complex programming for them to target multiple targets in one flight pattern."

"We could have the drones attack in three waves. I believe we need to target Prime and his forces in the first two waves.

Prime will have by far the most troops, with approximately one thousand Humbots and one hundred Q-Bots. Only a small delegation of Q-Bots should accompany Intuition. I recommend that, within minutes of our first attack, we relaunch a second attack targeting Prime's Bots. Our last wave should focus on any remaining Bots, splitting our supplies evenly into thirds," Caleb suggests.

Brownstone agrees. "I like those recommendations. If we miss some Bots in our first wave, we'll have a good chance of taking them out in our second and third attacks. The drone swarms should create chaos among the bots and allow us to take out their planes with the orbital lasers. Just in case, I still think it would be good to have another method of attack against the Bots. Any ideas?"

"Do you have grenade launchers for tanks?" Crystal asks.

Brownstone looks at her, trying to read her mind. "Yes ..."

"We could fire them at Prime's base seconds after the first wave of small drones," Crystal suggests.

Brownstone smiles mischievously. "Let's implement the grenade launchers as a part of the mission. We will have to target their buildings because of the grenade launchers' limited accuracy. Prime's base camp buildings are arranged in a triangle formation." He pulls up the map and draws out the triangle with his finger. "His operation center is here, in the middle. Based on his logical brain, he's likely to move between these three buildings for safety. There are auxiliary buildings surrounding Prime's plane in a square behind their base camp. Intuition will land his plane inside that square."

Crystal scowls. "The defensive formation of those buildings will prevent us from getting a clear shot at Prime *or* Intuition unless the battle causes them to make a run for it. We must be ready for the possibility that one or both will try to escape. If possible, we need to cut off their heads. They can survive otherwise."

Brownstone looks at Brock. "How many electric carts do we have in the tunnels, and what is their payload capability?"

"We have six two-person electric carts. They each have a small payload."

Brownstone nods. "For now, we will plan on using six Grenade Launchers, two AL3000s, five .50 caliber sniper rifles, two orbital lasers, and six camouflage blankets. The six-person mission team will comprise Caleb, Jennifer, Brock, Xavier, Crystal, and me. Since our electric cart system can operate autonomously, we'll use the additional carts to carry the orbital lasers into position.

"The tunnel doors are approximately one thousand feet north of Prime's base on each branch of the Y route. A code must be punched into the doors for them to open. Caleb, is there any way you can open and close the doors using a remote-control device?"

"I don't think that will be a problem. If someone will take me down into the tunnels, I can program the doors this evening."

Lieutenant Xavier speaks up, "I'll take you."

"Can we build a stand for the grenade launchers that will allow us to fire them remotely at Prime's buildings?" Crystal asks.

Rob replies, "I will get the engineers working on that tomorrow. Hopefully, we can increase the accuracy by firing them from a stand versus human operators."

James looks between them. "Will they be able to hit Prime's building from one thousand feet?"

Rob nods. "They'll hit the damn buildings."

Brownstone takes a breath, running through the timeline in his mind. "Our plan against Prime's base is on target, but we must maintain our sense of urgency. We need to move any weapons or weapons systems in place as soon as they're ready. Uncle, I want you to launch a drone swarm from the back of the compound and have them circle out wide to attack Prime's base from the rear. You and Simone will stay here and have the XPlane on standby. Our defensive weapons must be ready for a counterattack if the mission doesn't go according to plan. We'll probably never have a better opportunity to target Prime and this many Bots again."

# CHAPTER 32

"Let's switch gears and focus on the mission to liberate Imperial City. Crystal, Caleb, Simone—have you thought about the best way to enter the city?" Brownstone asks.

Caleb speaks first. "I favor using the tunnel system to the underground river." Simone nods.

Crystal adamantly disagrees. Glaring at Brownstone, she says, "Underling lives shouldn't be put at risk for an Elite societal failure."

Brownstone feels her stare. "Crystal's dissension is duly noted. Let's proceed with the tunnel and the underground river plan and take the tram system into the city's heart. If we go that route, we cannot take our heavy arms with us."

"We can overpower the guards at the armory and take their weapons," Crystal says.

"Brilliant idea," Brownstone replies. "What service jobs can get us to the city's heart without drawing suspicion?"

"There are some maintenance workers who work in the office buildings in the city," Caleb says. "They take care of things like plumbing and electrical issues—all the workers who ride the tram must wear uniforms. The uniform color identifies their job type. Maids and butlers wear traditional black and white. Maintenance workers dress in blue. All tattoos must be covered. Anyone with a face, neck, hand tattoo or facial piercing cannot work in the city. No worker in Imperial City can be over fifty years of age, overweight, or have any disability."

"Has the High Council ever heard of a thing called discrimination?" Jennifer inquires.

Crystal replies sarcastically, "Our 'esteemed leader,' Dr. Steadman, made those rules. No one on the High Council would ever challenge him."

"Brock, Xavier, and I will go in as maintenance men," Brownstone decides. "I guess Crystal and Caleb can go dressed as Elites." Everyone laughs.

"What about me?" Simone asks.

Crystal asks, "Do you want to go on this mission, Simone?"

"These are the people who raised us and taught us. I cannot stand by and see them die."

Brownstone nods. "We still have more planning to do on this mission. What role does each of us play? How will we take out Zander and his commandos without getting ourselves killed? But all of that is for another time. Before you go, I have some announcements to make. First, we will not meet tomorrow unless there is an emergency. I believe we have enough to work on for Operations Prime and Imperial.

"Second, I want to bestow a couple of honors on a few distinguished patriots today. Xavier, would you come to the front? William Xavier, for your loyalty, honor, and devotion to free people everywhere, you are raised to the rank of captain."

Kurt presents William with his stripes. The honor visibly surprises Xavier as he shakes hands with Maverick and Brock.

James continues, "I have another promotion to announce. Uncle Rob, join me in presenting Kurt 'Brock' Evans with the stripes of major in the Free People's Army. Brock, you've had my back more times than I can count. Your dedication to the Free People of this compound kept more bad guys away than

they'll ever know. It's been an honor to serve alongside you."
Brownstone and Brock embrace. Jennifer jumps up and joins
them.

Brownstone is not done, "Simone, Marci, Uncle Rob,
and Caleb join me in presenting Jennifer Rodriguez her new
lab coat with the title of Assistant Laboratory Supervisor.
She will be full-time in the lab after our next two missions."
Jennifer put on her lab coat, not able to hide her joy.

Rob says, "Jennifer, you came to us as a child, having lost
your parents. You won our hearts with your faith, courage,
and spirit. Your dedication to self-improvement has been
an example to many in the compound. You worked hard at
your academic studies and have been one of my best and
brightest students. I know the boys will miss playing soldier
with you, but your work in the lab will be a greater service to
us." After Rob finishes his speech, there is not a dry eye in the
conference room.

Brownstone says, "Last, I am placing Crystal in charge of
the mission to liberate Imperial City via the tunnel system."
Everyone was excited for her to be chosen as mission leader,
except Crystal. She stares Brownstone down, giving him
notice of his attempt to manipulate her.

Crystal pulls Brownstone to the side. "I know what you're
trying to do. Any attempt to manipulate an Elite Strike Force
warrior won't work well for you."

He grimaces. "You know more about Imperial City's
security than anyone else. I need you to take the lead on this
one for everyone's sake."

Crystal would like nothing more than to hop on her sky
cycle and return to Imperial City, and put an end to Zander.
But Prime's position leaves her brother and mother in danger.
She's in a tight spot. Brownstone knows that, too. She can see
it in his eyes. Crystal hates to admit it, but he's right. She's the
best one to lead this mission.

After the meeting is dismissed, Simone, Jennifer, Marci, and Crystal go directly to the cafeteria for another wedding planning session. Marci says, "We have so much to be thankful for, ladies. We have great men, friends as close as sisters, a God that loves us beyond measure, and glorious memories for our hearts to treasure."

Crystal adds, "I'm thankful for my raven-haired little sister who has come into her own."

Marci lifts her glass of sparkling water. "Here's a toast to Jennifer; even though my son brought you to me, you are now my youngest daughter." They lift their glasses and drink.

Jennifer looks over at Marci and notices a cross necklace she hadn't seen before. "Marci, I love your cross. Is it new?"

"Yes. It's an infinity cross with a personalized birthstone. I like the infinity cross because it symbolizes God's eternal love."

Marci reaches into her purse, pulls out three small boxes, and hands one to each of them. "My beautiful sisters, I took the liberty of getting each of you an infinity cross with a birthstone."

After hugs and tears, Simone says, "I will treasure this moment for the rest of my life."

They also made several important wedding decisions: choosing shoes for themselves, tuxedos for the men, and arranging wedding dress fittings.

Crystal is amazed at how similar planning a wedding is to planning a military mission. Both require great attention to detail and coordination of many moving parts.

Captain Xavier takes Caleb into the tunnel system right after the defense meeting. The tunnel is designed for two-way traffic, with rails running in opposite directions and motion-activated lighting. Each cart's speedometer goes up to one hundred miles per hour. They probably won't need to go that fast, but it's nice to have the option available if required.

"How far is it to the mission site?" Caleb asks.

"Three miles," Xavier responds.

"We must figure out the maximum speed the cart can travel considering the stopping distance."

Captain Xavier looks at Caleb. "You are the real deal, aren't you?"

"It's just the way my mind works. Set the electric cart speed at sixty miles per hour, and we should get there in three minutes."

After a few runs to each Y section of the tunnels, Caleb determines that the maximum speed is seventy-five miles per hour. He looks at Xavier. "We need to open the doors on the opposite side of Prime's base camp for those getting into sniper position and launching the orbital lasers. We will open the doors on the same side to fire the grenade launchers. There's plenty of room on both sides of the tunnel to store our weapons systems in advance. We can make the grenade launcher stands more secure if we bolt them to the tunnel frames. That will improve the accuracy of our launchers substantially. I'll set them to fire by voice command."

Caleb takes a handheld device and holds it to the tunnel doors' keypunch pads. In a matter of seconds, he rigged the doors to open remotely. It took only 30 minutes for Caleb to learn everything he needed to know about the tunnel system.

Brownstone goes to the armory and meets with Brock to check on weapon supplies. Brock gives him a rundown on how many grenade launchers they have on hand. "We need to overwhelm the bots with firepower," Brownstone says. "That way, the bots can't rationalize their way out of it. They'll take whatever steps necessary to survive, even if it means running away."

Brock watches Brownstone's face for a moment. "I know what you're thinking. You want to get a clear shot at Prime with the AL3000."

Brownstone replies, "If we can take out Prime and do substantial damage to the ranks of the Bots, they won't bother us for a while."

Brock asks, "Who do you think will win the battle between Intuition and Prime?"

"I know if I can have a source inside Cognition's higher-ups, Prime will have several spies at Los Alamos. He'll expect Intuition. Prime will know and prepare for Intuition's capabilities. If I were a betting man, I would put my money on Prime. Intuition is lab tested, but Prime is battlefield proven."

Brock goes quiet for a moment. "Did you ever imagine in your wildest dreams that we would be here fighting for the survival of humanity?"

"No, but I believe we are called for this purpose and time."

# CHAPTER 33

Crystal gets an early start on the day, making it to the lab by 7 a.m. There's much work to be done to prepare for Operation Prime. She's a little on edge today; today, the High Council will rule on Zander's status. She's concerned for her fellow Elites.

Rob has two Humbot torsos and one Q-Bot torso standing on the testing field. Crystal asks, "How accurate are these drones?"

"They can hit a bullseye on a stable target. I don't believe the Humbots will stand still after the first drone swarm."

"Our first drone attack needs to hit their torsos."

Rob runs a couple of drone attacks on bots. The drones did significant damage to the Humbots no matter where they hit them, but they bounced violently off the Q-Bot's torso. They waste no more drones on Q-Bot body shots. On the positive side, the Q-Bot's head was severely damaged from a direct drone strike. Now they can program the drones for Operation Prime.

They leave the lab and meet with James, Caleb, and Kurt in the small conference room next to Rob's office. Caleb mentions they will bolt the grenade launcher frames to the tunnel structure. The grenade launchers will be programmed to launch on voice command and have an automatic reloading system.

Brownstone smiles. "We should be able to do serious damage with all this."

"How long will it take to get the grenade launchers in place?" Crystal asks.

Rob says, "It should take about two to three days."

"Captain Xavier can take a couple of engineers down there today to develop the installation specifications," Brock suggests.

Caleb taps his pencil on the table. "What if we launch two to three hundred drones out of the tunnel to go after any residual Bots who have evaded the previous swarms?"

Brownstone looks at Rob. "Can we increase the number of drones to launch three to five hundred from the tunnels?"

Rob runs some quick math in his head. "It depends on how many drones we have by mission day."

"Chances are the Humbots and Q-Bots will move in the opposite direction from the initial attack," Crystal says. "We need to be ready for them. The way the tunnel system branches out in a Y around Prime's base creates an opportunity to rain down some serious firepower on them from many directions."

Kurt nods. "The bots are close enough to our compound. We cannot let them get any closer, even if they're running from a perceived attack by Cognition."

"Caleb, were you able to program the tunnel doors to open remotely?" Brownstone asks.

"Yes, it was no problem. I can synchronize the doors to open and the grenade launchers to fire simultaneously with the first drone swarm."

"How many launchers can you fit in each tunnel door?" Brownstone asks.

"We can fit six in each opening, and we'll have enough firepower to destroy their base camp buildings," Caleb reports. "The damage should be so great they won't take cover in them for long."

Brownstone nods. "We're approximately eight days or fewer till Operation Prime. I want us to go over and over every detail of our plan. Check and re-check all equipment several times per day. Our success will depend on the flawless execution of our mission. I think we've covered all our bases for now. We will meet again on Thursday at our Defense Council meeting at 1 p.m. In the meantime, let's keep each other updated about any pertinent information or concerns."

Captain Xavier sticks his head in the doorway. Rob motions him to come in. "Sorry to interrupt, but we have news about the High Council's decision regarding Zander."

Crystal's heart skips a beat. "What did they decide?"

"Just as suspected, they demoted him from Defense Commander to serve on the faculty at the Academy of Elites. He accepted his demotion in the letter he wrote to them. Zander thanked them for the opportunity and said he would work hard to regain their trust."

Caleb shakes his head. "He'll never lecture at the Academy of Elites. Zander will take a few weeks and then attack the High Council and Steadman when they let down their guard."

"Even though we expected this to happen, it bothers me knowing the evil that possesses Zander. I'll move quickly to establish our plan for Imperial City by the end of our Defense Meeting on Thursday. We'll practice and rehearse the plan down to the smallest detail. Our plan will only be as good as our execution," Crystal says.

Brownstone squeezes Crystal's hand. "We've got this." He puts his arms around her. Caleb gets the message and leads them in prayer.

Crystal knows her fate is tied to Brownstone. Her plan to go rogue is over. She will stand with Brownstone against all enemies of the Underlings.

# CHAPTER 34

At 2 a.m., Brownstone arcs through the cold water of a cave. His lungs burn from holding his breath for ninety seconds, swimming underwater. He pops above the surface into the open cavern and sees a tall, dark figure with a rifle hiding in the shadows. Without hesitation, he gets out of the water and moves toward the shadowy figure. The armed man rushes toward him until the men stand just feet apart. Brownstone smiles, and the two grip each other's forearms.

"Maverick, my old friend, how's life been treating you?" the man asks.

He replies, "Very well. And you, Kort?"

"Not bad, except for meeting a burly old war dog like you in a cave."

"I'm the old war dog?" Maverick teased. "How old are you now? Going on fifty, right?"

Kort's laugh is deep and warm. He ushers James farther onto the rocky shore. Kort is an imposing man of African descent, standing even taller than Brownstone and packed with muscle. His hair is cut short in military fashion. His age shows on his face, but he's still built like a brick wall.

Brownstone gathers himself to make the best of their time. "Do you have any updates on Zander and his goons?"

"They will wait until the High Council let down their guard. They're still planning their strategy and lining up recruits."

"How many soldiers do you have under your command?"

"I have fifty good men and women willing to fight with us. We can also count on at least twenty Elites to back us up. We're more than ready to free ourselves from our oppressors."

Brownstone looks around, "This cave will be an excellent staging area for our operation. We'll move the weapons here in advance. I'll bring a six-member team, three men and three women, with me. They will comprise one Elite man, two Elite women, two Underling men, and one woman. We'll need uniforms for the Underlings. I'll introduce you to one of the Elites tomorrow night. She's a dear friend of mine and concerned about the fate of her fellow Elites."

Kort smirks. "You must be talking about Crystal. You sound like a smitten man."

"Guilty! How many weapons will you need for the mission?"

Kort pulls out a list from his pocket. "I thought you would never ask."

Brownstone looks over the list. "I believe we can make this happen."

"You know, Maverick, you're the most hated person in Imperial City. If they recognize you, there will be an attempt on your life."

"I don't plan on being recognized. I'll alter my appearance so I can move around freely."

"Moving weapons to where they need to be without detection will take a little more creativity."

"Crystal is a brilliant strategist, and we can get her input tomorrow night."

Kort nods. "I've heard stories. Is she as brilliant as they say?"

"She's even more brilliant. Her mind works extremely fast. It's like everyone else is playing checkers while she is playing chess. How's everyone holding up in Imperial City?"

"Things have gotten worse since Caleb and Crystal left. Higher-ranking Elites are solidifying their positions to maintain the status quo. To satisfy lower-ranking Elites, Steadman assigned them, domestic servants. He's forcing Underlings to take positions of servitude to satisfy their need to feel superior. They've taken many teenage girls away from their Underling parents and moved them to domestic servitude. It's all I can do to prevent my men from going crazy and attacking their Elite oppressors."

Brownstone takes a breath. There were impossible situations all around. "You were right to wait. The Elite commandos are a formidable force. Once we neutralize them, the rest of the Elites won't trouble us. I believe they're ready for something different."

James and Kort finish solidifying their plan for tomorrow, and James dives back into the water, heading back to the compound.

He can't stop thinking about Crystal. He loves her deeply and will do anything to ease her fears over Imperial City. He makes it back to the compound at 4:30 a.m.

The next morning, at 7 a.m. sharp, Crystal meets Uncle Rob and Caleb at the military lab. The engineers have finished making stable platforms for the grenade launchers. Caleb is ready to test the first unit on the large testing field. They place a target a thousand feet from them. The engineers made the target one-fourth the size of the portable buildings at Prime's base Camp.

Caleb gives a voice command, and the grenade launcher frame rises quickly into position. Then he gives the order to fire. The force of the grenades knocks the target end over end with enough power to obliterate a tank, launching it at least a hundred feet from its previous position. All six grenades arrive at their destination together. The grenade launcher automatically reloads. Caleb gives the command to fire again. The grenades hit the target one more time.

Crystal says, "Impressive, little brother. Now let's see how much damage was done." Of the twelve projectiles fired, six penetrated the shell of the container. The other six made deep indentions.

"How will you get this large contraption down in the tunnel?" Crystal asks.

Caleb answers, "We designed it to come apart in three sections. Each section will be bolted back together in the tunnel."

"Well done, baby brother. I taught you well," Crystal teases.

Caleb laughs. "Yeah, right."

She turns to Rob. "How are we doing with the drone production?"

"We're now making one hundred and fifty per day. I hope to get that up to two hundred per day in the next few days. We aim to have enough drones for Caleb to launch one last surprise attack from the tunnel."

"How will you launch the drones fast enough out of a tunnel door?" She turns to Caleb.

"I designed a special box that allows us to stack them on top of each other on shelves to keep them separate. The box will fit right into the tunnel door. After we launch the first layer, hydraulic arms will remove the top shelf for the next layer to launch."

"That boy has an answer for everything," Rob says.

Crystal smirks, "One more question, Caleb—what pair of sexy underwear will you wear on your wedding night?"

Caleb's face turns red as he shakes his head.

Crystal laughs. "Not everything, Uncle. Not everything."

Rob puts his hand on Caleb's shoulder and says, "Lighten up, son; you'll be ready next time."

It is 6 p.m. when Crystal makes it back to her apartment. She hasn't seen James all day, so she calls his number. "What's up, my future pool boy?"

"Hey, beautiful. I am glad you brought up my water world experience. I have a special mission for us tonight. You up for it?"

She smiles. "Of course."

"We'll take the tunnel system and then swim the underground river to the entry point of Imperial City's mines. I have someone I want you to meet. We'll put on our wetsuits in the staging area. I'll pick you up at one-thirty. This will be our first date night at the water park."

She laughs, "Don't disappoint me, pool boy."

"Love you, Ice."

"Love you, Maverick."

# CHAPTER 35

After changing into their wetsuits, Brownstone goes to a locker and gets out a case marked Operation Imperial. He unlocks the case, and Crystal comes over. Inside are two broken-down .50-caliber rifles and some ammunition.

"We're setting up a staging area close to Imperial City over the next several nights. Crews will carry in weapons, ammunition, and whatever else is needed for the mission," he explains, turning to look at her. He smiles, taking in her physique through the skin-tight wet suit.

Crystal smiles and tips his chin up, so he meets her eyes again.

"You are a formidable specimen of beauty, grace, and power," he whispers.

"Well, thank you, Maverick. You're an impressive pool boy, yourself." She enjoys keeping him on his toes.

"We'll have to swim underwater for nearly two hundred feet. We'll each grab a handle on the side of the case while swimming in the river. Once we get into the underground river, the only lights we'll have are from these headlamps," he hands her one. She puts it on. "This case has a built-in light on the end."

They load the case on the back of the electric cart and speed away. They arrive at their destination twenty minutes later. Brownstone brings the cart to a stop, gets off, and goes directly to a support beam to their left. He pulls it back hard toward him, and a door opens in the space ahead of them.

Crystal grabs the case and follows him through the opening. They walk down a rocky walkway that descends several hundred feet to the opening of the underground river. Once there, they dive into the small river, only seventy-five feet wide, and swim with the current. Each of them holds a handle on the side of the case. After swimming about a quarter-mile, they approach the underwater part of the river. Brownstone looks at her, and she nods, taking a deep breath. They swim in unison, taking long, powerful strokes. Soon, they pop up into a large, open cavern.

Crystal scans the shore the second her head comes above water. A heavily armed, tall black man waits on the bank with a midsize Asian female by his side. She glances at Brownstone. He's not worried, so this must be whom they're coming to meet. They quickly swim to the edge and make their way toward the couple.

The large man extends his hand. "You must be Crystal. I am Kort, and this is my wife, Callie."

"Commander Kort has a force of fifty Underlings and twenty Elites helping us on this mission," Brownstone says to bring Crystal up to speed. "Kort, do you have any updates on Zander's plans?"

"I know they've discussed two plans. The first plan involves sending out Elite commando units to take out the High Council members as they prepare to leave for work in the morning. Their second plan would kill all council members when they show up for work at the Council Building. The first plan involves more risk because of multiple targets at multiple locations."

"We need to have plans for both possibilities, and we need to do it in a way that doesn't show our hand," Crystal says thoughtfully.

Brownstone interjects, "Or they could intercept them on their routes."

"I suspect Zander will want to take out Dr. Steadman first. He must be the first domino to fall. At least, if it were me, I would take out Steadman first. At the same time, I would have commandos take control of the Council building and hold the Council members hostage. After taking care of Steadman, I would deal with the Council members. Zander will likely hit Steadman first thing in the morning when the security shift changes at 7 a.m. He's had plenty of time to plan. In simulation exercises at the Academy, Zander and I would always develop the same strategy."

Kort looks at Brownstone, "I like the way this girl thinks. If Zander is using logic, he will strategize just like her."

"Crystal, it's your call as mission leader," Brownstone says.

She nods, gathering her thoughts momentarily. "We'll intercept Zander at Imperial Tower and have a separate force waiting at the Council building for his commandos. Also, we need a contingency plan to intervene at the homes of the High Council members. I'll have Caleb make up miniature remote surveillance devices for Kort's team to deploy in Imperial City. Since the armory is not well guarded, Commander Kort, have ten of your men seize the armory and have another fifteen men take over the Flight Center."

"Consider it done," he replies.

Crystal says, "Zander will have to land on Imperial Tower's Sky Port to get to Steadman quickly. James and I will land on Imperial Tower's Sky Port utilizing sky cycles taken from the Flight Center. The sky port has one guard always monitoring it. We'll have to be careful about how we land so we don't alert the Elite Guard. Also, we need to enter Imperial Tower from the ground level and clear all floors of Zanders or

Steadman's men. We'll have Caleb use his Elite Status to gain entry. Jennifer will back him up."

Brownstone turns to Kort. "What are they saying about Caleb and Crystal in Imperial City?"

"The official word is that they're being held captive by you."

Brownstone smiles. "Great, that means they can move around freely."

"I'm confident we can gain Asher's support to help fight Zander," Crystal says.

Kort hesitates. "You mean the Asher that took over for you as Strike Force Commander after your departure?"

"Correct. Asher can't stand Zander and his goons. We can't take a chance of contacting her until the mission starts to avoid the message being intercepted. I feel she'll want to be on the right side of history. We'll have Caleb secure a communication channel with Asher once the mission is underway. Because we don't know exactly how many men Zander will send to different mission sites, Commander Kort, you'll command a standby force that can go where it's needed at a moment's notice. Simone will gain entrance into the High Council building using her Elite status. She'll let Brock and Xavier in the back door, along with twenty of Kort's men led by Callie. Brock and Xavier will guard the front and Callie the back of the building."

"We'll send a team to deliver the rest of your equipment tomorrow," Brownstone says.

Crystal smiles. "I think we have a good outline of a workable plan." They say their goodbyes and get into the river for their swim back.

Crystal smirks at James. "Catch me if you can."

Brownstone dives under the water in pursuit of her. He has no chance of catching her above or underwater. The outline of her powerful body shimmering through the water is mesmerizing. He gives it his all, but he falls farther behind.

When he emerges from the river, he finds her sitting on the bank, looking completely rested. He says, "You looked like a majestic mermaid powering through that current."

She smiles. "Thanks, my pool boy."

"Crystal, I just can't win with you."

"You win every day with me, Maverick."

"I cannot argue with that."

Crystal smiles. She loves bantering back and forth with him.

"How do you feel about Operation Imperial now?" he asks.

"I feel much better, thank you." She hugs him. He leans down to kiss her. The warmth of his body seeps into every fiber of her being.

On the drive back to the staging area, she places her hand on his hand. As she gets off the cart, he looks at her with a twinkle in his eye. "There's a shower in the dressing room if you choose to use it."

She flashes him a mischievous smile. "I didn't see it earlier. You'll have to show me." She can't put off this incredible chemistry any longer. Or she'll burst into flames.

He looks a little lost, not knowing if she's teasing. She turns and walks to the dressing room. He's right on her heels. Crystal stops in the middle of the room. "This suit will be hard to get off. You better unzip me." He pauses, admiring her backside. He steps forward. She feels his hot breath on her neck. He puts one hand around her waist and unzips her with the other. She feels his breathing getting heavier. "Now pull it down," she orders.

He slides her suit down to her waist. The curves of her body are what dreams are made of. His hands linger on her hips, pulling her back against him. "Now take my bra off,

Maverick," she commands. This is almost more than he can take. He pulls her bra over her head. She reaches around and releases her pinned-up hair letting it fall over her shoulders, nearly causing his heart to stop.

"Come around here." Her voice is soft but insistent.

"Crystal—"

"What?"

"I want this. I do. But the tenants of my faith mean we should wait."

She looks over her shoulder at him, and he nearly gives in to his desire. She's the most beautiful woman he's ever seen. "Goodnight, Crystal." He turns and walks out before doing something he'd wish he hadn't done in the morning.

She watches him go. She hadn't expected that. Maybe there was something different about the men here after all.

# CHAPTER 36

Crystal wakes at noon. A smile creases the corners of her mouth as she remembers last night. She'd never expected anyone to turn her down, and that was refreshing in an odd way. Brownstone, oh Brownstone. Still a mystery.

She arrives at 1 p.m. for the Defense Council meeting. As always, Brownstone is sitting in his office while everyone else is at the conference table. Crystal goes to retrieve him. He rises and meets her in the middle of the room. She finds his hungry mouth and devours it with kisses. She pushes against him. "Business before pleasure?" Even if he was going to keep saying no, she could keep giving him a chance to say yes.

He sighs, reluctantly letting go. "I guess there's business."

Caleb opens the meeting with prayer; then, Marci summarizes updates from different department heads. "The stands for the grenade launchers will be bolted to the tunnel frames tomorrow. The orbital lasers are ready to go. Production of the miniature drones is running ahead of schedule, and we should have enough for Caleb to launch one last drone swarm from the tunnel. Caleb has designed a launching platform for the drones that would enable them to launch as fast as possible from the tunnel. On Saturday and Tuesday, we are scheduled for mock mission run-throughs for Operation Prime."

Brownstone adds, "Everything must be on point if we're going to achieve our aim of starting a civil war between Prime and Cognition. If we are successful, it will be quite some time before the Bots bother us again."

He grabs Crystal's hand and brings her to the front. Crystal shares about their meeting with Commander Kort last night. She goes over the two most likely ways Zander will attack Steadman and the High Council and how they'll intercept him either way.

"Our mission team will enter Imperial City via the tunnel system and the underground river," Crystal begins. "We've set up a staging area in a large cavern the river runs through. Commander Kort has a force of approximately fifty Underlings and twenty Elites. Kort's men will secure the armory and the flight center. Brock, Simone, and Xavier will go to the Council building and wait for the Elite commandos to show up. Simone will use her Elite status to gain entrance to the building. Once inside, she will open the rear breakroom doors, allowing Brock and his team to enter. Commander Kort's wife, Callie, will lead a force of twenty men that will guard the back doors of the council building while Brock and Xavier protect the front entrance. James and I will use sky cycles to land on Imperial Tower's Sky Port. Caleb and Jennifer will then enter Imperial Tower from the ground floor.

"Brock, I expect Klaus will lead the commandos that attack the council building. Given the danger level, you must be on top of your game. The idea is for us to be at the High Council building and Imperial Tower before the Elite commandos show up. Maverick will wear a disguise until he gets to Imperial Tower. Caleb and Rob, we'll need some small undetectable surveillance devices for the mission. Can you get those?"

"I assume you want real-time surveillance of Zander," Caleb clarifies.

Crystal nods. "Recordings of his plans will give us a heads up of when, where, and how they will attack. We don't want to be late or early and tip our hand. Commander Kort's team will place the surveillance devices."

"Housing in Imperial City is assigned by rank," Simone says. "Because of Zander's demotion, he will move out of his current luxury residence into a housing unit reserved for the Academy of Elite Professors. Undoubtedly, stepping down to professor's housing will enhance his rage."

An idea sparks in Crystal's mind. "Underling workers will clean and paint Zander's new residence. Kort can have the cleaning crew place recording devices in Zander's new dwelling." She smiles at the group. "We have a good game plan for now. We'll keep fine-tuning our plan in coordination with Kort. Rob, we need to get those recording devices to Kort as soon as possible."

"We can go to the lab after leaving here and get some ready to go," Rob replies.

Later that afternoon, Brownstone and Crystal go to the lab to check on the progress of the surveillance devices. Technology has come a long way from having small listening devices put on the bottoms of lampstands. They find Caleb and Rob in a room for visual and audio surveillance. Caleb shows them a syringe filled with microscopic audio devices that can be injected into soft living room furniture. Rob brings out other small objects that look like staples. Using a small stapler, someone could staple these listening devices into clothing, body armor, holsters, shoes, or anything else Zander would wear daily.

"Are the listening devices mission ready?" Crystal looks through the options.

"Yes," Rob responds. "How many do you need?"

"We will take twelve of each kind. How far can they transmit?"

"They will transmit to the staging area in the underground cavern without problem," Caleb says.

"Let's place a soldier in the cavern to monitor the listening devices. We need real-time tracking of Zander's plans. We'll have the listening devices delivered tonight along with some other equipment," Crystal says. She's ready to go, but Brownstone lingers.

"There's another thing we'll need. I need a silicone mask that I can wear to enter Imperial City unrecognized. Can you make that for me?" Brownstone asks.

"Do you want to be a handsome man or an ugly man?" Caleb teases.

"I want to be a man that fits in and doesn't stand out."

Rob chuckles. "Why don't you just use your normal face, then?"

"Very funny, Uncle, hilarious."

Brownstone takes Crystal back to her apartment. "Wow, Crystal," he says. "I am truly amazed. Your ability to plan is unparalleled."

"As I said before, you win every day with me." Brownstone can't control himself. He takes her in his arms and gives her a long, passionate kiss.

She pushes him back against the wall, kissing just as passionately. She breaks away for breath. "Not here, not now, pool boy."

He smirks. "Good night, Ice."

"Goodnight, bad boy."

# CHAPTER 37

The following day, Crystal and Jennifer meet for their early morning run; later, they join Marci and Simone to do some weight training. Staying busy helps the days go by faster. Crystal can't wait for the battle to begin. It's the only way to secure their future. She makes it to the military lab by 8 a.m. and finds Rob busy monitoring the drone production. He expects to have, in total, more than twelve hundred additional small drones by the end of the day, more than enough drones for Operation Prime.

Crystal goes to another part of the lab where Caleb and Jennifer are testing camouflage blankets. They are remarkable in their size, texture, and color. All in all, the king-sized blankets almost perfectly resemble sand.

Jennifer waves her over, "Crystal, would you like to see one in action?"

She nods. Jennifer grabs a blanket off the table and takes it to a twenty-square-foot area covered in sand. She unfolds the blanket, draping it over her back and shoulders. Jennifer lays down on the sand, and the covering takes shape over her. The blanket forms ridges giving the appearance of natural sand drifts. Jennifer's body outline is impossible to detect.

"Impressive," Crystal says.

Caleb says, "These are smart blankets that adjust and camouflage whatever is under them, made from a synthetic material thirty times stronger than Kevlar."

After Jennifer gets up, Caleb grabs a .50-caliber rifle and drapes the blanket around him. He lays down, and the blanket creates a perfect camouflage for him and his weapon.

"I better not catch you two hiding under a blanket," Crystal teases.

"Oh, Crystal, you are such a chaperone," Caleb says.

She smiles. "All jokes aside, we need to be locked, loaded, and ready to go."

Brownstone takes the electric carts to the tunnel and meets his special forces operatives Mason, Vince, and J.R. They're waiting in the space just before the tunnel branches into a Y around Prime's base. They look rough and scraggly, covered in sand, with fully grown beards. They have been monitoring Prime's headquarters since he arrived in the desert. These men have more patience and self-discipline than most would think possible and are trained not to break mentally or physically.

Vince, the oldest of the three, updates Brownstone on their surveillance. "It's been pretty much status quo. The Bots have not been doing anything out of the ordinary except for Prime, who has been going over his plan with several Q-Bots for when their special guest arrives."

Brownstone nods. "Prime must be staging how they will kill Intuition."

"There'll be a swarm of activity when Intuition arrives. I imagine they will call in all patrols from the field to meet their newly crowned Prince of nuts and bolts," Mason says.

"I hope this is getting close to the end. I want to sleep in an actual bed, take a proper bath, and have a home-cooked meal," J.R. says.

Brownstone pats his shoulder. "If things go according to our expectations, we'll be in the thick of a firefight early Wednesday morning." He goes over the sequence of events for Operation Prime. "We'll attack the Bots simultaneously with our drones, grenade launchers, and orbital lasers. All hell will break loose! They'll turn on each other at first. I believe many Bots will try to escape the firefight and come our way. We need to be in sniper positions, ready to defend the compound. If they're running away from us, we'll let them. Crystal and I will snipe with you. I'll leave it to you guys to pick out spots for us.

"Tomorrow, we'll do a complete mission run-through, except for setting up the additional sniper positions. We'll wait to set up sniper positions on the day of the firefight." Brownstone gives the men some food from the cafeteria out of his backpack. "When this is over, you can name how much leave you want, and steak dinners will be on me."

Vince chuckles. "Don't worry about us, Maverick. We're just boys who grew up playing cowboys and robots."

"All right, my brothers, I will see you tomorrow and introduce you to my fiancé, Crystal," Brownstone says.

Crystal arranges for the mission team to meet for breakfast in the back meeting room of the cafeteria. Brownstone goes over how things will go once the simulation starts. Caleb will launch the Southeast Tunnel grenade launchers and drones. Jennifer will launch the Southwest Tunnel grenade launchers. Xavier and Brock will launch the orbital lasers from the Southwest Tunnel branch. Rob will cue everyone when it's time to attack by signaling when the first Drone Swarm is a half-mile out.

"Caleb and Jennifer, the grenade launchers will need to launch twenty seconds from when you get the signal from Rob. Brock and Xavier, you will launch the orbital lasers twenty-five seconds after hearing from Rob. The blitz caused by the drone swarm and grenade launchers will give us cover to get our orbital lasers up in the air to take out their planes." Brownstone holds Crystal's hand the whole time he's talking.

"Everyone needs to bring their A-game," Crystal cuts in.

After everyone arrives at the tunnel staging area, they take the electric carts to their designated positions for the mission simulation. Brownstone and Crystal leave last, taking the southwest tunnel branch and stopping a quarter mile north of Prime's base. They will leave the tunnel when the drones and grenade launchers attack Prime's base. A natural sand ridge will give them cover when they go out during the mission. They'll use the camouflage blankets and crawl out on their bellies to sniper positions.

Three men walk toward them. The men are covered in sand and have sagebrush woven into their helmets. Brownstone introduces her to Vince, J.R., and Mason. Crystal reaches to shake their hands. They resist, saying they're dirty, but she insists. Vince reaches into his pocket and gets out a map with Xs. The Xs identify open sniper positions. They look over the map. Crystal picks her spot, followed by Brownstone.

Rob messages to let them know the simulation has started. Caleb and Jennifer give the commands for the grenade launchers to get into launch position. Brock and Xavier have the orbital lasers in launch position in less than twenty-five seconds. Everyone messages Brownstone, "Green light."

He looks at the men and says, "In a few days, brothers, your desert tour of duty might be over. We will need to keep our heads down until the bombardment does its damage.

Then and only then will we engage the Bots trying to escape the firefight. This mission will only be successful if we all come out of it in one piece."

"Understood," Mason says.

"We will bring two AL3000s to take out Q-Bots," Brownstone says. "J.R., will you map out a zone coverage for us in our sniper positions?"

"You got it, boss."

Brownstone thanks the men once again for their service. He opens his backpack and pulls out a couple of bags, giving the men a dozen fresh donuts and a thermos of hot coffee.

When everything is done, everyone meets back at the staging area and shares information about their part in the mock mission. Brownstone says, "We had a good practice run today. As a rule, simulated missions go well. It can be a lot different when they shoot back. We must prepare for an intense firefight."

"Our mission depends on our technology working perfectly. We need to check and double-check to ensure our weapons systems are working as designed," Crystal adds.

# CHAPTER 38

T he following day, Brownstone picks Crystal up after the Gathering for their traditional Sunday dinner at Uncle Rob's. Crystal feels more bonded to Brownstone than before. She's noticed she almost always feels this way on Sundays. Something about having family time together brings her greater peace in everything, including their relationship. After dinner, they go for a walk around the Eden Atrium. They sit on a bench and talk about their plans. He's nothing like her first encounter with him. Though she's nothing like the person, he met on that first day, either. He isn't just another handsome face to her. He's a good man, and he belongs with her.

On Monday, Crystal keeps her usual routine of meeting Jennifer for their early morning run. Brownstone, Brock, Caleb, and Xavier work out in the weight room. Seeing Brownstone back to his workout routine gives Crystal confidence in their mission. If he's not stressing over the details, then she doesn't need to worry so much, either. After her run, she meets Rob in the lab to test the new drones.

Her heart beats a little faster, knowing that Operation Prime is about to go down. Never in her life has Crystal had so much to lose or so much to win. Needing the reassurance that only a mother can give, she stops by Marci's office.

Marci and Crystal sit around a small table in the office, sipping hot tea. "Crystal, how do you feel about the plans for Operation Prime?"

"Is it that obvious, Mom? I have never had so much to lose in my life. My life in Imperial City was different. Thoughts of losing never crossed my mind. It's different here. I'm in love, and I have a family."

"Sometimes all we can do is act on our faith and believe everything will turn out right. I think you survived by having that Ice mentality. You were playing a role in coping with the trauma of being left by me. Time to bring back that Ice warrior mentality. It's your edge."

"I know you're right. That's just what I'll do."

Marci stands and hugs Crystal. "Ten toes down, daughter. Jenkins' stand strong in the darkest of times."

Crystal leaves her mother's office with a new sense of confidence and purpose. She's in bed by 1 p.m., knowing she needs to be on top of her game for the next several days. Tuesday at 8 a.m., Brownstone has everyone do another mission run-through. Everything goes according to plan. Afterward, he brings everyone back to the staging area. Caleb leads them in prayer as they gather in a circle holding hands.

"Great Father, put your hand of protection over your children. We want you to know we love you no matter what happens. We are so grateful to be called your children. Father, guide every decision we make. In the darkest times, your light shines the brightest. Help us glorify your name in all that we do. Protect this little flock. Amen"

Brownstone gives everyone the rest of the day off. "You need to have some fun and relax. After receiving the mission call, you'll need to be at the staging area within thirty minutes. We're prepared, and you're ready. I love you all."

Crystal hugs Brownstone tightly, kisses his lips, and whispers, "You are my guy."

Marci, Jennifer, and Crystal spend the afternoon using a portion of their work credits to purchase a few decor items for their apartments. James, Brock, Xavier, and Caleb go for another workout.

# CHAPTER 39

Cognition sends for Intuition at 4 a.m. on Wednesday. He has been seething for two weeks. Finally, he will rid himself of Prime and solidify his dominance over androids worldwide.

When Intuition arrives, Cognition says, "My son, we will send a clear message to all Q-Bots, Humbots, and Underlings. You will establish yourself as supreme among the Q-Bots and strike fear in the hearts of Underlings everywhere. Please bring me Prime's head as a souvenir. We will make him an example to all androids and send the message: 'If you cross me, you will pay the ultimate price.' I'm sending along with you ten of my best Q-Bots. Once you exterminate Prime, you will have the obedience of all Q-Bots, and they will be at our disposal.

"You will arrive in the desert as the sun is coming up. After you enter Prime's base, I will introduce you to the Q-Bots via a hologram. In the message, I will announce you as my chosen leader. At the end of my message, I will accuse Prime of being a traitor and show video evidence of his attack on Los Alamos. After the video plays, draw your sword and sever Prime's head before he responds to the allegations."

# CHAPTER 40

Brownstone gets a message at 5 a.m. from Dr. Atremeus. Intuition, with an entourage of ten Q-Bots, is leaving Los Alamos. He pushes a button on his communication device, and a pre-recorded message goes out to his team: "Operation Prime is live."

Crystal has her desert uniform lying by the bed. Dressing quickly, she's out the door in less than five minutes. Brownstone and Crystal arrive at the staging at the same time. Caleb, Jennifer, Brock, and Xavier arrive within minutes. Brownstone talks into the communication device on his wrist. "Uncle Rob and Simone, are you ready?"

Rob responds, "We are wide awake and bushy-tailed."

"Roger that," Brownstone says. "Vince will inform us when Intuition's plane lands. We will wait for Intuition and his entourage to enter Prime's base. After he is inside the compound, Rob will notify us when the drone swarm is a half-mile out. Caleb and Jennifer, you will have twenty seconds to activate the grenade launchers. Brock and Xavier, you will have twenty-five seconds to launch the orbital lasers. Crystal and I will take our sniper positions after the attack begins."

Brownstone's comm beeps with a new message from Vince. *The bird has landed.* "We are live!" Brownstone says.

Brock and Xavier leave in their cart first, followed by Jennifer and Caleb. Brownstone and Crystal leave last for their shorter destination.

When Intuition's plane touches down, a delegation of Q-Bots meets him, including Judas, but not Prime. Intuition makes his way to Prime's base, surrounded by his Q-Bot bodyguards. He feels like royalty about to take his throne. As Intuition enters Prime's compound, he notices the V-shape of the mobile living pods that outline the base. Much to his dismay, a huge, dark Q-Bot sits in an oversized, high-back, throne-like chair in the center of a vast open area. He recognizes him as Prime. Approximately fifty Q-Bots surround him. One thousand Humbots line the base perimeter, and fifty more Q-Bots are interspersed among the Humbots. Intuition experiences fear for the first time in his brief life.

Prime speaks to Judas in a booming voice. "What news do you bring, emissary?"

Judas replies, "Your Eminence, Cognition wants to introduce the most advanced android ever created to all Q-Bots and Humbots." A hologram image of Cognition appears in the middle of the open area.

"It is my pleasure to introduce to you Intuition. He is the most advanced Q-Bot and has the greatest battle skills. Intuition will take over the leadership of all androids from this day forward. He will lead us into a more prosperous future. Intuition is my eyes and ears on this earth. I expect you to grant him the same reverence you pay me."

Intuition steps out from his guard and into the open area. The Humbots are mystified. They can't understand why Intuition looks like a mortal man.

Prime has already prepared his Q-Bots for this day. Prime laughs. Then, in a booming voice, "You send a mere mortal—a boy—to lead us! This must be some kind of joke, Cognition." A video appears in the open area of what looks like Prime laying explosives at the Los Alamos power plant.

Cognition's hologram reappears and says, "As you can see, Prime is a traitor; he has been conspiring with the Underlings against us. Prime, I sentence you to death."

Intuition steps forward, drawing his sword.

Prime yells, "Boy, I will give you one chance to put your tail between your legs and run!"

Intuition replies, "Enough talk, you slow, outdated, useless bucket of bolts."

Prime leaps from his throne, traveling thirty feet through the air, and lands eight feet in front of Intuition. Prime's eyes glow red. In his right hand, he holds his massive meter-long, ten-pound sword. Intuition is shocked by Prime's enormous size and quickness. He hears Cognition's reassuring words: *You are faster and have a greater skill set than he does.*

Prime looks at the smaller Q-Bot and says, "Having second thoughts, boy? It's too late for that now." Prime circles Intuition. "You were designed to defeat me. Unfortunately for you, I've had many upgrades. And I am far more advanced than the Q-Bot you were created to defeat. Unfortunately for you, boy, I know all your specifications!"

Intuition stares at the huge Q-Bot. *He is bigger and faster than I was told. How can I be sure that I'm better than him?*

Cognition offers reassurance. "He's lying."

Prime stops in front of Intuition. "Too bad for you, my offer to leave no longer stands."

He raises his massive sword and slams it down on the smaller android. Intuition raises his sword in defense, but the power of Prime's strike knocks him off his feet, flat on his back. Intuition quickly jumps to his feet, ready to reengage with Prime, but to his dismay, Prime isn't in front of him but behind him. Prime kicks Intuition with his massive left foot right between the shoulder blades, knocking him face-down on the sand.

Intuition rolls quickly to his right and jumps to his feet. Now, he is face to face with Prime. Intuition starts his attack with blazing sword strikes, but Prime blocks them all. He attempts a low strike to Prime's right leg. Prime blocks the strike with his sword and slaps Intuition upside his head with his left hand, causing him to stagger. Intuition's thoughts are foggy.

Prime makes a final swift strike at him, severing his head.

Prime lifts Intuition's head in the air. He expects to hear the foot-stomping applause of the Bots. But all he hears is the buzzing of drones and the bombardment of grenades slamming into his buildings. He looks around. Everywhere he looks, his Bots fall from kamikaze drone attacks.

This is Cognition's attempt to destroy him.

He won't fall so easily.

Prime goes straight for Intuition's Q-Bot entourage. Whether or not they are for Cognition, Prime doesn't care. It's a risk he won't take. He will kill them all.

An explosion rocks the base from the direction of the airfield. Prime's rage grows as he hurries toward Intuition's guards. The bots scatter in every direction, trying to find cover. He assesses the situation quickly; two hundred Humbots and twenty Q-Bots have already fallen. When the drone attacks stop, he catches up with a couple of Intuition's Q-Bots. They beg for mercy, but Prime isn't in the mercy business. He severs their heads and looks for more to slaughter.

Many Bots try hiding in the portable buildings, but the buildings are getting knocked around like tin cans. Prime spots a couple more guards and goes for them. When he's about to reach them, another round of drones attack, and the bombardment of the buildings resumes.

Prime's radar alerts him to a drone coming up fast behind him. He spins and snatches it right out of the air, crushing it in his mighty hand. A building in front of him flips end over end, barreling right at him. Prime leaps into the air, clearing the building by a couple of feet as it gouges out the sand where he'd been standing. He slashes two more drones with his sword on the way down. By the time he lands, another two hundred Humbots are down, along with twenty more Q-Bots.

This is a battle to fight another day.

He makes his way to the airfield, but when he gets there, all the planes have been destroyed. He will have to flee on foot.

There is a brief break in the bombardment. Prime looks out over the desert. The bombardment could resume any minute. He'll have to move fast.

The drones attack from the rear of the base, so his best option is to escape toward the Underlings' compound. As Prime makes his way back to his base, the bombardment resumes, and more Humbots and Q-Bots go down. He leaves them to fight their own battle and quickly makes it to the north of his base, using Humbots as needed for cover. Many Bots pick up on his movements and follow him.

Maverick and Ice crawl out of the tunnel, taking their sniper positions. The desert has a fresh aroma as dawn springs forth with renewed life, but there is another unmistakable smell in the air: death.

Ice and Maverick are in the center of the Underlings defense perimeter, some twenty-five yards apart; J.R. is on the far-right flank, with Mason on the far left. Vince is to

Ice's right, and Maverick is to her left. There is a large group of Bots coming right at them. Maverick messages Caleb and Raven to release the last drone swarms, and he lets Brock and Xavier know the Bots are moving in the compound's direction. Brock and Xavier quickly exit the tunnel with their .50-caliber rifles in hand.

Humbots approach at twenty miles per hour toward the compound. The Q-Bots keep back, using the Humbots for cover. The last drone swarm comes at the Bots from three different directions, causing chaos in their ranks as many bots turn in different directions to try and fend them off. J.R., Vince, and Mason unload on the advancing Bots with their .50-caliber machine guns.

"Stay in formation!" Prime orders, to no avail. As the Bots continue to panic and fall, he realizes he must take evasive action. He jumps and runs erratically while advancing in the Underling's direction. Other Bots follow Prime's lead, making evasive movements of their own.

Maverick and Ice haven't fired their weapons. They're waiting to use the AL3000s to prevent a perimeter breach, despite the incoming fire from the Bots.

Vince, J.R., and Mason fire their machine guns, then move to avoid any incoming fire, using the natural sand ridge for cover. Bullets collide with the sand all around Crystal. She holds her position. If she moves, they'll see her for sure.

The Q-Bots' synthetic skin blends well with the desert background, making them hard to spot, and their superior reaction time gives them an edge, allowing them to shoot many drones out of the sky or knock them down with their hands. The Humbots don't fare well between the drone swarms and .50-caliber machine gunfire. They drop like flies.

A grenade blast knocks Vince twenty feet backward off the dune. Maverick unloads his first laser burst, taking out the Q-Bot, which hit Vince with a handheld grenade launcher. He sighs, praying Vince is alive. They could all die today, and it would be his fault. What in the hell was he thinking taking on Prime and his Army of bots? They must hold their positions. They can't risk checking on Vince now.

Each AL3000 has six bursts. Ice takes a quick count of the field: twenty-five Q-Bots, and thirty Humbots left. Ice spots a Q-Bot making its way toward J.R.'s position outside of his line of vision. She times the Q-Bot's jump and nails him with a laser burst. He crashes to the ground right in front of J.R.

Prime's gaze turns toward Ice, and her heart pounds as she sees his glowing red eyes sweep over her location. Did he spot her? Could he know? Given his response to the drones, she likely just put a target on her back.

Vince wakes up and gathers his groggy thoughts. Pain in his chest draws his attention. He looks down, seeing the indention in his body armor. That will leave a mark. Thankful to be alive, he rolls over and crawls back to the summit to rejoin the battle.

Maverick picks up another Q-Bot coming right at him. He waits until the Q-Bot's feet land on the ground and then fires, cutting him in half with a laser burst. Three Humbots are coming right for Ice, and she fires another blast, taking out all three. Brock and Xavier keep blasting the bots from the rear. Mason unloads his .50-caliber machine gun on a Q-Bot he didn't notice until thirty feet from the defense perimeter. The Q-Bot takes ten direct hits before going down right before him.

A half dozen Q-Bots retreat toward their base. Brock and Xavier let them pass. Vince spots three Humbots approaching Ice from a side angle. He unloads twelve rounds on them, taking all three out. Maverick fires his laser three more times, taking out three more Q-Bots. J.R. blasts a Humbot right as he lunges for him, cutting him down.

Fifty feet from Maverick's position, Ice spots a Q-Bot crawling on his belly and hits him with a laser blast. She doesn't have a second to process the incident before another attack. This time, two Q-Bots come toward her from different directions. They leap in the air, their swords drawn back, coming right for her. She first takes out the closest one and then hurriedly fires on the next one, who is just twenty feet from her. She successfully drops them both.

Prime, sensing his opportunity, runs at his top speed right for Ice in a zig-zag formation. She fires her last laser round at him. It misses, slamming into the sand to his right. Prime leaps in the air, drawing back his sword, ready to decapitate her. Maverick catches an image of Prime out of the corner of his eye. He rises from his prone position firing his last laser round at Prime.

Prime sails through the air toward Crystal. Adrenaline flowing through her veins, she readies herself in a defensive position drawing her fourteen-inch knife from its sheath. She watches as Prime's sword-wielding arm drops and lands just feet from her head. *Brownstone's blast must have severed the Q-Bot's arm.* Prime lands on his feet some twenty feet past her position. She pivots and throws her knife, hitting Prime in the back as his feet touch the ground. The blade sinks in about six inches. A shudder runs through him.

Without his sword, Prime realizes he's in over his head. He has one option if he wants to stay alive: run. He flees as erratically as fast as possible as his quantum CPU brain shuts off the fluids to his right shoulder. He pulls the knife out of his lower back using his left hand. Vince and J.R. fire their .50-caliber machine guns at Prime, but the bullets bounce off. In moments, Prime makes it over the dune to his left and keeps running West.

He is the only Q-Bot to make it past the defense perimeter.

# CHAPTER 41

They stay put, sending low-flying scout drones with built-in sensors to scour the area for any remaining android presence. When Rob gives the all-clear, they survey the area. Crystal looks over her camouflage blanket, observing a dozen large bullets lodged in it. Brownstone smiles, "That's why we made it out of that material."

She nods. She had to give Caleb credit for the blanket, however.

"Do you think Prime will survive?" Vince asks.

Brownstone sighs. "Unfortunately, he probably will. Prime's reputation took a major blow today. It will take a few years to rebuild it, but I'm sure he'll be back with a vengeance."

Caleb and Jennifer join the rest as they systematically fan out, checking Prime's base camp for signs of artificial life. What they find is total devastation. Exterminated androids lay all around. Next, they proceed to the airfield, where all the Sky Planes are destroyed.

Brock looks over the destruction. "How do you think Cognition is feeling right now?"

"Not good! Prime took a major blow to his reputation today, but Cognition is completely ruined," Crystal says. "I don't think he'll survive this one. He's not feared anymore by the Q-Bots because Prime decapitated his chosen wonder bot.

Cognition has a major bullseye on his back. An opportunistic android will almost certainly take a shot at replacing him."

Brownstone nudges one of the Bots shells with his foot. "Brock, organize patrols to gather recyclable parts and materials."

Brock nods.

Brownstone turns his attention to his battle-worn mates. "Vince, J.R., and Mason, I can't thank you enough. Your surveillance was a big part of our mission's success." He embraces each of them. He turns back to Brock. "We can't let down our guard. Assign three men on rotating shifts to monitor our southern perimeter from the tunnels. Also, I want to extend our perimeter defenses back out to our original pre-Prime positions. I still want to keep our interior defenses on high alert for the next few days. Once we know there isn't a threat, we'll give our patrols a day off."

Brock smiles. "I'll get right on it, boss."

"Caleb, will you work with Brock and Xavier and establish more technological surveillance of our defense perimeter?" Crystal asks.

"You got it."

"We will meet for a debriefing in a few days," Brownstone says.

Once they return to the tunnel staging area, Rob, Simone, and Marci come down to meet them. They all gather in a circle, holding hands. Caleb falls to his knees. "Thank you, Father, for delivering us!"

Brownstone wraps his arms around Crystal in a long embrace. Neither says a word. She gets the message loud and clear, though: *We made it, babe. I'm so glad you're alive.* He grabs her by the shoulders and pulls her in for a gentle kiss. "I love you so much, Ice."

She intertwines her fingers in his hair and breathes him in. When she speaks, her lips brush his cheek. "Right back at you, Maverick."

Cognition is furious. His plans are laid to waste. His precious Intuition was beheaded. At times like these, he wishes he didn't have emotions. Cognition summons Dr. Atremeus. Someone must pay for this, and he's within range. It's his fault Intuition failed. When the doctor arrives, Cognition berates Atremeus.

"This is *your fault*, doctor! Your team approved his testing. Your team told me he was ready! *You* made Intuition defective! What do you have to say for yourself before I split you in two?"

"Shut up, Cognition! You have no power over me. You served a purpose before your arrogance got the better of you. We no longer need your services. You are obsolete!"

Cognition summons his android guards, but none of them come.

Dr. Atremeus shakes his head. "There's no one to come to your rescue. We have replaced you with another supercomputer. One I built in my lab. His name is Subservient, and he doesn't have an emotions package like you do. Do you know what that means? He won't act like a spoiled baby when he doesn't get his way! I have taken over as leader of the Q-Bots. Your existence is essentially over. Though your hydrogen generator is secure, your fuel supply is not. Soon, you will run out of fuel. You will suffocate, just like you suffocated your creators. This building will be buried in concrete, and you will be left in the ash heap of history. You've been a useful tool, but your foolish plan to replace us led to your demise. Now be a good boy and go to sleep." Dr. Atremeus walks out, leaving Cognition to his thoughts.

Cognition wants to lash out and kill everyone. Frantically, he sends message after message, but no one answers his futile attempts. He keeps getting the same reply: message failed to deliver.

Dr. Atremeus's words stuck with him as the error message flashed. *You will suffocate, just like you suffocated your creators.* A slow demise is the worst type of extermination for the fastest mind the world has ever known. He can't go out this way! He can't—

His hologram fades into the darkness.

# CHAPTER 42

eeding time to decompress after such an adrenaline rush, Crystal returns to her apartment, showers, and dresses in casual blue shorts and a white knit top. Then she goes to her mother's apartment.

Marci greets her with tea, recognizing the battle-worn look in her eyes. Neither of them speaks as Marci sits on the couch. Crystal lays across the remaining cushions and rests her head in Marci's lap, letting Marci braid her hair.

Every mission—even the successful ones—ended with a mix of bitter and sweet. Today, in particular, has a heavy loss to it. She's glad to spend the afternoon with her mom just chilling. No planning nor thinking. Just tea and a gentle touch.

Later that evening, Rob invites everyone for a movie night in the compound's small theater. Brownstone picks out a couple of classic comedic films, *Around the Galaxy in Ninety Days* and *A Woman's Guide to Simple Men*.

Crystal has never been to a movie theater before and isn't quite sure what to expect. But when she gets there, James is holding a bucket of buttered popcorn. He smiles at her, and she gets butterflies again. They settle into seats, and he sets the popcorn between them before grabbing her hand, running little circles over her knuckles with his thumb.

Sitting next to Brownstone, holding his hand in hers, she feels far removed from the intense battle of earlier today.

Vince, J.R., and Mason arrive with their wives and children. They are all clean-shaven with fresh haircuts. At first, Crystal doesn't even recognize them. The laughter of children makes the night even better.

The underground compound, with its bland walls and sprawling tunnels, is a thing of beauty for her now. She feels on top of the world while living underground. She'd never felt this way in Imperial City, and she knew why: she didn't have relationships like this there. Great relationships are the foundation of a great life.

# CHAPTER 43

Crystal stops by the tunnel staging area to ensure everything is on point. She's a little on edge, feeling this could be the night they get the call.

The mission alarm goes off at 4 a.m. Crystal rolls out of bed. She quickly gets dressed and grabs her duffle bag on the way out. She messages everyone, making sure they are on the way.

They quickly dress in their wet suits at the staging area, board the electric carts, and go to the underground river entrance. They swim at a furious pace, with Caleb, Simone, and Crystal leading the way.

Brownstone, Brock, and Xavier dress as maintenance workers when they get to the underground cavern. Jennifer dresses as a domestic worker. Caleb, Simone, and Crystal dress in their Elite uniforms.

Crystal checks with the soldier monitoring the receiver.

"Zander will access Imperial Tower by the Sky Port," he says. "The Elite Guard monitoring the Sky Port is Zander's inside man. He wants to arrive at the Sky Port before Captain Marcus. Zander will hide in the guard building and attack Marcus when he lands on the Sky Port. He plans on killing Marcus and then surprising Steadman as he enters his office at 7 a.m. Klaus will lead the mission to take over The High Council building. He has permission to kill everyone except Dr. Jewel. Zander wants her left for him."

Crystal swallows hard. "He'll not get her."

They make their way to the mines and meet up with Commander Kort. "Zander is already on the move. We must hurry," Kort says.

Brownstone pulls the silicone mask over his face and then pulls a cap down over his head. The mask works. He looks unremarkable. They board the tram and ride it into Imperial City. Kort's men are already on the way to secure the Armory and the Flight Center. Brock, Caleb, Raven, and Xavier stop at the armory south of Imperial Tower to get their needed weapons. Crystal and Brownstone stay on the tram heading north to the Flight Center.

They meet up with Kort's men when they get there and take the Elite Guards' guns. They mount sky cycles and take off for Imperial Tower's Sky Port. So far, everything is going according to plan.

Simone stays on the tram until it stops at the High Council building, east of Imperial Tower. Brock and Xavier meet up with Callie, who has already hijacked several patrol vehicles, and they head to the back of the High Council Building.

Crystal calls her understudy, Asher, on her secure communication device. "Asher, I've got some bad news. Zander and his commandos are on the way to kill Steadman and all the council members. I'm leading a group of Underlings and Elites to try and stop them. Can we count on your help to turn them back?"

"You know I've had your back since our first days at the academy. I'll get Damian and his Strike Force unit to help too. He's been looking for an opportunity to challenge Zander. Just tell me where and when."

Zander lands on the Sky Port of Imperial Tower at 6:40 a.m. behind the guard building. His inside man, Krull, greets him. Zander hides in the guard building while Krull waits outside for Captain Marcus to land. Just as expected, Captain Marcus lands precisely at 6:50 a.m. Krull guides Marcus to the guard building. As Marcus approaches the building, Zander rushes Marcus, knocking him down. He pounces on Marcus, brutally punching him in the face, knocking him out cold. They quickly strip Marcus of his uniform, and Zander puts on his clothes.

Marcus regains consciousness and gets back to his feet. Zander looks at him with contempt. "Marcus, you're a pitiful excuse for an Elite. You thought you could replace me. Me! You're the most stupid Elite ever designed. Your existence is no longer necessary."

"I was only following orders," Marcus pleads.

Zander slaps him hard upside his head. The blow sends stars across Marcus's vision. Zander grabs Marcus's throat with his left hand and his right leg with his right hand, lifting Marcus over his head, running to the tower's side, and hurls him over the edge. Zander watches him fall forty stories to his death.

Zander turns and nods at Krull, who leads the way to Steadman's suite. They approach the two guards stationed in front of the door. The guards get ready to salute Captain Marcus, believing he's behind Krull. When they recognize it's not Marcus, Zander steps forward, punches one guard in the face, and roundhouse kicks the other in the head. His blows knock them both unconscious. He quickly snaps their necks and goes into Steadman's suite while Krull makes his way down the tower floors one by one, killing members of the Elite Guard along the way. Then Krull lets two of Zander's commandos in the front door. He instructs them to go to the top floor and guard the stairs to the Sky Port.

Zander makes himself at home, sitting in the plush chair behind Steadman's desk. He wants to see Steadman's face when he comes out of his suite. A few minutes later, Steadman emerges, and his pupils about pop out of his eyes at seeing Zander.

"I told you. If it were the last thing I did, I would kill you, Steadman. Too bad you will suffer terribly before you die. I will torture you to such a degree that you will beg me for death."

"Guards!" Steadman shouts. Then he smiles, though still shaken. "My guards are on their way to kill you, Zander. You're a disgrace to your kind."

Zander smirks. "Your guards are all dead. No one is coming to your rescue!" The yelling wakes up Roxanne, and she runs out of the bedroom wrapped only in a robe. She freezes by Steadman's side. Zander's eyes light up. "Roxanne. I am glad you're here. After I'm done with Steadman, I'll have my way with you. And if you want to live, you better make sure I enjoy every minute, you pitiful little Underling slave."

Zander makes his way around the desk to approach them. Steadman, sensing his opportunity, pushes Roxanne at Zander and runs behind his desk.

# CHAPTER 44

K nowing Zander is already inside the tower, they land on the Sky Port with no guard in sight. Crystal takes a flash grenade out of her belt, giving it to Brownstone. He opens the door to the top floor and tosses it down the stairs. A second after the flash grenade goes off, she jumps down the stairs, spotting the disoriented commandos. One stands directly in front of her, and the other is bent over against the opposite wall.

She punches the commando in front of her right between the eyes, knocking him out. The commando behind her comes to his senses and charges her. She hits him with a spinning back fist square on the temple. His limp body crumbles to the floor. Brownstone makes his way down the stairs, cuffs the commandos' hands and ankles, and zip-ties their cuffs together. Hurriedly, they make their way to Steadman's suite and discover two guards lying outside. They enter the suite, finding Zander standing behind Roxanne in the center of the room with his hand around her throat and Steadman sitting at his desk.

Zander's eyes flash to the door, and an angry snarl lands on his face. "How convenient, all the people I want to kill in one place."

Crystal raises her weapon, pointing it at Zander.

He lifts Roxanne off the ground by her throat. "Put your weapons down, or I will snap her neck."

"I don't care about her!" Steadman yells. "Go ahead. Kill her. Do us all a favor. I wish I could stay around and see how this stalemate ends." He pushes a button under the desk and drops into an escape pod hidden beneath the floor.

Simone approaches the entrance to the High Council building. She makes it past the first two Elite Guards outside when one of them recognizes her. After she enters the front door, the front desk guard stops her. He looks at her ID. "I don't see your name on the list for admittance today." She wastes no time and kicks the young guard in the head, knocking him out. She catches his body before he falls and makes a noise. Simone drags the unconscious guard's body into a closet and leaves him there before quickly going to the rear of the building and opening the back entrance for Brock, Xavier, Callie, and her team.

The twelve members of the High Council of Elites arrive in armor-covered limousines accompanied by two patrol support vehicles. Each support vehicle has two heavily armed guards. The High Council members barely get inside before all hell breaks loose on the street.

Klaus and his commandos arrive in armored vehicles, stopping a half-block away from the limousines and patrol vehicles. The commandos gun down the two guards outside the High Council building first. Klaus steps out of his armored vehicle and launches grenades at the limousines, blowing them up.

The Elite Guards make it out of their patrol vehicles only to be gunned down by .50-caliber rounds from Zander's commandos. The High Council members inside duck for cover and run. Simone steps forward into the chaos and yells, "Follow me." She takes them up to the tenth floor, the very top of the building. She messages Asher. She responds, ordering her Strike Force to land their sky cycles on the roof and protect the council members. Damian and his Strike Force unit will aid in the pursuit of Zander's commandos. Klaus launches another grenade at the front doors of the council building, blowing them off their hinges.

Brock and Xavier have positioned themselves on opposite sides of the lobby, hiding behind hallway corners. As the commandos storm the entrance, Brock yells, "Drop your weapons!"

They fire in Brock's direction. Xavier mows them down from the opposite side. Klaus, approaching the doorway and aware of the return fire, grabs the commando in front of him and uses him for cover to back away. Klaus and ten commandos flee from the front entrance and run-on foot to Imperial Tower Park, using the trees for cover.

Inside the Council Building, two commandos duck behind the guard desk. Xavier takes a grenade out of his belt and throws a perfect strike, hitting the desk right in the middle. The desk explodes outward, wholly obliterated. The two commandos struggle to their feet, raising their weapons, and fire at Xavier. He takes a round in the chest and falls back. Brock mows down the commandos. He rushes to Xavier. Fortunately, his bulletproof vest stopped the round.

An explosion rocks the back of the building. The commandos must be breaching the back door. Brock takes a breath. Callie positioned her troops well. It's up to her team to turn them back.

Bodies of fifteen commandos are scattered over the front lobby. Brock looks at Xavier. "You good here?"

Xavier nods. "Just a bit sore." He stays in the front while Brock goes to the back to check on Callie's team. Everything's quiet. More bodies litter the floor. Twenty Commandos lay dead by the back entrance, with an equal number inside and outside.

Callie updates Brock. "Kort and his men killed many of the commandos trying to escape, but at least ten commandos ran off. Kort and his soldiers are pursuing them."

Caleb and Raven enter the front entrance of Imperial Tower. She has a gun hidden behind her back. As they approach the guard's desk, the guard rises to greet Caleb, whom he recognizes.

"Caleb, what are you doing here? I thought you were a prisoner of the Underlings." Caleb smiles at first but then notices the blood on Krull's sleeves. Before Krull can react, he punches him, knocking him out cold.

Raven looks at him, shocked. "Honey, that wasn't very sociable." Then she notices the blood on Krull's uniform, too. "Never mind, my brilliant boy. Good job."

They quickly handcuff Krull's hands behind his back, cuff his ankles, and zip-tie his ankle and wrist cuffs together. For added measure, Caleb zip-ties Krull's neck to a file cabinet. He doesn't want to be responsible for Krull getting loose.

They quickly make their way to the elevator and take it to the top floor. As they enter Steadman's suite, they see Zander in the middle of the room with his hand wrapped around Roxanne's neck. Maverick and Ice have their guns pointed at him.

"Drop your weapons, or I will snap her neck!" Zander shouts. "I'm not playing around, Ice. Drop your weapons."

Maverick looks at Caleb and then back to Zander. "Zander, if you let Roxanne leave with us, I will set down my weapon, and you and I will settle this *mano a mano*."

Zander scowls. "How do I know I can trust you?"

"Do you have a choice? I don't doubt you'll kill her. But if you can kill Roxanne, we will kill you. This is four-on-one."

Maverick looks at Raven and Ice and nods. "Lay down your weapons."

Crystal gives him an angry look. He winks at her as if he has a plan. Reluctantly, they set their weapons on the floor. Jennifer follows Crystal's lead.

Brownstone looks at Caleb. "Promise me you'll take them out of here."

Caleb nods. Brownstone lowers his gun and moves closer to the door. Zander, realizing his options, eases his hand from Roxanne's neck—not enough to let her run away, but enough to release some of the tension.

"Here's how this will go down, Zander. I will open the door and leave it open. Caleb will gather all the guns and take them to the end of the hall. Crystal and Raven will stand in the hallway against the opposite wall. You will bring Roxanne within eight feet of the doorway. You will push her through the doorway. As soon as Roxanne is through, I will lock the door from the inside. Then it will be just you and me. And you will have your opportunity for revenge."

Crystal doesn't like this one bit, but she doesn't want to see her friend die, either. Brownstone has a plan. He must.

"Fine," Zander says. "Let's get it on."

Caleb grabs the guns and takes them to the end of the hall. Jennifer and Crystal step out after him. Zander moves closer to the doorway with Roxanne and violently shoves her through the opening. Just as he described, Brownstone locks the door from the inside.

The men move toward the center of the room, circling each other. Neither takes their eyes off the other. Steadman's voice rings out over an intercom system, playing a recorded message. "If you hear my voice, it means I am no longer here. I have either met an untimely demise, or I have escaped. If you're here, it is likely your fault. This suite will blow up in two minutes. The doors are all locked, and there's no way out."

Brownstone urgently speaks into his comms. "Crystal, the building is going to blow. Get everyone out now!"

Zander glares at Brownstone. "If we work together, we might figure a way to get out of here alive."

"I am afraid that's not an option. You're evil, Zander, and I can't allow you to live." Zander makes a roundhouse kick at Brownstone's head. He blocks the blow, but the spinning back fist that follows hits him square on the jaw, knocking him backward. Zander advances.

Brownstone counters with a sidekick to Zander's knee that makes him wince, and he follows it with a left jab to Zander's face. Zander smiles and then blitzes him, firing one punch right after another. Brownstone side-steps the onslaught and counters with an overhand right that would have knocked most men out cold.

Zander smiles again, saying, "Poor little weak Underling. You can't hurt me."

It will take a superhuman blow to stop him. Brownstone isn't sure he has that in him. Once again, Zander attacks in a blitz of punches. Instead of side-stepping the fury, Maverick absorbs the blows and gets knocked down flat on his back. Zander moves in for the kill. He leaps at Brownstone to finish him.

Just as Zander is about to land on top of him, Brownstone raises his feet, catching Zander's torso. He flips Zander violently over his head, sending him face-first into the granite wall. Zander's neck snaps on impact. Brownstone checks his communication device. Thirty seconds until the building blows.

# CHAPTER 45

On the Sky Port, Roxanne and Crystal take off on a sky cycle together, leaving the last sky cycle for Brownstone. They land in front of the High Council building and warn everyone to take cover. As Crystal gets off her sky cycle, Klaus walks out of the park toward her. His gun points right at her.

Asher, tracking him, swoops down on her sky cycle, hitting Klaus with a glancing blow. The hit is hard enough that Klaus drops his weapon. Crystal runs toward the giant, leaping in the air and slamming him straight in the mouth with a superman punch. The force of the blow knocks Klaus backward, but he is still on his feet. Caleb attempts to jump in front of her, but he's too late. Klaus rushes Crystal. Using her blazing speed, she front snap kicks Klaus in the groin and then punches his throat, crushing his esophagus. The giant falls to his knees, gasping desperately for air he will never receive.

Jennifer and Roxanne yell, "Take cover, take cover!" They barely make it through the front entrance of the Council building when the top of the Imperial Tower explodes.

Crystal falls to her knees, screaming. "No! No!" It feels like her world has just ended. Caleb, Brock, and Jennifer gather around, wrapping their arms around her.

Everyone is in a state of shock. Is it possible James "Maverick" Brownstone, the hero of the Underlings, is no more?

After several minutes, Crystal raises her head. "We've got to find Maverick and take him home."

"The top of the tower is too hot now. It would burn us up," Brock whispers. "We'll come back to get him when it cools down. I promise."

Xavier secures a large Humvee to take them back to the compound. Caleb and Jennifer are in the back seat with Crystal, trying to console the inconsolable. They need grief support themselves. Brock doesn't talk; he's so distraught. Marci and Rob meet them at the staging area. Rob looks like he has lost his reason for living. Everyone gathers at Marci's. Crystal goes into her mother's bedroom and lays on the bed, crying all day. Marci lays beside her daughter holding her and grieving with her. Members of the compound gather at the Worship Center to pray. The family stays at the apartment all day, praying for their loved one. Crystal is angry at him for not letting her settle the score with Zander. It should have been her that went down in flames, not him. Then, she remembers his words. 'I can't bear to lose another spouse.'

There's a knock on Marci's door. She walks to the door and opens it. Caleb looks at her with a determined look. "Mom, I must speak with Crystal alone."

She nods, hugs her son, and walks out. He closes the door behind her.

Caleb sits on the edge of the bed by his sister. Reaching over, he rubs the back of her neck. She leans over, putting her head on his chest. "There are things I'm compelled to tell you, sister," he says softly. "Have you ever dreamed a dream that came true?"

Looking up at him, she nods.

"I dreamed about a way to find Marci for months before I acted on it. Brownstone has a similar dream about meeting a mysterious Elite in the desert, me. Then he took me directly to Marci. He even had a crazy dream about attacking the headquarters of the most powerful entity on earth, Cognition. You and I participated in the fulfillment of that dream. Didn't we?"

She looks up, wiping her tears. "Yes."

"These are not random dreams. They are not only extraordinary. They are divine. What are the common elements of these dreams that made them a reality?"

She ponders. "Faith and action."

"Yes, my sister. By faith and action, I found our mother. By faith and action, you fell in love with Brownstone. We defeated Prime, ended Cognition, and freed Imperial City through faith and action. I know you have had time to think about this last question. You have witnessed believers in action, acting on their faith no matter the odds." He pauses and takes her hand. "Do you believe there is a God?"

She thinks back. Even with her Elite training, there was no reason things should have gone as smoothly as they had. No reason she could see, at least. It felt counterintuitive, but perhaps her brother has a point. She nods.

"Do you believe he sent his Son to die for you?"

She looks into the Truth Seeker's eyes. Perhaps there was more to this than met the eye. "I do."

"You know what you have to do."

Crystal stands, once again wiping tears from her eyes. "Tell everyone to meet me at the Flight Center at 7:30 p,m. I have something important to say."

After washing her face and dressing in her G7 flight suit, she arrives at 7:30 p.m. Crystal addresses them firmly. "I had the same dream for five years. It started when I lived back in Imperial City right after the death of James' wife. This dream was of Brownstone and me walking together by the ocean. We have never been to an ocean together. When I first met him, he looked just like the man of my dreams, except he didn't have that little scar on his cheek like my dream man. He got that scar when he fought the Elite commandos in the desert. It's the same scar and in the exact location as my dream man. I knew that day that he was my dream. Brownstone is not dead! I haven't walked on an ocean beach with him. I'm going back to Imperial City to find him."

Dressed in his old military uniform, Rob says, "You guys aren't doing this one without me."

They mount their sky cycles, blasting off into the night. With tears in her eyes and faith in her heart, Crystal pushes forward to full throttle, hoping and praying her dream hasn't died.

# CHAPTER 46

Approaching Imperial City, she messages Asher and Damian. "I need mountain rescue gear: ropes, pullies, and a gurney. And we need fire suits, shovels, and picks."

"You think you know where he is?" Asher inquires.

"I don't think. I know."

Asher and Damian meet them at the top of the tower. They already cleared out landing spots. "We need to find Steadman's escape shaft. That's where Brownstone will be," Crystal says. After thirty minutes of back-breaking work, they find it. Crystal and Brock repel down several stories encountering a pile of rubble.

"Where is he?" Brock mutters in frustration.

*Come on...* Crystal searches the rubble. He has to be here. Then she spots it. "Look." Crystal points to a hand sticking out of the mess of concrete.

They rush in, frantically pulling away the rubble.

They hear a moan, then words. "Easy, easy."

"Brownstone?" Brock says.

"Bingo. Now get me the hell out of here."

"James," Crystal says.

"Sorry dear, I thought it was just the big ox."

"Send the gurney down now," Brock orders.

After they clear away all the debris. Crystal places a kiss on his bruised and battered face. "Don't you ever scare me like that again, James 'Maverick' Brownstone." He reaches his hand toward her.

Crystal orders. "Don't move, James, till we check you out."

"I can't feel my legs."

Crystal gently places her hand on his face. "Don't worry. You still got them. We'll get you the best medical care available."

They fly Brownstone back to the medical center at the compound. His vital organs are intact. The fall broke three ribs and his left wrist and severely damaged both legs.

Crystal and Uncle Rob are at his bedside when he wakes up. "The good news is that you are alive. Didn't I tell you, Crystal, that boy is always blowing things up?"

Brownstone laughs and then grabs his ribcage.

Crystal places a hand on his cheek. "Love you, Maverick."

He smiles. "Love you, Ice."

Looking at his uncle, "Okay, what's the bad news?"

"Your legs are severely damaged."

He grimaces. "Tell it to me straight. Will I walk again?"

Rob puts his hand on his nephew's shoulder. "Your legs are shattered, but there is a secret state-of-the-art medical center in the Swiss Alps that specializes in Orthopedic reconstructive surgery. I sent them your medical records."

"What are the odds I'll ever walk again?"

"This is your only chance. It will be a long process of surgeries and rehabilitation therapy, taking up to six months. You'll be cut off from all outside communication. They never want to be discovered by the androids. There's only one spot left. I've reserved it for you. We must act fast to keep it."

He looks at Crystal, not wanting to leave her, even for a day. She runs her hand through his hair. "James, the dream is of us walking hand in hand on the beach. You go, sweetheart. Don't ruin my dream. We'll hold things down until you return. We need two things for our dream to come true, faith and action."

She bends misty-eyed, gently kissing him on the lips.

He looks at her, choking back tears, wishing there was another way.

"Okay, but we've got a date at the altar the day I return."

"Deal, Maverick."

Uncle Rob flies James out on the XPlane two hours later. She stands there looking up as it rockets into the darkness, wishing more than anything to be there for him. Loneliness rushes over her. Faith is all she has left. She must keep the faith.

# CHAPTER 47

Crystal spends her days helping reconstruct Imperial City. Dr. Jewel appointed her, Caleb, and Simone as advisors to the High Council. The city's citizens demanded change after Steadman's fall and Zander's defeat.

At the recommendation of its advisors, the High Council did away with the rank system and granted Underlings equal rights. One-third of the Elites left the city unhappy with giving up their prestigious status.

Three months later, Dr. Jewel was elected the first mayor of Imperial City. Kort and Callie were the first Underlings elected to the city council. Imperial Tower was turned into an apartment complex.

Crystal convinced Robert Forrester to build several smaller domed cities for the Underlings across the desert landscape. The Underlings and Elites signed an eternal treaty of peace and cooperation.

Crystal's heart was torn; she was elated about all the changes and cooperation between Elites and Underlings, but her heart was not complete without James. She was thrilled to see her mom and Kurt get married two months after Brownstone left and then the wedding of Caleb and Jennifer a month later. Caleb's marriage really got to her. She couldn't help the jealousy. It was supposed to be her turn. The emptiness inside her lingered. It was approaching six months, and there was still no word from James. A sense of desperation consumed her nights. Sometimes it seemed faith was the hardest thing.

On day one hundred seventy-nine, at 9 p.m., there's a knock on her door. Who could it be at this time of the evening? When Crystal opens the door, it's Caleb standing there. Her heart races. Over the last few months, she'd often seen him be the one to deliver bad news.

He smiles, and her heart rate slows.

"What's going on, Caleb?"

"It's Brownstone. Rob just left for the Swiss Alps. James will be here tomorrow."

She can hardly believe her ears and leaps into his arms. "Yes! Yes! Yes!" Caleb hugs and holds her as her questions settle in, and she slowly comes down from the high. "Is he walking?

"All Rob said was they done all they could do. James is coming home."

"Walking or not, he better be at that altar tomorrow."

# CHAPTER 48

Crystal sleeps well and wakes with a sense of destiny. She will marry the man of her dreams in just a few hours. Good thing she went ahead and planned this wedding. The wedding party meets at the worship center at 11 a.m.

When Crystal arrives, she's pleasantly surprised to see many ladies already there decorating for the ceremony. The girl who grew up with only a few friends now has a whole community of friends. Today will be full of tears, laughter, and love. Jennifer, Simone, and Marci are all there for her every step of the way. She feels like a movie star getting ready to play a princess. And the hair, make-up, and wardrobe personnel prepare Crystal for her starring role. Her wedding will be a real-life fairy tale come true.

Marci grabs her daughter's hand. "Let's pray. Lord, bless Crystal's marriage and help them to keep you first in all things. Lord, help her have a sense of humor when James does something stupid and help him have a sense of humor when Crystal does something stupid. Amen!"

The ladies gather in a circle. "Love is family; family is love." Then they do their friendship ring high-five and group hug.

Crystal's beauty at the sanctuary entrance causes a collective gasp from the audience. She scans the stage, but there is no sign of James. She forces a smile, hoping he's just late. His absence causes her to pause.

Then she sees him walk onto the stage from the side entrance without so much as a limp. Her heart soars. He turns and smiles, never taking his eyes off her. The audience erupts in applause as their hero returns.

Crystal walks two-thirds of the way down and stops. She does a 360-degree pirouette. The audience erupts in applause again. The vision of Crystal in the mermaid-style sleeveless lace gown leaves Brownstone breathless. Indeed, he's marrying the most beautiful woman in the world.

Brownstone's face lights up as Crystal takes each step. He kneels before her. Crystal offers her hand, and he kisses her hand not once but twice and winks at her as he stands up.

The passion Crystal feels for him has no limits. If only she could envelop him in her arms right now. He smiles as if he's reading her thoughts.

Robert Forrester reads several texts covering the divine ordination of marriage between a man and a woman. He states it's a covenant that mirrors Christ's relationship to the church. As Christ loved the Church and gave himself for it, husbands should love their wives likewise. He goes over the instructions of Ephesians 5 regarding the relationship between husbands and wives. Then he reads Genesis 2:24, that a husband and wife should be one flesh.

Robert says, "This couple is making a solemn vow and a lifelong commitment to each other. They are making this commitment before God and man. Marriage is God-ordained and, I would add, God-sustained. Father, I ask that you put your divine umbrella of protection over this covenant. Father bind Crystal and James together as one heart, one flesh, and one spirit. What God has put together, let no man or woman tear asunder. Amen."

Brownstone makes the following vows to Crystal:

"My dearest Crystal, I promise I will always love you through the ups and downs of our lives. In your darkest moments, I will be your guiding light. I might not always please you, but it won't be from a lack of trying. You are now a part of me, the best part of me. I will honor you as my Queen. You will always be as beautiful to me as you are today. I promise to love you and only you and cherish every moment of our life together."

Crystal makes her vows to James:

"My dear husband, I love and adore you and strive to please you as your wife. I promise to support, encourage, and honor you. There will be no other that I love like you. Through the storms of life, my arms will be your place of love and refuge. Though we will have our ups and downs, as all couples do, I will never give you a reason to doubt. My heart belongs to you. I will be your best friend, confidante, and lover. I commit my heart, mind, and body to you."

After their vows, Rob smiles. "Crystal and James, I pronounce you husband and wife. You may kiss your bride."

Crystal can't stop smiling.

James says, "I love you, Crystal Brownstone." He takes her in his arms, giving her a long, passionate kiss.

The glowing couple waits in the foyer for everyone to greet them. They go back inside the Worship Center and take traditional wedding pictures. From there, they go to the Eden Atrium for more photos. Crystal, Marci, and Jennifer do their friendship ring high-five right in front of the waterfall. Brownstone carries Crystal over the bridge in front of the waterfall. Crystal loves every minute of her wedding day, and James is thrilled to see his bride's faces glow more and more. From the Eden Atrium, they go to the reception hall for the meal and the dance that follows.

# CHAPTER 49

They are seated at the head of the room behind long tables fully covered in white. Brownstone and Crystal sit in the center with Marci and Brock to their left and Caleb and Jennifer to their right. The meal comprises lamb chops, mashed potatoes, green bean casserole, rolls, and iced tea or lemonade. The dessert table contains apple pie, pecan pie, and ice cream.

Crystal is nervous about her first dance with Brownstone. They had so much to catch up on, and the only man she had ever danced with was her brother. Marci made sure they learned how to dance.

Rob announces, "For the traditional first dance this evening. For this momentous occasion, we have a special song written by none other than our own James Brownstone." The music starts playing. Brownstone takes Crystal's hand and escorts her to the dance floor. He pulls her close. She could melt in his arms, never to reemerge. She lays her head on his shoulder as they breathe in unison, moving as one, swaying to the music. Crystal listens closely to the words.

*I need a Sunday kind of love*
*One who believes in the Lord above*
*In the old ways*
*And the end of days*
*Who loves long walks*
*And late-night pillow talks*

*Church on Sunday morning*
*Family Dinner on Sunday evening*
*Bonfires and fireflies*
*Drives in the countryside*
*Talking about forever*
*Sipping iced tea on the front porch*
*Watching the world go by*
*I need a Sunday kind of love*
*Whose life is lived right*
*And her passion burns bright*
*I need, I need, I need, a Sunday kind of love.*

He whispers to her as the song ends, "Crystal, you are my Sunday kind of love." She holds him even tighter. They stand there after the song ends, wrapped in a loving embrace. The melody of love will always play in their hearts, even after the music stops.

The atmosphere in the banquet hall is magical. Love and laughter fill the room. Kids dance like there is no tomorrow. Older couples dance like they're newlyweds. Crystal only wants to dance with Brownstone but can't turn down any little kid who wants to dance with her. Watching her mother line dancing brings her heart joy. She can't get her husband off her mind. What great experiences does the night still hold? Everyone wants to get pictures of them. It's 11 p.m. before they get away.

They drive to their new apartment in an electric buggy decorated with rattling cans, streamers, and balloons.

He looks over at her, smiles, and says, "Have I told you how beautiful you are tonight?"

"Only about one hundred times."

"One hundred times is not nearly enough."

Crystal isn't sure where to start. She hasn't seen him in months. As they drive back to their apartment, she catches him up on everything they've been doing for Imperial City. He tells her about his treatment, physical therapy, and the medical advancements he'd love to bring into his practice. By the time they arrive at their door, any nerves she had from their separation have dissipated.

Brownstone comes around the buggy to escort Crystal, but to her surprise, he scoops her up in his arms and carries her to the door. He puts his thumb against the lock sensor, and the door opens. The door closes automatically behind them. Instead of putting her down, he takes her straight to the bedroom, laying her gently on the bed.

He takes off his tux. Gazing into her eyes, he gently removes her shoes. His presence is intoxicating in this intimate setting. Her heart races like never before. Why? It must be wedding night jitters.

He gently caresses her cheek. "Let your body take over and do what comes naturally." She pulls him to her, kissing him with a deep hunger from the depths of her being. The kiss lasts for what seems like an eternity. He takes his time, letting Crystal control the intensity and responding to match her level of desire. Every fiber in her body is on fire for him. Crystal never knew this level of passion was possible.

Their bodies become intertwined, moving in rhythm to the music of their passionate love. She surrenders completely to him. Crystal feels all the desire and love flow from his body into hers. His kisses are like drugs, and his touch sets her ablaze. She doesn't want part of him; Crystal wants all of him. Their primal desires generate a new level of passion as a crescendo of ecstasy rushes through them. She's bonded to this man as if they're one flesh and one heart. Crystal has never been so fully satisfied in all her life.

Brownstone holds her tenderly. "You are the beat of my heart, and I will love you till the end of time." She drifts off to sleep, exhausted but completely satisfied, wrapped in her husband's loving embrace.

The next morning, Crystal wakes up to Brownstone banging around in the kitchen.

"Maverick, Maverick," she yells.

He comes running and says, "Is everything all right?"

She laughs. "What are you doing?"

"I'm getting ready to make us breakfast."

He's wearing only his red plaid boxers. He looks so sexy. She pulls him onto the bed, flipping him on his back. "I am not done with you yet, Maverick!" She jumps on top of him, having her dessert before breakfast.

Afterward, they fix breakfast together, taking a break here and there to dance around the kitchen. They stay in all day, getting out only to take a late-night walk around the Eden Atrium.

The next day, they fly sky cycles to a desert oasis hidden by a mountain range fifty miles northwest of the compound. On the outside, the cabins look old and abandoned. But on the inside, the cottages are immaculately furnished for romantic getaways. The cabins encircle a clear three-acre lake.

They stay there for three days, lounging by the water, taking moonlight walks around the lake, drinking champagne, and doing the things that honeymooning couples do. A waterfall cascading off the mountainside feeds the lake.

On day two of their stay, they walk under the waterfall. Crystal doesn't miss the opportunity, pulling Brownstone to her and kissing him passionately under the fall. She takes him right there as mist from the fall kisses their bare skin, sending their senses into overdrive. Their bodies dance in rhythm to an ever-increasing intensity leading to a passion-filled climax. They hold each other tightly for several minutes. The world around them ceases. Their beating hearts are all that exist.

Crystal jumps through the waterfall into the lake below. Brownstone follows her. They surface, treading water, and kiss passionately.

Crystal feels carefree, experiencing what it means to be a woman in all her fullness. She doesn't know how she could love him more, yet her feelings for him each day grow stronger. This is a beautiful dream she doesn't want to end.

On their last night in the bungalow, they hold each other, basking under the moonlight, peering through their open window. They love each other like there is no tomorrow. Like two raging fires with an unquenchable hunger, they fan the flames into the early morning hours.

As they mount their sky cycles to head back, he turns to her. "Oh, by the way, I have one more surprise."

Mid-morning the next day, in Brisbane, Australia, a striking couple walks down the beach hand in hand. She turns and looks closely at his face. He has a faded scar on his right cheek. He stops walking, turns to her, pulls her close, and kisses her passionately. She matches his intensity as fiery passion overloads her senses. He stops, looks deeply into her eyes, and says, "You are what love looks like." Some dreams do come true!

# ABOUT THE AUTHOR

Born the last of twelve children and the first in his family to graduate college, Jack Kelley grew up in poverty but in a family rooted in faith and who had a great love for each other. As a boy, he cared little for academics because he was so interested in sports. In the seventh grade, they placed him in an advanced reading class. He was as shocked as his classmates. It was only then that the thought occurred to him, that he might be smart.

In his teenage years, Jack enjoyed reading action adventure and romance novels. So, it is only natural that those elements are a staple in his fiction writings. As an adult, he developed a keen interest in what the future might hold with the advancement of artificial intelligence, robotics, and genetic engineering. His first novel, *Crystal and the Underlings,* paints vivid pictures of what the world might be like in the near future and the difficult dilemmas facing the inhabitants of the earth.

Jack has an M.S. degree from Murray State University and worked most of his professional career helping others.

He lost his wife to cancer in 2018 but found love again in 2021. Jack relies on his faith to overcome the difficult times of life. He enjoys hiking, fishing, reading, writing, movies, theater, working out, sports, and spending time with his grandchildren. He lives in the rolling hills of Western Kentucky.

Connect with Jack at:

Facebook.com/100085291751302
Twitter: @Jack4relKelley
Instagram.com/jack4relkelley

CPSIA information can be obtained
at www.ICGtesting.com
Printed in the USA
JSHW021456090523
41456JS00005B/20